THURSDAY'S CHILD

BY

M. A. WRIGHT

Thursday's Child
By M. A. Wright

This book was first published in Great Britain in paperback during July 2023.

The moral right of M. A. Wright is to be identified as the author of this work and has been asserted by them in accordance with the Copyright, Designs and Patents Act of 1988.

All rights are reserved and no part of this book may be produced or utilized in any format, or by any means, electronic or mechanical, including photocopying, recording or by any information storage or retrieval system, without prior permission in writing from the publishers - Coast & Country/Ads2life. ads2life@btinternet.com

All rights reserved.

ISBN: 9798399355740

Copyright © July 2023 M. A. Wright

Dedication

In loving memory of the late

Carrie Valerie Smith

Who fought a valiant battle but sadly lost

10th September 1956 - 29th July 2023

A donation from every book sold will be sent to the

Sue Ryder Thorpe Hall Hospice, Peterborough

Thank you for buying this book £2.00 from every book sold will be forwarded to

Sue Ryder Hospice

M. A. Wright
Wrightma1944@gmail.com

Happy Birthday Mum,

lovely Story & great that its raising money for this Charity

Sam xxx

PROLOGUE

LONDON DECEMBER 1885

At five a.m. on a freezing, cold Thursday morning in December 1885, a tiny baby girl was delivered of its mother, Selena Carney-Tompkins. The baby girl was silent as she slithered her way into the world, and was whisked away by the so-called midwife, to the annoyance of Sarah, Selena's former nanny now companion.

Selena lay exhausted as Sarah hissed instructions to the woman to strike the baby's bottom and massage its heart, only to be ignored as the woman hurriedly left the room.

Whilst Sarah attended Selena, assuring her the baby girl was going to be all right, Sarah fretted at the midwife's strange behaviour. By the time she had finished preparing Selena to welcome her husband with the news, the midwife walked back into the room looking serious and shaking her head. The smile that had been on Sarah's lips slid away.

'Can I see my baby?' Selena asked weakly. 'I know Gerald was hoping for a boy, but when he sees her, he will love her just as much.' she continued dreamily.

'Just one moment Miss Selena, I'll.......I'll be back in just one moment.' Turning, Sarah walked towards the midwife and taking her roughly by the arm, pushed her out into the corridor.

'Oy, get your 'ands of me!' the woman spat at her.

'Who are you? And where is Mrs Carson the midwife Mr Carney-Tompkins engaged?'

'I don't know nothin' about no Mrs Carson, all I know is I was told to come 'ere as there was a girl what needs delivering of a babby.'

'But who sent you?'

The woman shrugged. 'Some posh woman, paid me an all so you don't need to give me nuffing, unless you wants to of course.'

'Pay you! Where's the baby? I bought that darling girl laying in that bed into the world nineteen years ago and I promised her late Mama I would always take care of her, so where's the little lass she's just delivered. Where is she, what 'ave you done with her?'

'She's dead! You old hag. That's what I was about to tell ya when you hassled me out of the room. She's dead.'

'But.......but, she can't be. Many a baby is born quiet, you just have to smack its backside to make it take its first breath, massage its little chest, breathe life into its little mouth. No, no, no, I don't believe you.' By now Sarah had tears of despair running down her cheeks and was in terror, knowing the longer the little mite was left unattended, death would be her fate. But Sarah wasn't giving up yet. She didn't trust this woman, though she couldn't think for the life of her why she would want to hurt the baby and in turn devastate Selena, a young girl she didn't know, not to mention her beloved husband Gerald. How to tell Selena. Sarah went to find Gerald and tearfully told the story.

It would be many years before the mystery would be revealed. In time, the couple would come to accept the still birth of their first child. Though the story of why Mrs Carson was told she was not required for Selena's birthing remained a mystery. Mrs Carson, when approached had produced a letter telling her she was no longer needed. This letter had not been written by either Gerald or Selena. When asked about the disappearance of the child's body, Mrs Carson confirmed that it was not unusual for a midwife to dispose of the body of a stillborn, especially if it had been deformed. This was done to ease the mother's stress, she explained, though later, the swaddled body of a baby was produced and laid to rest in a small white coffin.

Unbeknown to the grieving parents, earlier that evening, two women met at the appointed time on the edge of Old Nichol, a notorious slum in the East End of London. A heavily veiled woman stepped down from a carriage, in her arms a bundle. Ginny, not her real name, came out of the shadows.

'Ginny?' The woman hissed. Ginny nodded but said nothing. The woman thrust the bundle towards her. 'Here, take it.' Ginny hesitated. This whole thing stank of criminality and poor she may be but........ then again Ginny had been offered money, good money, and when you were as poor as she was.......she thought of her own little family and the dead baby that she held in her arms, ready to do the swap with the live one the posh lady held out to her. She thought of her daughter, starving back in the hovel she called home, no wonder the baby her daughter just delivered was born dead, but would her daughter really want this one in its place? Still, she was receiving good money to take it. Reaching out she went to take the bundle then withdrew her arms.

'Wai'd a minute, where's the money?' she demanded.

'It's here, in my reticule but until you take this off me, I can't reach it.' the woman said angrily. She spoke with a posh accent, so she was obviously not a servant. This woman was making sure no one would know of what she'd been up to this night.

Tentatively, Ginney reached out, handing over her dead granddaughter and took the proffered bundle. Inside the shawl something moved, and a soft mewling sound came from it. 'Here, quick, take it.' The woman was now referring to the pouch of money which Ginny could hear a jingling of coins inside. 'If you don't want to keep it, tomorrow, take it to the workhouse and say you found it lying beside its dead mother, then leave, and don't you ever speak of it again, do you hear me?'

'Oh I 'ear ya all right.' But the posh woman was already climbing back into the carriage which brought her. Wonder what the driver thinks of all this, Ginny mused, but where money was concerned, it was best not to know.

Arriving back home, Ginny woke her daughter who had recently given birth. ' 'Ere, put this poor little sod to yer breast.'

'What! What the 'ell,'

'Done argue, jus' do it.' Her daughter obediently took the child and after a bit of a struggle, got the child to suckle.

'Where d'you get it from?' She asked her mother. ''nd 'ow d'ya expect us to keep anover kid?' Ginny shook the pouch of coins.

'Doin' some rich cow, a favour, so done ask questions, an' done never speak abart it neiver or I'll bleedin' scalp yer.'

'Well, I don't want it! If I can't 'ave me own kid I don't want thisen!' and dragging the child from her breast, she pushed it into her mother's arms.

As dawn broke the next morning, Ginny took the baby and headed in the direction of the workhouse but as she approached, she looked around at where she could leave it. She hadn't thought to bring a box, and if she left her on the steps, it could be sometime before she was found. It was freezing, snow still lay on the ground, the child could die, would die. Poor little mite. As poor as she was, Ginny could not leave the baby to die. And then there were questions. Oh, she knew what she was supposed to say, but it wasn't easy. Turning, she looked around for somewhere to leave her, somewhere where the child would be found quickly. Then she saw it, the church steeple, of course, why hadn't she thought of it before, the church, better still the vicarage.

She moved quickly, slipping, and sliding in the slush, gripping the bundle hoping she wouldn't fall and the child would stay sleeping.

At last, she reached the Vicarage. Looking up, she could see no lights in the windows, though there was bound to be a servant already at work. Quietly, Ginny unlatched the gate and crept up the path. There was an enclosed porch which luckily Ginny was able to open the doors too. Gingerly she lay the bundle down, then pulling on the doorbell, she turned and scuttled back down the pathway just in time to hide in the hedge as the front door opened. Ginny watched as the maid looked about her trying to see who could have rung the bell. Ginny prayed for the maid to look down. Just as she was about to go back inside and close the door, the maid did look down. Ginny saw her gasp and bend to pick up the child. As soon as she'd gone inside and closed the door, Ginny was off down the road not caring now if she slipped, she just wanted to get as far away as possible and put the whole episode behind her.

Inside the vicarage, Maisy ran with the baby to the kitchen. 'Mrs Morris, Mrs Morris, look what someone's left on the doorstep.' Maisy hurtled into the kitchen, startling the cook who was busy preparing breakfast.

'Maisy, Maisy, for gawd sakes girl calm down, you'll wake the 'ole household, what you got there?'

'A baby Mrs Morris, a baby. I found it on the doorstep. I was in the parlour setting the fire when someone rang the doorbell an' when I went ta see 'w'o it was, there was no one there so I was 'bout to close the door when I 'eared a noise an' looks dan, an' there it was. See it's wakin' up.'

'Oh, my gawd' Mrs Morris said. 'Give it 'ere. Go to the nursery and get a bottle, then go and gently wake the mistress an' tell 'er what's 'appened. I'll warm some milk.'

Elizabeth Milton the vicar's wife was followed swiftly by her husband the Reverend Mark Milton on hearing the strange news Maisy had excitedly reported. Not waiting to dress, the pair slipped on dressing gowns and hurriedly entered the kitchen to see Mrs Morris cradling a baby in her arms whilst feeding it.

Elizabeth's face softened as she looked upon the tiny little face with its eyes closed, the baby sucked noisily on the bottle. Tiny little hands escaped from its covering, its fingers eagerly trying to hold on to the bottle. 'What is it?' she asked Mrs Morris

'It's a baby.' Mark whispered to which Elizabeth, raising an eyebrow replied.

'Well, I can see that dearest, what I meant was, is it a boy or a girl?'

'Oh, I don't know Madam, I haven't 'ad time to look. Poor little thing was so 'ungry, I just got on feedin' it.' Cook replied.

'Quite right Mrs Morris, quite right.' Elizabeth agreed.
Mrs Morris shifted the baby to her shoulder to burp the child saying. 'Sorry Madam but with all the excitement I haven't finished cooking breakfast.'

'Don't worry Mrs Morris. Why don't I take the child and give it a bath and a change of clothes, I must have something from the children's baby clothes that will fit, then you can get on with breakfast.'

'Yes Madam.' Mrs Morris happily handed over her charge, more than happy to be getting on with cooking. What a ta-do!

Upstairs Mark had already retrieved the baby bath from a cupboard in the nursery and Maisy had brought warm water from the bathroom, towels, soap and flannel. Elizabeth joined them and undressed the child, gasping when she saw it was a girl. 'Oh Mark' she whispered, tears spilling from her eyes. Mark knew exactly what going through her mind. 'Do you think, could this be...?'

'The hand of God?' Mark enquired. 'Who knows, they say God moves in mysterious ways.'

'Oh Mark, a little girl.' As Elizabeth gently picked up the child to bathe her, she remembered the two little girls she'd given birth to who had not survived. True they had three strapping healthy sons, but what mother doesn't dream of having a daughter. 'Look Mark! she is new-born. She still has the umbilical cord attached. Who could have given her away, it's shocking! Wicked!' Mark touched her shoulder.

'Someone who no doubt was desperate.' He said quietly.

'Oh, look Mark, see. There's a little mark on her shoulder, it looks like......good heavens. Mark, am I going mad or does that look like...the star of Bethlehem.'

'Good heavens, I think you're right. Well, that should make it easy to find her mother.'

'Oh No!' Elizabeth rounded on him. 'Mark, we can't give her back, this child wasn't wanted. For whatever reason, she stands a better chance with us.' As Elizabeth took a now clean baby from the water and wrapped her in warm soft towels, she sang sweetly to her. Mark watched, his heart heavy.

Knowing how much his wife wanted the child he knew it would be wrong not to try and find the baby's mother and offer help to her. Elizabeth was a wonderful mother to their three sons, but he knew how she longed for a little girl.

But who knew, perhaps when found the mother would be happy to let them have the baby if she wasn't able to keep it, but they must report it and perhaps as Elizabeth said, let God have his say. Mark got in touch with the police in case anyone had reported a missing baby, he also put-up notices, he had to start somewhere. He called in their doctor to examine the little girl who said she was in remarkable shape considering, and that he thought she could not be more than twenty-four to forty-eight hours old. He suggested taking her to the orphanage, but Mark and Elizabeth refused. No, the baby would stay with them until the mother was found, and if she wasn't, well.........

'I suppose we should give her a name, temporarily, we can't keep calling her "The Baby" and "The Child".' Mark said.

Elizabeth thought for a moment. 'Thursday, yes, that's right. Today's Friday and the doctor said she was probably born about twenty-four hours ago, so that would be yesterday, Thursday, I shall call her Thursday. I think she was born on Thursday. "Thursday's child has far to go".' she quoted.

CHAPTER 1

HARROGATE, YORKSHIRE
APRIL 1881

The last of the mourners had left. Upstairs in her boudoir, fourteen-year-old Selena watched as the last carriage trundled down the driveway and out of the gates. There came a gentle knock on her door. 'Selena, Selena my dear it's Papa.' turning the doorknob, he gently opened the door and slowly entered, opening his arms to his young daughter.

Sobbing, she ran to him throwing herself into his arms and crying inconsolably. It was over, Mama was gone, now life would have to start anew although nothing would ever be the same again, Selena was going to have to face it.

'There, there Princess, please my dearest, dry your eyes, Mama would not want you to cry so hard. It's true you will miss her, *we* will miss her, but your Mama was a wonderful woman, a Lady like no other and we should remember her with love and laughter, knowing she would want our future to be full of life and happiness. *That*, would bring her peace.'

Selena's tears subsided as she lay her head on her father's chest, taking comfort in his arms. Gently, he took her by the shoulders and looking into her eyes, those beautiful deep brown eyes so reminiscent of her mother's it made him swallow a sob that threatened to have him break down. Stroking the red gold curls which had escaped from the little lace cap she wore he noticed the smattering of freckles her distress had brought to the surface. What a beautiful child she was and what a beautiful young woman she would soon become, and that day was not too far away. When the time came, he would make sure she made a good match, money and title would not play any part of his or her choice. He wanted for her what he had, had with her Mama, love. Now, a wealthy, well respected wool merchant, John Elliot had decided it was time they should shortly make their move.

In October eighteen-eighty he had met a fellow wool merchant, one Gerald Carney-Tompkins. Unlike John, Gerald had come from aristocracy though previous ancestors had destroyed and abused the wealth, leaving Gerald's father a legacy of debt. His father had done his best to rebuild the family's position and had just about managed to hold on to their position in Society, which was important to him, not so to Gerald. Gerald had seen an opening in the wool trade and over the years had learnt from the sheep farmers the importance of breeding which sheep for their fleece and those only for meat. He'd learnt from the wives the techniques of spinning, dyeing and weaving and gradually opened a small factory which later became a larger factory it was then he'd met, by accident, John.

John had been on a business trip to London trying to gain appointments to show his swatches of wool designs to the London tailors. On hearing his Northern accent, the tailors stuck their noses in the air and dismissed him. It was in one of these tailors, where Gerald happened to have visited with a view to ordering a new outfit, he'd been lucky enough to catch a quick glance, as John tried to display his samples.

After John's hasty departure from the tailors, Gerald quickly took his leave running into the street, looking up and down, trying desperately to see which way this strange little man had gone.

Annoyed at the way the tailors had treated the man, Gerald was now angry at having lost the chance to get a good look at the man's wares. Disgruntled, Gerald headed off to the Black Bull tavern for some lunch. Imagine his surprise when entering and looking around for a free table, he saw the man he'd been looking for. Smiling to himself and chuckling that this was fate and could only be a good omen, Gerald approached him.

'Excuse me Sir, may I join you?' John looked up pleased to see a gentleman who seemed to be not only polite but friendly. He'd been in London for three days and had been unable to gain any orders for his cloth which sold well in the North, but John knew he had to expand, and London was the place to be, but it seemed only if you had the right accent.

'Of course, please.' John replied.
Gerald knew he had to be honest with this man, plain speaking was what was needed here, he was sure of that.

'My name is Gerald Carney-Tompkins and like you Sir I am a wool merchant.' He held out his hand. John stared back at him.

'How the heck did you know what trade I'm in?' John asked surprised. Gerald interrupted him, smiling. 'Forgive me Sir, I happened to be in the premises of the last tailor you visited and luckily caught a glance of the samples they'd so rudely dismissed. I was not able to get a proper look but what I did see excited me and I tried to find you, but you had gone. Then as luck would have it, or was it fate? I was drawn to the very same tavern for lunch and low and behold, there you are!' He was laughing now, jovially. As his words sank in, John began to relax. What had he said, this toff, he was excited on seeing Johns samples?

'And you say you are a wool merchant?' said John unsure where this was leading.

'That's right. Though to be fair, I've never seen anything like your samples. If I'm not mistaken, there seemed to be some fine samples and colours so vibrant.'

John nodded slowly, unsure. Was this man trying to steal his designs? 'Can I ask, if you say you are a wool merchant, what do you want with me?'

'Nothing crooked I assure you. No, on the contrary, I think I can help you, introduce you to a tailor who would appreciate your cloth, and if I may be so bold, offer to help in other ways, perhaps join forces? What do you say?'

John did not know what to say but was already taking a liking to this gentleman. He decided to introduce himself and listen to what Gerald Carney-Tompkins had to say. 'The name's John, John Elliot and I hale from Yorkshire. I have for some years built up my business in Yorkshire and Manchester but of late think I need to expand, so here I am down in

London and not doing too well I am afraid.'

'Let us order some lunch.' Gerald said 'Then we can get to know each other. I can recommend the Beef and Oyster pie, and I can suggest a good ale, brewed in this very house.'

'Sounds good to me.' John agreed.

Having given their order to the young girl, Gerald turned to John. 'Now John Elliot from Yorkshire, tell me all about yourself.

'Not much to tell really. Name's John Hadley Elliot, aged forty-six, born and bred in Yorkshire, on a sheep farm. Brought up with sheep breading, shearing, spinning, dyeing and I was lucky enough to inherit a small team of cottage workers from my uncle when he died. Not long after, my wife's parents died and left a small legacy and we decided to invest it and start a small factory. Over the years, as the profits came in, we put 'em back into the business and it grew.'

'You say you are married? Have you sons?' Gerald asked.

John shook his head. 'Sadly no, though I do have a beautiful daughter Selena who has just turned fourteen.' He was silent for a moment and Gerald sensed there was more to come, something of importance so he kept quiet and waited. 'Thing is, my wife's terribly ill. Not expected to make a recovery........... Should not be here really but she was insistent, said as how I still had a business to build and a daughter to be cared for.' Gerald nodded his understanding.

Their food and tankards of ale were placed in front of them, and they began to eat. During the meal, Gerald told John about his background and how he felt they could work well together. After they had finished their meal, He offered to take John to meet the brothers Cohen, Jewish tailors who were not afraid to push the boundaries of fashion.

That had been six months ago. Since then, Gerald had visited Yorkshire twice and John had been back to London, visiting Gerald's factory.

His introduction to the brothers Cohen had been phenomenally successful and he was now sending regular orders of his cloth to them.

Then Mary took a turn for the worse, and John refused to leave her. There would be plenty of time for business when Mary passed but whilst she lived, he would never be far from her side. Gerald fully understood this and marvelled at the devotion his newfound friend and partner had for his wife. It was the sort of marriage Gerald hoped would one day be his, but at twenty-six years of age, he had not met anyone with whom he wished to spend his life with.

But now Mary was gone, and it was time for John to push forward with his plans to move to London. He had not mentioned any of this to Selena. How would she take it? When he had originally decided on what he would do when Mary had departed, he had thought it would be good for Selena, that she'd welcome living in London with all the fashions and social life to be had, but now, he wasn't so sure. Of course, for their first year they would still be in mourning, and he didn't intend moving for a least six months. Hopefully, this would give Selena time to adjust. They would have to find somewhere to live, arrange for their home in Yorkshire to be cared for, and he hoped to keep a skeleton staff here as they would be coming back from time to time. He thought the servants he had in mind would be pleased, after all it would mean less work for them. And they wouldn't have to worry about finding new employment. Servants not required to remain in Yorkshire would be offered employment at the London house, if they wanted it. But none of that needed to be discussed just yet, there was plenty of time in the future. In the meantime, he knew he could go to London whenever he was needed and Selena would be quite safe there with Sarah, who had not only brought her into the world but had remained as her nanny and lately companion. Sarah had also nursed Mary, so she was more family than servant.

Below stairs the small staff were clearing up after the funeral tea. Mrs Harris or Cookie as she was referred to by Selena, was the cook/housekeeper. There was Anna who was the general servant but no butler, John thought they were not grand enough for that, just Bill Turnbull who was a handyman, jack of all trades. Then there was Albert Briggs the gardener who was helped by Billy Martin a young simpleton but a good youth, and lastly the groom and coachman William

Hargreaves.

John had thought he would take William and Sarah to London and asked William if his wife would like to come as cook/housekeeper as he knew she had often helped in the kitchen with Mrs Harris when they'd had dinners and parties in the past.

He had thought of promoting young Joseph Turner to manager at the factory in York. He would need someone to take control if he were going to base himself in London, and Joseph had been trained in all departments and now ran the office. Overall, it was all coming together, he just hoped when all those he placed in various places, would approve, he liked to have a happy staff.

Sighing heavily, he poured himself a whisky and soda and settled in front of the dying embers of the fire, it had been a long and traumatic day. Tomorrow he would wake up to what was to be the first day of the rest of his life and if he were honest, he was dreading it. For all his thoughts and plans of a life without Mary, it was heart breaking and torturous. Finishing his whiskey, he got to his feet and went wearily to his bed.

Upstairs, Selena lay thrashing about in bed, unable to sleep. Her mind was in turmoil, what was to become of her. She knew Papa made frequent trips to London, though not so much in the last three months as her Mama had been so ill. But what now? Would Papa want to go to London more often? and if he did, would he ever consider leaving Yorkshire and moving permanently there? Slipping out of bed, she pulled on a shawl and went to the window to look out onto the gardens and across to the moors spread out before her. There was a full moon so she could clearly see the rolling hills and hear the feint baa-ing of the first new-born lambs. How could she ever get used to living anywhere other than this, her home, the only home she had ever known or wanted to know.

She had heard tales of London, read about it in story books and it all sounded rather scary to her, not the sort of place she'd want to visit.

Papa had talked about somewhere he called the' East End' and she had heard him relaying tales of dire poverty and squalor to Mama. She had heard about the slums of Manchester but never thought that such places existed in London where England's dear Queen lived. She shuddered at

the thought.
No, if Papa ever mentioned living in London, she would put her foot down, she would be quite content living here with Sarah and Cookie.

Six weeks later John took his leave for London, and to Selena's relief said nothing about living there. He had suggested before his leaving that she might like to look at her Mama's wardrobe and jewellery and give thought to how they may dispose of the items, his suggestion made her feel sick, and a sadness once again engulfed her. And this is how Sarah found her, sitting on the floor, in her Mama's boudoir surrounded by gowns and in floods of tears.

Sarah sat down beside her and let her cry it out. When her tears subsided, Sarah suggested they put away Mama's belongings and leave it for another day. Downstairs in the warmth of the kitchen, Cookie made hot chocolate and plated up sticky gingerbread which Selena and Sarah tucked into. They agreed it was too soon to do anything with her late Mama's possessions. Instead, Sarah suggested a brisk walk into the village as she needed stamps and thought the fresh air and exercise would do them both good.

It was now the middle of May and her beloved Mama had been gone over a month. The daffodils were dying off but, in their place, bright colours of tulips competed with daisies, bluebells and blossoms on the trees in shades of deepest pink to creamy white. Selena could not resist smiling as wrapped up against the chill air, she looked about her, absorbing the beauty of nature.

Arriving at the village post office, Selena and Sarah were greeted with warm affection and soon enthralled with all the latest gossip. As Sarah waited in the queue for her stamps, Kitty Hargreaves, William's wife approached her.

'So, Miss Selena, what d'you think of your Papa's idea of moving to London?' The smile slid from Selena's face. 'My William's quite excited aboot it, 'specially as your Papa's offered for me to go wi' 'im, and for me to be cook-housekeeper d'you know!' Seeing Selena's reaction, a look of horror crossed Kitty's face and she put a hand to her mouth. 'Oh, my goodness Miss! What 'ave I said. Did yer not know? Oh, I'm that sorry, oh me and me big mouth. Forget I said anything. Please don't say I said anything, or your Papa might change 'is mind, I don't want to get our William int' trouble Miss.'

Selena pulled herself together as by now everyone in the post office, including Sarah, had turned to look at Selena waiting for her to confirm or deny the rumour.

'Em, well, em, I'm not sure about all the arrangements.' And turning to hide her embarrassment, she fled out the door, shortly followed by Sarah. 'Did you know about this?' she demanded of her companion. Sarah shook her head.

'Best not fret lass, your Papa's probably not made his mind up himself yet. It's only been six weeks since your dear Mama passed so I expect he's just thinking about it.'

'Hmm, thinking about it he maybe, but enough to mention it to William, and him to his wife!'

Sarah didn't know what to say and now she was worried too. What would become of them all if the Master did take off for London. Selena was in no mood for the congenial conversation they had been having when they first set out on their walk, now she was in a hurry to get back home.

On arrival, Selena slipped off her cloak and handing to Sarah ran swiftly upstairs, closing the door firmly on her boudoir, which sent the message, do not disturb, loud and clear!

Sarah headed off in the direction of her private sitting room, what was she to do? She could not ask the Master; it was none of her business. Then again, it could affect her. She thought of talking to Mrs Harris with whom she'd always got along with, even considering their relationship more of a friendship. But then if she had not heard anything and spoke to the Master, Master may take a very dim view of what he may consider gossiping. Sarah was in a quandary but decided not to do or say anything to anyone. If Selena wanted to broach the subject on her Papa's return, and she was sure she would, that was her business, perhaps then Master would put them in the picture. Until then she would go about her usual chores, acting as if nothing had changed.

CHAPTER 2

MAYFAIR, LONDON 1881

John had spent three days at the home of Gerald where he had been made welcome each time he'd visited London. After the first initial visits when he had stayed in hotels, Gerald had broached the idea of an official partnership and John had welcomed the hospitality offered.

Not only had the pair become firm friends but respected business partners. This visit had been the first since Mary's passing and Gerald was keen to bring John to a decision of moving permanently to London. This evening, Gerald decided to broach the subject having not spoken of it during the first three days since his arrival and he was aware of Johns hesitancy regarding the upheaval in Selena's life. Since joining them together, the two businesses had picked up at a speed with previous tailors now eager to purchase the cloth they had once spurned, but Gerald and John were not having any of it and since John's idea of designing and making what he termed as 'Off The Peg' garments and employing their own machinists, Gerald needed his partner with him more and more.

After a leisurely evening meal, Gerald mentioned the matter of property. 'I've had a bit of luck recently regarding a house which is shortly coming onto the market.'

'Oh?' John said, 'Are you thinking of buying?'

'Not for myself but I thought you may be interested. It's a rather nice villa in a good part of Knightsbridge. Six bedrooms, water closets, a library and study, drawing room, lounge, formal dining room, small breakfast room and of course servants' quarters. It overlooks Hyde Park where the ladies take carriage rides, including our dear Queen. I have taken the liberty of speaking to the owners, informing them of a purchaser, though I did not mention names and stressed that for family reasons, it may be convenient to rent for six months to settle said family. After which I was sure the gentleman concerned would be happy to purchase. What do you think? Would you at least like to view?'

This had all come as a shock to John. Yes, of course he knew the time would come when he would have to start seriously not only thinking about the move but doing something about it. It was not fair to keep Gerald dangling. Once again, his thoughts turned to Selena, was it too soon? he feared it was. Suddenly an idea came to him, a compromise of sorts, after all if the villa was a good buy, then he wouldn't want it to slip through his fingers.

'I think you may be right Gerald, regarding the renting. As you know, I am very conscious of uprooting Selena too early, and we are only at the start of out period of mourning. A move like this I fear would be too much for her, but that does not mean I could not take it on as a rental with a view to purchasing. Yes, yes, I think it may be an excellent way of easing Selena into the move. She could come with me on my occasional trips here, Sarah I am sure would enjoy the change of scenery and after a few months she might like to invite one or two of the local ladies to take tea with her in the afternoon, I'm sure that wouldn't interfere with her mourning.'

Gerald was pleased with John's response and said if he would like to view and discuss arrangements before he returned to Yorkshire, he would at least be armed with details to impart to Selena on his return.

Two days later Gerald and John stood outside an imposing Victorian villa. The small garden either side of a brick red tiled pathway was immaculate, with neat lawns edged with shrubs and bushes just starting their spring to summer flowering. Black railings a top of a small brick wall gave the gardens security and seclusion. John was impressed.

'How much did you say he was asking?' John asked Gerald who on mentioning a figure smiled as he heard John's sharp intake of breath.

'But this is London.' Gerald reminded him realising his friend would be comparing it with prices asked in Manchester and Yorkshire.

'Yes, I suppose it is, and it certainly is a beautiful place.'

'And wait until you see inside. It has been tastefully decorated and is to be sold complete with furniture.'

'Really! Why is that?'

'The owners are emigrating to America.'

'My goodness me, well that really is a bargain isn't it.'

'Indeed, it is, one thing less for you and Miss Selena to worry about. Oh, and by the way, some of the servants are going with them, but a couple who do not relish the journey are not, so if you require extra servants, they would be happy to accept employment, and this means they come with good recommendations and references.'

'Mm, you have thought of everything Gerald. I think I would be a fool to walk away from this.' Gerald smiled and patting John on the shoulder, opened the gate.

'Then let us go inside and announce ourselves.'

The front door was opened by a sweet young girl in a grey dress over which she wore a crisp white apron. On her head she wore a frilly white cap and bobbed a curtsey when Gerald announced themselves. Taking their coats and hats and placing them on the coat and hat stand, she replied 'Yes Sirs, master's waiting for you in the drawing room if you care to follow me.

The young man who greeted them when they entered the drawing room surprised John at his youth, until he explained the property had belonged to his late parents now deceased. It had been left to him, but he was selling to fund his family's new life in New York where he had been offered a position in the world of finance.

Moments later the same young maid returned, and after knocking, trundled in with a trolley of tea, coffee, hot chocolate, and a selection of muffins.

John accepted the tea, Gerald the coffee and their host, who they now knew as Mr Jameson, chose the hot chocolate.

Having put Mr Jameson in the picture regarding his move to London and the fragility of his young daughter after the recent demise of John's wife, Jameson was more than happy to agree to a period of six months renting and a purchase thereafter.

Mr Jameson took John around giving him a guided tour of the house and gardens at the rear, and as he stood listening to the peace and quiet, a black bird high up in a Sycamore tree, trilled away. John knew Selena would love it here, given time.

The rooms were all of good proportion and in immaculate condition. The kitchen was of good size and his introduction to the cook and a mention of three other maids, who all bobbed curtsies, made John feel very much at home.

Discussions took place concerning monthly rental and a purchase price, which when John considered this included furniture, carpets, and window drapes, concluded it was very reasonable. Mr Jameson had already had his solicitor draw up papers for each agreement and John duly signed them, witnessed by Gerald and Mr Jameson's butler who it appeared was travelling to America with him. They discussed the servants who would not be leaving, and John asked if Mr Jameson could draw up their names and what role they played and let him have this before he returned to Yorkshire. He would then be in touch regarding which of the servants he would be able to employ.

By the time they returned to their factory, John was feeling so much more relaxed, and the move felt less traumatic than he'd previously feared.

More orders had been received while they had been absent, and an application from a young lady, who'd heard about John's idea of his 'Off the Peg', was requesting a chance to show her ideas for ladies' wear. 'Lady designers? What next?' Gerald asked.

'Well,' John replied. 'Why not. At least we could see her, look at her ideas, it wouldn't hurt.'

'Nothing ventured.' Gerald said.

'Exactly!' laughed John.

'Oh, I can see we are going to have a fine old time you and I John. I feel rejuvenated since we got together, I knew the day we met it was fate, I felt it in my bones, and now I know I was right. I think you and I are going to shake up the world of fashion! Now, when are you going to make this move? I need you' he said laughing. Gerald's excitement was infectious, and John knew he was right. It had been fate and yes, he too was eager to make the move and start this new adventure. Suddenly he felt happier and more content, certain in which direction he was going. He had had a wonderful marriage, but Mary was gone, and suddenly his loss and grief felt less. He knew Mary was saying ' Let go John, make your new life with our daughter.'

The date John had agreed with Jameson to take on the house would be the first of July so that gave him three weeks to sort out servants in Yorkshire and London, pack up what needed to be taken with him to London, confirm Joseph Turner's appointment as manager to his Yorkshire factory, and last but not least, convince Selena it was a good move.

To talk Selena into this, he'd derived a plan. It was simply to suggest she accompany him to London for a week's holiday, two if possible. He hoped with a bit of help from Sarah, Selena would start to look at her new home with some interest. A carriage ride in Hyde Park one afternoon might help, it would if the Queen happened along. But if Selena knew she could return to Yorkshire whenever she wanted, it might in time convince her that London really did have lots to offer. It was a long shot, but one which John thought worthwhile rather than forcing her against her will.

Four days later John took his leave of Gerald and headed home to Yorkshire but not before he and Gerald had interviewed a delightful Miss Amelia Johnson, a no nonsense thirty-five-year-old spinster with a talent for drawing, and not only drawing but designing. John had been impressed; Gerald concerned because she was a woman. 'But who better to design for the ladies, but a lady!' John had declared. 'Come on Gerald, you followed your instinct when you came after me, a man whose wares had been shunned by half the tailors in London. Follow my instincts now, after all you liked my cloth so I must have some idea. Why don't we give her a try, I must say I liked some of what she showed today, she has potential. What do you say?'

'Mm, I'll think about it.'
'Well don't think too long, we might lose her.'
Gerald nodded his head thoughtfully. Slapping John on the back he said. 'Okay my friend, you win. I will write to her saying that we were impressed but that you must return to Yorkshire, but on your return to London we will invite her to discuss some form of arrangement. There! How does that sound, no commitment, but a carrot of possibility.' John shook his head at Gerald's guardedness. It was the best he was going to get out of him now but at least it would hopefully keep Miss Johnson from showing her ideas elsewhere. And right now, he had a train to catch.

Arriving home, John was greeted with a sulky daughter which was unusual as Selena had never been a moody child. Perhaps this had something to do with going from a child to a young woman. John was too deep in thoughts of London to ponder further.

At dinner, Selena still looked cross, and John was about to ask her if there was something worrying her when she burst out. 'Well, when were you going to tell me? I am your daughter, yet all the world seems to know of your plans except me!' she cried angrily.

John was stunned, never had he ever witnessed such a tantrum displayed by her. He gathered his thoughts, trying to make out what she could be alluring too. Could she have found out about the house? But how. 'Come now Selena, whatever are you talking about?'

'Oh Papa! I am not a child!' At this, John raised an eyebrow. 'And don't you dare make fun of me!'

John held up his hands in surrender.

'Okay my darling. Now, why don't you calm down and tell me what it is that I have done or not done. And please Selena, stop raising your voice, it is not ladylike.'

Selena took several deep breaths, her lips tightly pressed together. 'While you were away, Sarah and I took a walk into the village and entering the village shop and post office, encountered William's wife who told us..........'

'Oh.' John interrupted.

'Exactly Papa, Oh indeed! I see you are not going to deny it, you know exactly what William's wife told me'.

'Yes, my dear I think I do, but I must tell you that when I spoke to William I was only......testing the waters shall we say, nothing specific, just an idea......'

'Well, it may have been an idea to you, but to William's wife it sounded like a definite plan! Can you imagine my humiliation when I, your daughter knew nothing of your plans, or were you leaving me behind?'

'No, no, of course not, I would never leave you behind. It was just......well, you know for some time I have known that to expand my business, I would have to live in London. All this toing and froing is not good for me or for the business. But I had to put all that aside when your poor Mama was so terribly ill. I could not bear the thought that something might happen to her and I would not be there to comfort her, so I shelved all my plans. But now......' He fell silent as both he and Selena remembered the sad demise of her Mama. Selena was calmer now when she spoke.

'I know Papa, and I am sorry I was so cross with you. But it just came as such a shock.'

' Let us finish our meal congenially then we can talk fully.

Later as they sat together, John told her about the house which Gerald had come across and how nothing had been planned, it was just one of those things. But as soon as he had seen it, he knew it was too good an opportunity to turn down and when Mr Jameson agreed to John taking it on a rent to purchase later, John felt he had to accept. 'I'm sure you'll love it, Selena. It's in a beautiful part of London, overlooking Hyde Park where ladies take carriage rides even the Queen, so I'm told. But the beauty is that whilst still in mourning, you can spend time here in Yorkshire and perhaps pay the occasional trip to Knightsbridge? It will give you time to adjust. What do you think? Will you try it?'

'And what if I do not like it, what if I never like it?'

'Then I will have no choice but to let you stay here. After all, I will not be taking all the staff as I shall want to return from time to time to check on my factory and workers here.'

Selena, slightly mollified, thought this over.

'Why don't you think about making a trip with me to London in September, for your birthday? I know it will be a low-key affair, but we can have a small gathering, Gerald, and perhaps by then I will be able to introduce you to a couple of young ladies your age who once out of mourning, would be able to introduce you to a wider circle. You must not think of cutting yourself off completely Selena, life does have to go on and your Mama would not want you to grieve for ever.'

Selena smiled sadly, nodding her head in agreement, there was such a lot to digest.

The following morning, before leaving for his York factory, John asked Mrs Harris to assemble all the staff in the drawing room at noon. Seeing the look of concern on her face, he smiled reassuringly. 'Please do not concern yourself Mrs Harris, it is nothing to worry about, just a few changes but nothing which will harm any of you. I understand there have been certain rumours flying about and I wish to set the record straight, so none have cause for concern.'

'Yes Sir.' Mrs Harris replied, sighing with relief, for she had been worried about her job.

In York, John was greeted with delight. All his staff, no matter what position they held, were always treated with concern and respect. John, an unusual employer, would remember if someone's husband or wife had been ill and ask after them. He would ask after someone's wife expecting a baby, then congratulate them. At Christmas there was always a little extra in their pay packet, unheard of and despised by other employers, but John took no notice of the snide remarks made in the company of those. He knew he had the right attitude and that he would get far more productivity willingly, from his workers than others did.

As he sat with Joseph catching up over a pot of tea, duly brought to him as soon as he sat down, the young man he'd left in charge reported on orders and work in general. Satisfied at what he'd heard, he asked Joseph to sit down and join him with a cup. There was something he needed to discuss with him and for now, he needed Joseph to keep it to himself as it was a case of irons in the fire not yet finalised. Joseph was intrigued.

John explained about his need to spend more time in London and his plan to live there and to this end was in the throes of purchasing a house. He assured him he would not be and never would be selling his Harrogate house in Yorkshire. This was his home, born and bred, and one day, God willing, he hoped to retire there. In the meantime, he needed to be in London but would from time-to-time visit.

'So, we now come to this factory.' John said 'As you know I have been leaving it in your capable hands, and extremely pleased at the way things have been going and knowing my workers are all happy is important to me. So, soon, I will be away for longer periods, though you can always contact me if you have any concerns. But I think it only fair to put your position of acting manager on a more permanent footing. I am therefore going to make you my official Manager, which should be shown in your remuneration for the extra responsibility. What do you say to that?'

Joseph was staggered but overwhelmed. 'Mr Elliot Sir, I hardly know what to say.'

'Well say yes lad if you want the job.' He replied jovially.

'Yes Sir, yes Sir, I am honoured, and I assure you I won't let you down.' He said jumping up from his chair and shaking John's hand excitedly.

'Good, good. And I know you will not let me down or I would not have offered it. Now, just remember, keep it to yourself, just until I have had a chance to speak to the workers and of course my staff at home. Unfortunately, there have already been rumours flying which unfortunately my daughter got to hear of and terribly upset she was too. So, I am off now to speak with the house staff, then I will return later this afternoon to inform the workers. Could you have them assembled by four-thirty for a meeting but tell them it's nothing to worry about.'

'Yes Mr Elliot of course Sir.'

'There was another matter I wanted to run past you, get your opinion on. When I was in London, a young lady approached my partner and myself, with a request we look at some of her ideas on fashion design, ladies wear you understand. Whilst my partner was not convinced, I liked the idea and saw enormous potential. I am calling it 'Of the Peg' garments made up in bulk ready to sell if you just walked in off the street. Imagine, I think it could catch on and of course it would not be as expensive as going to a dressmaker. It would give the less well off, the ordinary homemaker a chance to purchase fashionable attire at reasonable prices, what do you think?'

'I think it would be a wonderful idea Sir.' Joseph replied frowning. 'But who would make the clothes?' He asked.

'Ah, but that is where not only the ordinary lady would benefit, but ladies who already make their own clothes in their own homes. We would create an area in our own factory where they would come and work for us, making up such garments and getting paid for it.' He finished triumphantly.

A beam of a smile spread across Joseph's face. 'Now that is revolutionary if I maybe so bold to say.'

'You may indeed young man, you may indeed. Only keep that to yourself for the moment also. When I return to London next week, I hope to convince Mr Carney-Tompkins that we should put this idea into action as soon as before anyone else gets wind of it.'

'Yes Sir, yes Sir. We are looking at exciting times ahead Sir, how clever of you to think of this. You are on to something.'

'Well to be honest, it wasn't so much my idea as the young lady with the designs, Miss Amelia Johnson.'

'Yes, but you saw the prospects and had the vision to take it forward Mr Elliot.'

'Yes, you are right Joseph, you are right. Now then, I must be off, and I will return by four-thirty.'

When he had gone, Joseph sat down, staring out of the window. What a morning. First his promotion with extra pay, now this new idea, just wait until he told his mother. Hopefully, Mr Elliot would announce this at the afternoon's meeting, then he would be free to tell his Ma about all of it.

Joseph wondered if Mr Elliot would talk about the garment making? he hoped so as it would bring such hope to the community and much needed extra money into the homes of so many.

'Papa, where have you been, everyone is gathered in the drawing room, you're late' Selena admonished him.

'Yes, I know, I am sorry. Got a bit carried away in my meeting with Joseph. Anyway, I am here now.'

When John opened the drawing room door, the mumble of voices stopped. 'Good afternoon, everyone, so sorry I have kept you waiting. I promise not to take up any more of your time, I am sure we are all wanting to get to our luncheon. Now, some of you have no doubt heard rumours of a move to London for my family. This is true in part, but I wanted to explain and put your minds at rest that no one is going to be out of a job.' He then went on to explain about his move to the London house and his continued visits to his Yorkshire home and Selena's preference to only make small trips to London during her continued period of mourning. He laid out the staffing for Harrogate and London and assured them that in the event of Selena at some point making her home more permanent in London, there were no plans to sell his Yorkshire home as this was earmarked for his eventual retirement.

There were sighs of relief all round and the meeting broke up as everyone scurried back either to their work or to take their break. John and Selena retreated to the dining room where the maid immediately brought in their first course.

'What did Joseph make of your plans Papa?' Selena asked.

'He was incredibly pleased, especially as it involved a promotion and a small pay increase.' John continued telling her that he had discussed the garment making with Joseph who thought it an excellent idea. He was pleased when Selena showed interest in this, and surprised when she said she would like to meet Miss Johnson and wondered if it would be possible to invite her to Selena's birthday in September. John thought it an excellent idea and hoped this was the first sign that Selena was looking to the future.

At four-thirty prompt, John was back at the factory and as promised, Joseph had gathered all the workers for the meeting. Having reassured them there was nothing to worry about, for some there was still speculation. So, it was a great relief when they heard it from their employer's mouth, that the speculated move to London, was not going to put them out of work, on the contrary they had the feeling there was more good news to come, but what, he was not yet able to divulge but soon hoped to do so. They trooped back to work relieved and excited knowing there was more good news to come. Some tried getting Joseph to disclose information as they were sure he was privy to such, especially when it was announced that he, Joseph, was no longer acting manager but manager in full right. No one begrudged him his promotion and Joseph remained tight lipped.

The weeks flew by and when he was not in the factory, John was at home packing and deciding what should be taken and what of his personal possessions should be left.

William's position for the present would be that he remain in Harrogate as Selena may require his services. When William broached the subject of a possible move to London in the future, and that of his wife, who was keen for a position, John was honest with him and saying that yes, William would be required to make the move when Selena decided to go, and although John may take on the present cook in London, he was sure his wife's assistance would be welcomed and she would be able to make the move with her husband.

Satisfied that everyone, Selena, servants, and workers were happy and content with the arrangements, John headed back to London to assume residence in his new home.

CHAPTER 3

Gerald welcomed his friend and partner back with open arms. He had been mulling over Miss Johnson's ideas and had concluded John may have a point. As a result, he had written to her saying they were interested and he would contact her when Mr John Elliot, his partner, returned from Yorkshire. John was pleased when he heard this as he'd been concerned, he may have an uphill battle to convince Gerald it was the way forward.

John spent a couple of days at Gerald's home then on the first of July, as arranged, moved to his new home at twenty-two Park Avenue. The servants assembled in the hallway at ten o'clock on the dot, all eager to see what kind of employer this strange man with the funny accent, would make. He seemed a most unlikely employer, more like one of them. He spoke to each one as though they were his equal, was this a trick? they wondered. The only servants that hadn't left for America were Mrs Bailey the cook, three below stairs kitchen and parlour maids, a boot boy and a gardener and his apprentice. After greeting all of them he asked them one by one to come to his study and inform him of their duties and if they wanted, to ask any questions regarding their employment with him.

It was all very strange but within the month, they were beginning to get used to the new master's ways and all agreed he seemed like a good employer with an easy manner.

When Mrs Bailey asked if he would be employing a housekeeper, John had a sudden thought and replied. 'In time Mrs Bailey. When my daughter joins me, my groom William will come with his wife who will take on that role. Until then, may I presume upon you to take that on, on a temporary measure. I promise you I will not be entertaining at any great length as I am still in my period of mourning.' He hoped William's wife would be happy with the position, as he felt Mrs Bailey may bridal at the thought of having another woman in her kitchen, other than the maids already there. Mrs Bailey was quite happy to accommodate the new Master.

'I thought we might have an informal discussion with Miss Johnson one evening, get something organised.' Gerald said one morning to John. Looking up from the figures he had been studying, John agreed. 'May I be so bold as to suggest we christen your new dining room with its first dinner party?'

John frowned. 'Oh, I don't know about that Gerald, I am after all still in mourning.'

'Well, I wasn't thinking of anything frivolous, more of a business dinner, you know, get to know Miss Johnson better and officially offer her a position of designer.'

'Oh, I see, yes, yes, you are right. And the sooner the better or she may go elsewhere.'

Gerald nodded. 'So, shall I send a message inviting her, say for Saturday evening? I will send a carriage for her, what do you think?'

'Em, yes, I think it a particularly clever idea. I will speak to Mrs Bailey this evening.'

'By the way, have you heard from your daughter since you arrived?'

'Yes, yes Selena writes regularly. I think she's actually missing her old Papa, but she seems to be looking forward to coming here in September, which reminds me, I must write to William and ask him if his wife would like the position of housekeeper, if so, it may be prudent for them to travel down with Selena in September.'

Amelia Johnson was thrilled to receive the invitation to dine with Mr Gerald Carney-Tompkins and Mr John Elliot at twenty-two Park Avenue, Knightsbridge on Saturday the 3rd of August. A carriage would be sent for her at seven o'clock and would be at her disposal at the end of the evening. If she would care to bring some of her ideas and designs, the gentlemen would like to offer her a formal proposal to join their establishment as chief designer.

Amelia spent the next few days and nights feverishly gathering her designs, making notes of questions to ask and information to give and finishing off one of her latest gowns a cross between a day dress and a dinner dress. She had chosen a material which looked the colour of ruby wine yet when you moved it showed shades of blue. It was not quite off the shoulder but caressed them like a shawl. Not having a maid of her own who could dress hair, she called in a coiffure for the evening, she wanted to look her best, look professional.

When the carriage arrived, Amelia ran downstairs, snatching up her cloak and purse. Her mother was knitting and father already dozing in his rocking chair. She smiled excitedly at them as her mother wished her good luck and said to enjoy herself, they were immensely proud of her. Their general maid was waiting with the door open holding out Amelia's evening gloves. 'Have a good evening, Miss.'

Arriving at number Twenty-two, Amelia was helped down from the carriage and before she had reached the front door it was opened and there stood her two hosts waiting the greet her. Taking the portfolio from her, they ushered her into the lounge for pre-dinner drinks. As Amelia rarely took alcohol, she asked for tonic water. Talking to both gentlemen, she found was easy and comfortable. She knew Mr Carney-Tompkins was aristocracy, but he was like no one she had ever met before. He, like Mr Elliot treated her as an equal, they did not dismiss her as some silly female.

'What took you into design Miss Johnson.' John asked her.

'I sort of fell into it.' she replied hesitantly. 'My parents are very elderly and not in good health though they try hard not to show it. They had almost given up hope of having a family, so I was a bit of a surprise when I appeared late in their life but welcomed, oh yes very much welcomed. It is for that,......and other reasons, I have never married, preferring to take care of them as they took care of me.'

'Very laudable of you, I'm sure.' John said.

'When I was younger, a lady used to come to our house to make gowns for myself and Mother, and she used to leave scraps of material for me to make clothes for my dolls. That is when it all started. As I grew up, I started drawing garments that I dreamed of wearing, mostly ball gowns but later day wear. When our dressmaker passed away, Mother was in a quandary. She is a rather private person and was worrying about trusting another dressmaker and I suggested I sew her something.' Amelia laughed, 'I must be honest, my first effort wasn't exactly haute couture, but Mother said it was wonderful and encouraged me from then on to make her clothes and mine. Obviously as time went on, I grew better, which I hope you will agree.'

'Did you make the gown you are wearing?' Gerald asked.

'I did Sir.'

'Oh, come now I think we can dispense with the formalities of 'Sir' Mr Gerald, and Mr John I think as we will be, I hope, forming a working relationship.'

'Of course, thank you and you must call me Amelia.'

Just then dinner was announced. Over dinner the conversation turned to fashion ideas and the fashion industry. They were surprised to learn that 'ready to wear' had started with the Americans when they'd made uniforms for their soldiers, and as Gerald pointed out, men's wear had been available 'off the peg' as John like to call it, for some time, so why not women's.

After a pleasant dinner, they took coffee in the lounge and Gerald mentioned the business side of the arrangement he and John wanted to offer her.

She would have her own office, have free range of design ideas, though Gerald and John would have the final say. She would be contracted to them and only work for them unless at any time she wished to leave their employ. The remuneration offered almost made her gasp it was so generous and unexpected. Her hours or work were agreed, and she assured them her parents were able to be left as they did have a general maid and cook.

John spoke about his daughter Selena, and how he had recently lost his wife, and asked if Amelia would care to join them on the evening of Selena's fifteenth birthday. Although Amelia was somewhat older than Selena, John felt she might make a particularly good friend for his young daughter. Amelia was a steady, sensible, and caring young woman and he felt they would get on well together.

When they said goodnight, it was agreed Amelia would start work on Monday when they would have her contract ready to sign. Overall, it had been a successful evening and as John thought of it, the start of another adventure.

At the beginning of September, Selena started to get excited. She had missed her Papa more than she had realised. Yes, he had gone away many times in the past on business, but it had only been for a few days or at the most a week, and she always knew when he was coming home. His living in London now felt quite different and she didn't know how she was going to feel when after her birthday celebrations, she would be coming back to Harrogate without him. But then the thought of leaving her beautiful Yorkshire would also be a wrench. Oh, what to do?

She was looking forward to meeting Miss Amelia Johnson the lady designer her Papa had taken on. What must it be like to work in such a position alongside someone like her Papa and Mr Carney-Tompkins?

Sarah came bustling in one morning breaking into Selena's thoughts. 'Now Miss Selena, have you thought of what you are going to wear to your birthday dinner?'

'Mm. If I am honest, I am getting fed up with white, pale lilac and grey. Is that very disrespectful of me?'

'No lass, you're only a young girl your Mama would've understood. Em, I've an idea...I hope you won't be offended........come with me lass.' Selena followed Sarah out into the corridor but hesitated when Sarah opened the door of her Mama's dressing room. 'Come on lass, I think your Mama would approve of what I'm about to suggest.'

Following inside, Sarah went to the windows and opened the curtains. Selena stood watching and wondering what she was about to be shown. Sarah was rummaging in the closets, looking for something. 'Ah, here it is.' she said and drew out a hanger on which the gown underneath was covered with a sheet. Removing the sheet revealed a dress of cream silk, modestly cut with tiny pale pink rose buds attached and a wide sash of a slightly deeper shade of pink. 'We can take the rose buds off and change the sash, so it is more in keeping with your situation. What do you think?'

Selena stared at the dress. It really was a very pretty dress. 'But would it fit me?' she asked uncertainly.

'If it needs taking in, I can do it' Sarah said. Selena stood looking. Somehow, it did not feel right, which she knew in her heart was silly. What was the point of leaving Mama's things just to rot away, and wouldn't it be a bit like paying a tribute to her late Mama, to wear one of her dresses on her birthday? Still feeling a little reluctant, Selena agreed to try the dress on. To her surprise, the dress fitted like a glove, so all Sarah had to change were the rosebuds and sash which she swapped and replaced with pale lavender flowers and a sash of the same colour.

Three days before her birthday, Selena, Sarah, William, and his wife Kitty, all boarded a train for London. They would have gone by carriage, but John suggested the train to avoid stopping over at Inns on the road. He too could not wait to see his daughter whom he had missed. He was hoping it would not be too long before she agreed to make the move though he felt he would have to wait until she felt her mourning period was over. His mind drifted back to the previous September and Selena's fourteenth birthday, which had passed almost ignored because her Mama had been so ill.

John was at Euston station to meet them when the train pulled in and was thrilled when he saw his daughter alight from the carriage looking so grown up. Even in these few short months, she had matured. He supposed it was partly due to her being an only child and losing her Mama at a momentous time in her life as she went from child to womanhood. But there seemed to be a new maturity to the way she carried herself. He smiled as child or young woman, she still could not resist waving and running into his arms as soon as she spotted him.

'How was your journey?' he asked them collectively when they gathered around him. Selena had found it exciting, as had William but Sarah and Kitty had not been impressed, like a fire breathing monster they stated.

They took a carriage home but first, partly to mollify the two older ladies, John asked the driver to take them on a little tour of London. This did the trick, and they were in awe when he pointed out the Tower of London, the Houses of Parliament, St Paul's Cathedral, whom he proudly informed them was first built by King Erken Wald in604 AD, the later one designed by Christopher Wren and Robert Hooke. He pointed out Madam Tussauds which had opened in 1835 and promised to take the ladies to see the wonderful wax works. But the best was driving down The Mall and looking at Buckingham Place. John told them of the spectacle of The Changing of The Guard which had moved from St James Palace to Buckingham Palace when Queen Victoria moved in in 1837.

'My, my Papa, have you been doing any business since moving to London?' Selena joked 'Or just immersing yourself in London's history?' Everyone laughed but agreed, it was a fascinating city, and they were all looking forward to exploring it. John was pleased at the reception he was getting. and to know the more interest Selena could show, the sooner she may consider her move, he just hoped Sarah would still be happy to accompany her.

Their arrival at twenty-two Park Avenue was greeted in awe. Having seen how crowded, and in some parts dirty, London could be, they were pleasantly surprised. The Villa, as they were often referred too, stood on a leafy street, overlooking the beautiful Hyde Park. The gate opened onto the brick red tiled pathway and the gardens either side still had the last of the summer shrubs and flowers in bloom. The door was opened by George Wright, the footman, who John had kept on as footman and general help. John had explained he had no use of Butlers or Valets, and George was more than happy to work with this new employer as being a northerner, he seemed a lot more relaxed than some. Standing beside him was Mrs Bailey the cook who was nervous at the thought of meeting the woman who was going to be the new Housekeeper. John had explained to all the staff that when his daughter eventually joined him, she would be bringing Sarah, her companion and William the groom and his wife Kitty who was to be the new housekeeper. The three maids Clary, Cilla, and Brenda, smartly dressed in dark grey, with sparkling white aprons and mob caps, smiled brightly and bobbed a little curtsey when introduced. Selena was pleased the servants did not look down on them. She had had a horrible feeling that not being gentry, servants in London may look down on them she had heard tales of such treatment.

John asked George, Cilla, Brenda, and Clary, to help William take the ladies luggage to their rooms. He then gave Selena, Sarah, and Kitty a tour of the house, including the kitchen, much to Mrs Bailey's surprise, who bobbed another little curtsey.

He left them in their rooms to freshen up and said tea would be served in half an hour. Later, he showed William and Kitty to their accommodation which they were pleased to see was a small apartment over the stables, which were empty at present as the horses and previous groom had gone with Mr Jameson to America. For this trip though they were not on duty but guests getting used to the idea of London life, so they would stay in the main house. Kitty liked the idea of being a housekeeper, for which she secretly found exciting.

Over the next few days, John left Selena and Sarah in the capable hands of William to escort the ladies to wherever they wanted to go. At first, they found the hustle and bustle of London streets overwhelming and a little frightening but after their initial shock, they soon got used to it.

Though Yorkshire and Manchester had its fair share of factories and slums, all the ladies had been shielded from these. Perhaps it was because they had always been accompanied by Selena's father and Kitty by William, who knew where not to go in the North. Whereas in London, William was not so knowledgeable and therefore they occasionally found themselves in less salubrious areas. On one occasion they came across a place called Soho, where there were so many languages spoken and so many cafes and restaurants all selling foods from foreign countries, you almost felt you were in another country. The ladies found it a bit intimidating, William on the other hand was fascinated but soon had to retrace their steps as the ladies felt uncomfortable.

One evening Selena was thrilled when her father announced he was bringing home the following evening, Gerald, and Miss Amelia Johnson the designer they had employed and whom Selena was looking forward to meeting. Miss Johnson was neither servant nor gentry, so Selena was hoping she could make a friend of her despite the age gap.

Kitty Hargreaves decided one evening after dinner, to pluck up the courage and go down to the kitchen and ask Mrs Bailey when it would be convenient to have a chat with her during this visit. She wanted Mrs Bailey to know, Kitty's title of housekeeper, should not intimidate her and she hoped they could work well together and become friends. At the end of the day, she and William were the same as all those currently employed by Mr Elliot. In the event, Mrs Bailey suggested Kitty join her in her sitting room at three-thirty the following afternoon for a cup of tea.

Both women were nervous wondering how the meeting would go. When Kitty entered Mrs Bailey's private sitting room, she had the impression the older woman was a little bit prickly and knew she had to let her know that she, Kitty, was not about to start throwing her weight about.

Kitty was a quiet, easy-going sort of woman, so on entering, she gave Mrs Bailey a warm smile, and looking around congratulating her on making such a cosy, inviting room. Next, spying the delicious looking Victoria sandwich, she enthused, which did the trick as visibly Kitty noticed Mrs Bailey relax. 'Have a seat Mrs Hargreaves, would you like some tea and cake?'

'Oh, my goodness Mrs Bailey, would I? It looks amazing. So how long had you worked for the previous lady and gentleman?' she asked, cunningly hoping to give the lady time to talk about herself, always a good move Kitty thought. And it worked.

Mrs Bailey it appeared had worked first as a parlour maid, then a house maid and eventually, after being taught by the previous cook, she herself had taken over as cook and had done the job for the past twenty-six years. When the old couple died, and Mr Jameson returned from America, she and the other servants were really worried as to what was to become of them. After Mr Jameson announced he was selling the house, they all worried they may be put out of work when the new owners brought in their own staff. 'Imagine our surprise when Mr Jameson told us Mr Elliot offered to keep any servant who did not want to go to America. We could remain here and work for him. Of course, we did not know what kind of employer he would be, but so far, he's been a real gent and a pleasure to work for.' Kitty smiled. Now it was her turn, and she was pleased to note Mrs Bailey had thawed. Having complemented Mrs Bailey on her baking she began by asking.

'Mrs Bailey, do you think it would be too forward of me to suggest when in private we could be less formal? My name's Kitty.' Kitty held her breath, had she gone too far?

'Why Mrs... Kitty, I think that is a lovely idea and I'd be delighted. My name is Marie, and when you start your employment here, if there is anything I can do to help, please don't hesitate to ask me. Now tell me about yourself.'

Kitty told Marie about the years she and William had worked for Mr Elliot and the late Mrs Elliot and how devastated they had all been on her demise.' Such a lovely lady, so kind and caring. Of course, my husband William has worked for them longer, I only worked occasionally helping their cook, Mrs Harris, when they had parties or large gatherings.'

'So, you've never been a housekeeper before?'

'No, so I could well be asking you for advice.' This was said once again to put cook at ease and to confirm Kitty, was not going to get above herself.

'Did you not have a housekeeper in Yorkshire?' asked Marie in surprise.

Kitty shook her head smiling. 'No, when Mrs Elliot first married, she wanted to run the home herself, she wanted it to be just that, a home. Sadly, when she took ill, she only wanted those she knew, around her.

Thursday's Child

And as there were no longer any entertaining to be dealt with, Cou Mrs Harris and I managed if Mr Elliot ever had to entertain business associates to dinner, or Selena's birthdays, which Mrs Elliot would never allow those to be overlooked, though the last had been a quiet affair.'

'I should think not. She seems a lovely young girl, Miss Selena.'

'She is, very down to earth, well-mannered, and considerate. She will be missed in the town and surrounding villages. Speaking of which it is her fifteenth birthday Saturday week, yet we have no plans. As you know it's only a few months since her Mama's passing and Selena is keen to keep it low key. Perhaps you could advise?'

Marie Bailey sat up straight, pleased she had already been included in the plans for Miss Selena's birthday. 'Perhaps you could ask her what she would like, and if she wants to talk to me, I could always join you to offer some ideas.'

'I think that's a wonderful idea Marie, I will speak to Mr Elliot and then Miss Selena. Well, I mustn't keep you any longer, I know you have the evening meal to prepare but even whilst we're here as supposed guests, please don't hesitate if I can help in anyway, it must be an awful lot of extra work having us all here. Right, well thank you so much for our chat and the tea and cake, I feel so much easier now about our move.'

'It was a pleasure Kitty, it's put my mind at rest as well, knowing that you and I are going to get along very nicely. I can also pass this on to the others, who will be thrilled about our chat.'

CHAPTER 4

ST GILES, LONDON APRIL 1886

Reports to the police and notices placed around the streets, brought no information on the baby girl left on the Vicarage doorstep.

As time went by, Mark watched as Elizabeth and the boys bonded increasingly with the baby each day. He worried if this day would be the day when there would come a knock on the door with news of the real mother being found, and worse still, the mother herself wanting her baby back. Even the boys had begun to refer to the baby as "their little sister."

Four months had passed and there was still no news. One morning Mark made the decision, something had to be done regarding Thursday. To wait indefinitely was torturous, the longer the situation went on the worse it would be if the real mother did turn up. And how would they know if some strange woman claimed to be the mother, was the real mother? Also, there was the child to consider. The longer Thursday was in their care the worse it would be for her to be torn away from the Milton family, apart from Elizabeth, the boys too would be devastated. He would approach the local magistrate for advice.

When approached, the magistrate simply shrugged his shoulders disinterestedly. 'What do you want me to do about it? He asked.

Mark explained his concern if the real mother turned up to claim the child, they as a family would be devastated, and what of the child? What sort of place would she be taken back to?

The magistrate stared back at him. 'So, I repeat, what do you expect me to do?'

'Just tell me if I would be breaking any laws by keeping her, and how can we make sure no one can ever take her away from us?'

'There are no laws you would be breaking as there are not any covering this situation. Children, unwanted, illegitimate are regularly passed on or end up in an orphanage or workhouse. So, if you want it, keep it.'

'The child is a girl, a baby girl, not an *IT*!' Mark retorted angrily.

Bleary eyed, the magistrate stared back at him. He had little time for the clergy at the best of times, and this morning with the hangover from hell, he had even less for this pompous do gooder.

'Got a birth certificate, have you?'

'No, of course I do not have a birth certificate, I told you, the child was left on the doorstep of the vicarage!' Mark was becoming increasingly angry at this man's insolent attitude.

'Then I suggest you get one. Of course, it would make matters better if you put your name to it as the father, are you the father?' He asked with a nasty smirk.

Mark almost exploded at the insinuation. 'No! I am NOT the father, and how dare you insinuate such, such……., I am a man of the cloth! And I have a loving wife and three wonderful sons. How dare you Sir! How dare you!' Mark could not tolerate the magistrate's behaviour any further and turned, slamming the door behind him. Good job the door closed behind him, so the vicar did not hear the magistrate's remark. 'The Vicar he doth protest too much.' laughing at his crude insult.

Later when Mark told Elizabeth of the meeting with the magistrate, she felt part relief and part worry. 'So, you mean we must get a birth certificate for Thursday?'

'Yes, so it seems. This will ensure no one can ever claim her and take her away from us.'

Elizabeth bit her lips, frowning. 'But what if the mother was a good woman?'

'What good woman leaves a child on the doorstep of strangers?'

'Yes, but what if she was stolen?' Elizabeth said.

'And if she were stolen, don't you think it would have been reported to the police? And when they heard our story, do you not think they would not have come running to our door?'

Elizabeth nodded. 'Yes, you are right, of course you are right. So, what do we have to do?'

'Well, we have to go along to the registrar and register Thursday as being ours.'

'But she is not ours, how can we say she is?' Elizabeth said, the dishonesty as she saw it, concerning her.

'I don't like it any more than you do but it is the way things are done, according to the magistrate.'

'Oh.' was all Elizabeth could reply.

Mark went to get paper, pen, and Ink. 'So, when we go, we must make sure of the facts as we know them. Her name? What are we calling her?'

'Well, we've always called her Thursday.' Elizabeth smiled. 'Thursday's child has far to go.'

Mark nodded slowly, thinking. 'Yes well, I suppose that is as good a name as any. But if she had been born to us, she would not have only one Christian name, would she? She would have others, so what do you think, what other names shall we give our little girl?'

'What about, Elizabeth, and Mille after my mother and Rowena, after yours. Yes, Thursday, Elizabeth, Mille, Rowena Milton!'

'Brilliant.' Mark printed the names. 'Date of birth?'

'Well, we called her Thursday as that was the day, we thought she'd been born.' Elizabeth went to look in her diary, skimming back through the pages. 'Ah, yes here it is. Saturday the twelfth of December, I wrote only this.

I did not have time to write in my diary yesterday as in the morning the strangest thing happened. Our maid woke us in a terrible state saying a baby had been left on our doorstep.... so, if that was the Saturday, Friday was the day she'd been left, so Thursday, which would have been the tenth. That is it. Thursday was born on Thursday the tenth of December eighteen-eighty-five. Although it could have been the Wednesday, I suppose....'

'Unlikely.' Mark said. 'Doctor said as the umbilical cord was still fresh, the child could only be hours old.'

'That's it then, the tenth of December.'

The following morning, Mark and Elizabeth took baby Thursday and visited the registrar. He was not impressed at the lateness of the registration and scrutinised the couple suspiciously. It was only when Mark made to loosen his coat collar, exposing his vicar's collar, the man relaxed, accepting their excuse of Elizabeth having been extremely ill during and after childbirth. When mentioned it was their fourth child, the registrar was heard to mutter something along the lines that, 'better not have any more then.' Mark ignored him but the remark caused a hot flush to the cheeks of Elizabeth and fury at the man's rudeness, but they wisely kept their council.

Pleased to be out of the office, Elizabeth and Mark hurried home. They hoped not too much would be made of Thursday's arrival and continued stay at their home. Hopefully, given time, people would soon forget. If necessary, Mark would request to be moved to a different parish. There was only one last hurdle, and that was the boys. How to explain Thursday was now theirs, the little sister they had already come to love. Harry was the eldest at ten, he was old enough to understand some sort of explanation, Edward was eight, he should also be able to understand but Theo was only five. If they said nothing to Theo, he would just accept Thursday was still there, and in time would not remember a time when she had not been.

There was of course Maisy and the cook Mrs Morris, but Elizabeth and Mark were sure they would just accept Thursday was staying, just staying.

CHAPTER 5

PARK AVENUE, KNIGHTSBRIDGE
SEPTEMBER 1881

The birthday party had been a tremendous success and Selena had enjoyed it far more than she thought she would, despite it being low key. It was only towards the end when Papa had made a short speech saying how proud he was of her and how her Mama would be looking down on her, that made her remember. Mama was not there and would never be with her to celebrate all other future celebrations. An uncomfortable hush descended over the gathering and John realised that perhaps it had been inappropriate to have said what he did at that precise moment. Maybe it should have been said in private. The party had been a small gathering with Gerald and Amelia, and unusually included three servants, William and his wife Kitty, and Sarah, Selena's companion. Luckily, Amelia, dear Amelia as Selena thought of her, having quickly made a good friend of her, came to Papa's rescue.

'Well now, I do believe Mrs Bailey has a surprise for us.' She nodded to George who opened the dining room door with a flourish, as Brenda pushed in the trolley on which was a beautifully iced cake complete with fifteen candles which shocked and, for a moment frightened the assembled gathering. Mrs Bailey quickly stepped forward to explain.

'Please don't be scared, the candles have been sent by Mr Jameson from America as a birthday wish to Miss Selena. Apparently, the person whose birthday it is has to make a wish, and not tell anyone, then blow out the candles in one breath, 'tis a tradition in America, s'posed to bring good luck.' she announced proudly.

'Well come along Selena, I will stand by you, so you won't be in any danger.' Gerald said getting up and moving around the table, so he was beside her.

Selena stood up, slightly nervous but as Gerald stood beside her, she looked into his face and into his eyes, smiling. With Gerald by her side, she felt very brave and moved towards the cake. Gerald's heart had suddenly given a gigantic thump, which shook him as he reached out, placing his hands on Selena's shoulders. 'Don't forget to make a wish, and do not tell us. It must be a secret.' he said smiling down at her.

Selena shivered at his touch and knew at once what her wish would be and there was no chance of her telling anyone. Closing her eyes, silence fell around the table as her guests watched fascinated with this new ritual. Suddenly she opened her eyes and with a huge puff, blew out all fifteen candles in one go. There were cheers of 'bravo' and laughter and clapping, as Mrs Bailey held out a large knife. 'This is the finale bit of the ceremony; you must make the first cut. Mr Carney-Tompkins, would you help Miss Selena, knife's bound to be bit heavy.' As Selena slid the knife into the cake, with the aid of Gerald's hand over hers, a thought ran through both their minds, is this what it would be like cutting the cake of a wedding?

Later, as Selena and her Papa said goodnight to Gerald and Amelia, whom he'd brought and promised to escort home. They both thanked them for coming, and for their gifts and making Selena's fifteenth birthday such a happy one. Gerald had been kissing the hand of Selena when the words 'fifteenth' hit him like a sledgehammer. Of course, she was still a child, well almost, but she was on the brink of womanhood. Gerald stood tall clasping John's hand thanking him for the invitation and hoping he had not noticed the attention his partner had paid to his young daughter. He would have to pull himself together he admonished himself, what was he thinking of, there were years between them, far too many years. He should not even be thinking such idiotic, romantic thoughts, whatever would John think, he hoped he had not noticed. In the darkness of the carriage driving home, he flushed with embarrassment until he realised Amelia had spoken.'

'I'm so sorry, I was far away.'

'I said what a lovely party it was, exactly right I think under the circumstances.'

'Oh yes, I agree, exactly right. I believe you have formed quite a friendship with Selena.'

'Yes, we have. Mr John was worried she would find it difficult to make friends in London, so despite our age difference, he encouraged me to visit while she is visiting.'

'Age difference? Yes of course. But do you think that matters? Surely someone, a bit more mature is a good thing, a wise head.'

Amelia nodded. 'Yes, but one could also say that a more mature person could also be a danger to a young innocent girl, especially if one was not......how can I put it....'

'I know what you mean.' Gerald said kindly rescuing her from saying anything indelicate.

'And you Miss Amelia, is there no beau in your life, or am I being indelicate?' He asked laughing.

'Oh no Mr Gerald. I have quite given up any thoughts in that direction. I have a mother and father whose health requires me to look after them, oh please do not feel sorry for me. I have wonderful parents, whom I love dearly and enjoy being with. They themselves are concerned for me but I tell them, I am very content and happy with my life, and it is true. Though I must be honest, the opportunity you and Mr John have given me, well, I cannot tell you what joy it is to see my creations taken seriously. And I know my mother and father are relieved I have an interest outside of home.' As the carriage drew up outside Amelia's home, she turned to him. 'Thank you so much for this evening, Mrs Bailey even gave me two slices of cake for Mother and Father, wait until I tell them about the party. I will see you on Monday morning Mr Gerald, and once again thank you so much for this evening.' As the driver helped her down, Gerald inclined his head. What a genuinely nice young woman, but then he thought of the other young woman, girl, who'd stolen his heart that night. Where would it all end?

A few days later, John took Selena, Sarah, William and Kitty, to Euston station. Selena had surprised the staff in the London house by going below-stairs on the day of her departure, thanking them all for looking after them and making her visit a happy one. She would, she told them, look forward to the time she would return to make London her home, in the New Year, she added.

Kitty had said her goodbyes earlier and despite being treated as a guest over the last few weeks, had already been accepted by the other servants who agreed, they looked forward to working with her. Likewise, William was on good terms with Bert the gardener, his apprentice Ben and George, who all said they too were looking forward to having another man about the house. To many women 'ere Ben had joked which had earned him a clip round the ear by Mrs Bailey.

Selena was surprisingly sad as they journeyed home, but thinking about it, it was her Papa she was going to miss. He would not be home until Christmas he'd told her, which had surprised her, but she understood, he couldn't keep coming to Yorkshire especially now as he had a reliable Manager in Joseph.

When she mentioned her sadness to Sarah, her companion had suggested they concentrate on making plans for Christmas. This gave Selena a thought, which she voiced to Sarah. 'Do you think Papa will bring Mr Carney-Tompkins for the festive season?' Sarah turned in surprise and was about to reply, when she caught the dreamy look in her mistress's eyes. She froze in horror. Surely Miss Selena had no romantic notion in his direction, the man was years her senior. Why he must be in his twenties at least, far too old for such a young and innocently brought up young girl. 'Did you hear me Sarah?'

'Yes, I heard you Miss.....and I've really no idea. I 'spect the gentleman would have lots of offers for the Christmas season, him livin' in London.' Selena's face fell.

'Oh, do you think so?'

'Shouldn't wonder Miss Selena. Now, how about we start planning what we are going to do over Christmas?'

'Mm, yes.... I suppose so. But before we do, I think I will write a letter to Papa, as soon as we arrive home, just to let him know we arrived safely and look forward to seeing him in December, though it does seem an awfully long way away.'

Selena did write to her papa, but she also suggested he may like to bring Mr Gerald for Christmas, if he had no plans of his own.

The following morning, Selena suggested to Sarah they walk into the village and post her letter. Four days later she had a reply and bursting with excitement she read that Gerald had been delighted at the invitation to spend Christmas in Yorkshire.

Gerald had been struggling with himself ever since Selena had returned to Yorkshire. Before her birthday, when in her company, he'd just seen her as a delightful child, but now, suddenly she seemed to have grown up, blossomed into a young woman overnight. He had to keep reminding himself she was only fifteen. He almost felt scared as her father was his partner, and a particularly good partnership it had become. They both had their own strengths. If John ever got to feel Gerald had feelings for his daughter, what would he think? On the one hand he may be horrified, he dare not think his attentions would be welcomed, it was impossible, Selena was too young. Perhaps if she were older…then it came to him. Finishing school. If John could be persuaded to send Selena to a finishing school, it would give Gerald time to get over this silly fantasy, for surely that was all it was. And if he still felt the same on her return?

It was the idea of finishing school which made Gerald accept an invitation from Mr and Mrs Simpson -Wardour. Their daughter Jane had attended finishing school in Switzerland, prior to her coming out. Under normal circumstances, Gerald would have excused himself from their invitation as he'd had a rather embarrassing time with Jane.

The Simpson -Wardour's were a social climbing couple, intent on marrying Jane off to any man who happened to have a title. Jane however, had other ideas and made a beeline for Gerald whenever they met at any social event. She'd become even more insistent as her coming-out drew nearer. It seemed Miss Simpson-Wardour was determined to ensnare Gerald during her season, title or no title but luckily for Gerald, when her parents got wind of her infatuation they soon put a stop to it, warning Gerald off. When Gerald informed them, they had no need to worry as their daughter held not the slightest attraction for him, they were livid.

Now it seemed they were eager to invite him, as they saw it, to rub his nose into the fact Jane was becoming engaged to none other than Lord Cornelius Du-Barry. This overweight, penniless, fifty-two-year-old owner of a crumbling Castle, somewhere in the Scottish Highlands, was more than happy to take Jane's hand. Especially as with it came a very handsome dowry, which would not only shore up the Castle walls, but go a long way to clear his debts. It was his title which attracted the Simpson-Wardour's.

Initially, Jane had been quite flattered at his Lordships attention, though when the notion of marriage was put to her, regretted encouraging him. She was adamant she would not marry him. Tears, tantrums and threats of killing herself followed until her father proposed, unbeknown to Cornelius, that Jane should marry him, give him a couple of heirs, then she could divorce him, her father would see to that. By this time, he was sure that Cornelius would have spent enough of the Simpson-Wardour money, but Jane could still retain the title of "Lady" and the children would be in line to inherit the Castle. The Simpson–Wardour's had always fancied themselves in a castle.

When Jane heard that Gerald had accepted the invitation, she was excited and fancied that perhaps he'd had second thoughts and was green with jealousy and about to declare undying love and whisk her off to Gretna Green to marry her. Of course, it did not happen. Gerald spent the evening discussing the merits of different finishing schools with her Mama. Jane was apoplectic with rage when she also discovered he'd been making enquiries on behalf of Mr John Elliot for his simpering daughter Selena, who she'd seen out and about during Selena's recent visit to London. To add insult to injury, he had the audacity to approach her and

Cornelius when he took his leave, to congratulate them on their engagement!

Mrs Simpson-Wardour had at first been aloof, but as the conversation progressed, it was obvious to her that his enquiries concerned a young woman, and although he did not allude to any names, it was obvious it was the daughter of his new partner. He was the wool merchant Gerald had recently teamed up with. "Trade", she'd sniffed. Gerald Carney-Tompkins never would amount to anything, she thought. No, Jane had done well for herself and her family. Now society would have to look up to the Simpson-Wardour's when their daughter was a "Lady". Somehow, Mrs Simpson-Wardour was able to forget that her husband's money came from trade, all be it overseas!

Gerald had been thrilled to receive the invitation from John to spend Christmas with them in Yorkshire. On his few visits, he'd been surprised how much he had enjoyed the area. Before visiting, he'd always thought of Yorkshire as a wild, inhospitable part of England, but John and Selena had shown him the beauty of the undulating hills and valleys of the Dales, and the harsher Moors, but both had a beauty he'd never realised and it fascinated him, and Harrogate, where their house was, was stunning.

He wondered if Selena would ever be happy if she had to settle permanently in London. In the meantime, he felt Selena would benefit from a spell at a finishing school, though how to broach the subject to John without seeming to be telling him how to bring up his daughter, would have to be done sensitively.

The opportunity came unexpectedly when John, in conversation, asked how his invitation to the engagement party had gone.

Gerald, pulling a face, laughed. 'Oh, you know how these things go,'

'No, I don't. Remember, you're talking to one of the Hoi-Palloi! Trade my man, the dregs of Society, according to Society. Though what they would do without us I would like to know. In fact, what would the Country do without us? After all, it's trade that keeps people employed and the money they earn feeds families, which in turn pays rent to landlords' etcetera.'

Thursday's Child

Gerald patted him on the back. 'You are right my friend; you are so right. But that simple analogy passes many of them by.'

'But not so when one has a title and no money and another has money but no title, then it seems "Trade" suddenly goes unnoticed.' Gerald smiled, nodding in agreement. 'God help me for snobbery!' John continued, though he too was laughing at the ridiculous notion.

'And where would you stand if it were your daughter looking to marry?' Gerald asked lightly.

'Selena? Good lord, she is but a child, only just fifteen.'

'But emerging as a young woman. It won't be long before a gentleman may see your daughter as a possible bride. She is after all.......not only going to be a beautiful young lady on the outside, but she has a delicate persona about her. She is gentle, kind and extremely intelligent. I think she will one day make someone an excellent wife.' Gerald stopped here, thinking if he continued to verbally show his admiration for Selena, he may give the game away.

'Good heavens, do you really think so?'

'I do.'

'Oh dear. I had never thought of it like that.' John said thoughtfully. 'I suppose if her Mama had lived it would have been a quite different story. You don't suppose I've been holding her back, do you? I mean, I'd hate to think I'd neglected her growing up, been selfish thinking only of business.'

'John, John, John, my dear friend. Don't fret, you have done a wonderful job bringing Selena up, she is a well-adjusted, down to earth, young woman. She has a kind heart, and I have glimpsed a sense of humour despite her present situation. No, I don't think you have neglected her, but there is something I think it may be wise to consider. It came to me when I was at the engagement party of Jane Simpson-Wardour. I was in conversation with her mother who informed me of Jane's time spent at a finishing school in Switzerland, according to her it had done wonders for her daughter.'

John frowned. 'Really? And what do they learn at this finishing school?'

'Well, whilst one cannot fault Selena's manners, if she is to mix with Society in the future, which is bound to happen if she makes her home in London, there are certain rules of etiquette to be observed and I'd hate for Selena to ever be............'

'Poked fun at or ridiculed?' John interrupted.

'Quiet. Though to be honest, I think Selena is perfect as she is. But I think a spell away may protect her in the future.'

John nodded thoughtfully. 'You are right. I should talk to her. Perhaps when I return for Christmas, and when you come up you will be able to answer questions, she may have that I do not have the answers too. How would I go about finding one of these schools?'

'As a matter of fact, I noted the details of the one Jane Simpson-Wardour went too. If you like, I could send for their brochure, then you can take it to Yorkshire and Selena could browse through it.'

'Excellent idea Gerald, excellent.......' They were interrupted with a knock on the door by Amelia, and it was back to work.

In Harrogate, the weeks had flown by. Sarah had done a wonderful job of keeping Selena occupied with plans for Christmas. They'd spent hours making Christmas decorations, an idea brought about by the Queen and Prince Albert and making and buying presents and wrapping them.

Selena had been visiting some of the local elderly neighbours who found the wintry weather hard to deal with. She'd shopped for some and helped cook for others. The village school had had its nativity play and there were rehearsals taking place at the village hall for a pantomime which was to take place after Boxing Day.

Many of these festivities had also been introduced by the Queen and her Consort, Prince Albert who'd brought these over from Germany. These had soon been copied by those who could afford it, and to a lesser degree for those who couldn't. Mr Charles Dickens, now a popular published author, had his stories read publicly at Christmas, especially *"A Christmas Carol"*. Everyone delighted in hearing about the horrible Scrooge, who'd got his comeuppance.

Selena planned a special Christmas for Papa as this would be their first since Mama had passed and although Papa was in mourning, he wasn't strict and felt they had to get on with life, Mama would have wanted that. Also, with Mr Gerald staying, she wanted to give him an enjoyable time not a sombre one. Gerald, Gerald, she tried saying it quietly to herself, when would she be able to say his name without the formality required? Selena hugged herself, giggling about her little secret.

John arrived home three weeks before Christmas as he wanted to spend some time at the Yorkshire factory and catch up with Joseph. Things were going so well in London and Amelia had come up with the most amazing suggestion. At first it seemed ridiculous, but she was sure, a show of their outfits, where young ladies could walk up and down, could be well received, and she suggested approaching one of the new London stores
Gerald and John agreed Amelia could approach Whitley's of Bayswater and were astounded when she returned with an agreement and an appointment for her two bosses to meet with Mr William Whitley the founder. In the end it was agreed that Carey-Tompkins & Elliott would present their first "Off the Peg" range at Whitley's in the Spring of eighteen-eighty-two.
When Papa told Selena the news, she was extremely excited and wondered if she hadn't been too hasty rejecting the move to London. It would also mean she would be able to see more of Gerald. Then Papa presented her with a dilemma.
'Selena, I have a suggestion to make.' John said after dinner one evening.
'Oh?'
'How would you like to spend a year in Switzerland?'
At first the idea sounded exciting, Selena had never been abroad, although she'd read many books about other Countries, and Switzerland sounded and looked like the fairy tale she'd seen in pictures. But then her thoughts turned to London. She had almost made up her mind she would like to return there when Papa went back in January.
'Oh.' was all she could reply.
John didn't know what to make of her reply. 'What do you think?

Gerald suggested it may be good for you, for when you join me in London. Give you some ideas about what to expect when mixing in London Society.' Selena was shocked. Gerald had suggested Papa send her away for a year! In a foreign Country! What was he thinking of? Had she got it wrong? Had he been amusing himself, laughing at her girlish infatuation? Well, she would show him.

She cleared her throat so Papa wouldn't detect a note of upset in her voice. 'Gerald suggested it did he? Well, yes, I think it might be a clever idea, after all, when I come to London, I wouldn't want to embarrass either of you with my course country girl manners. Yes Papa, I think I would like to go to Switzerland very much, very much indeed. And now I think I will go to my bed. Good night, Papa.' And with that she was gone. John sat speechless at his daughter's obvious displeasure. What had he said to make her react so angrily? And the way she'd used Gerald's name, not Mr Gerald but Gerald. There was a familiarity about her tone. It was a mystery. It might be a clever idea to have Amelia speak with her. Then it came to him. Why not invite Amelia for Christmas. Why not invite her parents as well. That was it. He would write immediately and invite them and ask Gerald to accompany them when he travelled.

John decided not to mention Switzerland again to Selena, but he did speak with Sarah who at first was surprised but when he suggested she went with Selena as companion, thought it would be a pleasant experience for Selena.

After a few days, when Selena continued to sulk, John decided it would be a clever idea to inform her of the invitation he'd extended to Amelia and her parents. Selena seemed slightly mollified by this news and knew she would have to be happy and welcoming, anything else would make Amelia and her parents uncomfortable. As for Gerald, well she would certainly let him know what she thought of his little scheme to get rid of her for a year.

Just before they arrived, Selena confided in Sarah, her Papa's suggestion of finishing school and was surprised and at first a little angry, to discover she already knew about it. However, when Sarah told her, her Papa had suggested she should go too, Selena was a little more understanding. Especially when Sarah explained about all the fun she would have meeting with other young ladies her age, then of course there would be a chance to meet socially some young gentlemen. After all they would have to practice their social skills.

Mm thought Selena. Mr Gerald hadn't thought of that, perhaps she should inform him of this and point out how nice it would be to mix with "younger gentlemen" with the emphasis on "younger".

In the event, Selena threw off her mood in time to welcome their guests when they arrived for Christmas. Amelia had been thrilled to receive the invitation for herself and her parents to go to Yorkshire. They had never been this far north, and had eagerly read books about the area, absorbing the pictures. The scenery on their journey had not disappointed and having left the train at Manchester, had completed their journey by coach as William had been sent by John to meet them at the station.

By the time they arrived in Harrogate it was dark, and they were all tired, cold and hungry. As William drove the coach up to the front door, John was the first to appear, followed by Selena and the servants, all eager to get their guests inside by the warmth of the fire.

As William and the others took luggage to the rooms allocated to the visitors, downstairs in the kitchen, Mrs Harris was busy heating up the lamb hotpot and cutting large chunks of warm freshly made bread. As soon as it was ready, she sent word to the Master. John had revived the ladies with a glass of sherry and the gentlemen with a whisky. When dinner was announced, they all trooped into the dining room, although the Johnson's Amelia's parents, and Amelia, felt so tired they didn't think they'd be able to eat a thing, but the aroma of Mrs Harris's cooking soon had their mouths watering.

When the spotted dick, a fruity suet pudding, was placed in front of them, no one could refuse, especially when it was laced with the creamy yellow custard. Everyone declared it was the best meal they'd had for a long time and soon retired to their rooms with instructions from John not to rise early in the morning and to treat his home as theirs.

Selena retired soon after their guests, having kissed her Papa goodnight and bade Mr Gerald a curt goodnight. She'd barely spoken a word to him from the moment he'd arrived. Her cool interaction with him left him bewildered and bereft. What had he done to deserve her behaviour? He felt quite sad, so much so that he felt he had to speak to John, although he risked John's curiosity at his concern.

'Ah...I'm afraid dear Gerald, I may be to blame for that. As I said in my letter to you, I have discussed with Selena the opportunity for her to spend a year in Switzerland, and I fear I mentioned your input. I think she now blames you, sees it as you think she needs polishing or some such nonsense. I've tried to explain but she would have none of it, although she did simmer down when I said Sarah would be going with her. That's when I thought perhaps Amelia could talk to her, tell her what a brilliant opportunity she was being given.'

'I see. So that's why the invitation to Amelia and her parents.'

'Well, yes. I knew Amelia would not leave her parents at Christmas, so I thought why not? It would be a good opportunity for Amelia to talk to Selena and a pleasant change for Mr and Mrs Johnson.'

'Quiet. Although if you don't mind my speaking to Selena in the morning. I would hate for her to get the wrong idea. I wouldn't want her to think I was trying to get rid of her. After all, we will all be working and mixing a great deal in the future, and I would like us all to get on and be happy in each other's company.'

'I agree. Take her for a walk in the morning, weather permitting and clear the air.' John said.

Gerald said he would but at the same time hoped John would never regret encouraging him. As he bade his friend and partner goodnight, he wondered just what he could say to Selena to convince her he wasn't being unkind or dismissive without giving the game away about his true feelings.

The following morning was Christmas eve and after breakfasting, Gerald asked Selena if he could have a word with her. She refused saying she was taking Amelia to visit some friends in the village. Amelia looked surprised at this and shrugged but went and collected her hat, coat, and boots. Gerald was about to say he'd go with them but out of earshot, asked Amelia if she could put in a good word for him over this finishing school business. 'Ah,' said Amelia as the penny began to drop. She smiled encouragingly at him, patting him on the arm. 'Don't worry, I'll try and smooth things out, and as she won't be going until next September, after her sixteenth birthday, I think she will have a different attitude by then.'

As they headed in the direction of the village, Selena pointed out the school where she'd been educated, the church they attended and told Amelia stories about some of the residence, some funny some sad. Amelia kept trying to bring the conversation round to talk about Switzerland but every time she did, Selena somehow batted it away. As they strolled out of the village and walked along a country lane, Selena suddenly stopped and pointed out the hills and mountains in the distance, capped with snow. 'Isn't that just the most beautiful sight you've ever seen Amelia?'

Amelia stared at the view, when surprisingly, a lump came to her throat and tears sprang to her eyes. 'Oh Selena, it is...........if I ever lived here, I don't think I'd ever want to leave.'

'Why Amelia, I think you've fallen in love!' Selena joked with her friend. Through the tears, Amelia started to laugh. 'Oh, dear me, what a silly romantic fool you must think me.' She said wiping the tears away.

'Wait until I tell Papa, he will be thrilled that our Yorkshire has kidnapped you.' As the girls stood silently taking in the views, Amelia suddenly felt the time was right.

'Selena, may I talk with you, woman to woman?' Amelia asked.

'Of course, what is it?'

'Please don't think I'm interfering, and I may be wrong. But there is something I think you should know. That is of course if you haven't already guessed.' Selena frowned. 'Oh dear...' Amelia said. 'I hope I haven't got it wrong, but how do you feel about Gerald? What I mean is, do you, could you ......is there a chance, when you're older of course, you may find him a possible suitor?'

At this Selena tried to hide her face but not before Amelia saw a flush to the young girl's cheeks. Amelia put an arm around her shoulders whilst taking in the winter scene before her. Trying to comfort her she said. 'If it's any consolation to you, I do not believe Gerald is trying to dismiss you, on the contrary, I think he's trying to save you and give you time to know and understand your feelings. To be sure of the commitment you both could make given another year or two. Do not forget, Gerald is a good deal older than you, for him it would be so easy to declare, but you are so young and have had no experience of life as a young woman. He sees this opportunity of a year at finishing school as a chance to experience life away from home and after a year apart, well who knows. But if you both feel the same, that year apart will have proved you were meant to be.'

The words from Amelia were like music to Selena's ears. Slowly she turned. 'Do you really think he feels like that about me?'

'From what I have seen, yes, I think he does. But of course, he must be careful. I don't think now your Papa would welcome his attentions towards you, you are still his little girl. But given a year at Finishing School, your Papa will see the difference. You will have turned seventeen and he will see the little girl who went away, has come back a young woman, ready for the next step in life, marriage and motherhood.'

Selena was thoughtful, taking it all in. Holding out her hand to Amelia she said. 'Come on, we'd better be getting back, your mother and father will be wondering where we are.'

As soon as they returned, Selena excused herself from Amelia, going in search of her Papa. She found him in his study reading the paper. When she entered, she was pleased he was alone?

'Is Gerald not with you Papa.? She asked in a pleasant, easy-going tone. John raised a quizzical eyebrow, humorously. 'Noooo, Gerald is it now?'

'Yes Papa, you may not have noticed, but I have grown up.' John inclined his head still smiling. 'I have been having a talk with Amelia, about Finishing School. From what she tells me it could be quite fun, enlightening, although as she said she did not have the chance to go but has known others that have. She feels that it could help me when I move to London in the future. It appears they have some funny notions about certain types of behaviour, which could spare my blushes, being a Northerner. Although I think *WE,* could teach them a lot! And as I will not be going until next September, I will have time to get used to the idea.'

John laughed lightly, this daughter of his had a very dry humour and he was sure that in time, she would put a few people in their place. Being a Northerner was not something she would ever be made to feel ashamed of. 'So, it's alright if I go ahead and make arrangements then?'

'Indeed, it is Papa, but I would like you to discuss it with me along the way. Now, I must go and find our guest as I wish to have a word with him.'

'Fine. When you do find him, you might like to mention mass to him on Christmas morning. I've spoken to Mr and Mrs Johnson and despite the cold, they are looking forward to the occasion.' Selena gave a prim little nod of acquiescence and went in search of Gerald. As she walked through the hallway, Selena caught a glance of him through the window, walking back down the driveway, he had obviously been for a walk, good she would catch him before he entered the house. What she had to say to him was for his ears only. Snatching up a wrap from the hall stand, she ran quickly out of the house, running towards him.

Seeing Selena coming through the door and making a bee line for himself, Gerald halted, was he to get a further angry retort? he hoped not. So, he was surprised to see a bright smile light up her face as she hurried towards him. Once again, her very movement towards him made his heart dance. Oh, he so wished he could take her in his arms, but he must remain in control of his feelings. Removing his hat, he greeted her, relieved to see she no longer looked cross. She stopped abruptly in front of him.

'Mr Gerald, Gerald, I can call you Gerald can I not?' without waiting for a reply she continued. 'I went for a walk with Amelia this morning, we had a long discussion about my attending a Finishing School in Switzerland from next September, and I must say it does sound interesting. If I am to marry on my return, I must be ready and know how to entertain, I should not like to embarrass my husband or let him down in any way.'

Gerald was taken aback by this last. 'You are to marry on your return?'

he asked uncertainly

'Yes of course. So, I shall go, and when I return you have my permission to ask Papa officially for my hand, as I am accepting your proposal as of now. Until then, we may not speak of it again.' Gerald was left open mouthed as Selena turned to walk away, only to stop and turn back to him. 'Oh, and by the way, Papa asked me to remind you about tomorrow morning mass'. And off she marched leaving an astonished Gerald who started laughing. His laughter followed her, but he could not see the grin spreading from ear to ear as his future wife marched back to the house.

The Christmas festivities passed all too quickly. It snowed again when they went to mass on Christmas morning, but the little party including the staff thoroughly enjoyed it, this was the real start of Christmas.

On their return, Mrs Harris, with the help on this occasion of Sarah, flew into action in the kitchen. Anna, the Elliot's maid arrived with jugs a warmed spiced red wine and plates of spicy mince pies.

There was much talk about the service, little bits of light gossip and lots of laughter when Anna appeared and said Luncheon was served. They all trooped into the dining room and an array of dishes, with golden roast potatoes, sautéed red cabbage, carrots, parsnips, peas and beans which had been bottled by Mrs Harris in the summer

John stood proudly sharpening his carving knife as he carved first the goose, then the beef. They helped themselves to all the vegetables and rich thick jugs of gravy, and everyone agreed, Mrs Harris had excelled herself. When she later entered with the flaming plum pudding after the main course had been cleared away, followed with jugs of thick cream, they all patted their stomachs declaring they couldn't eat another thing, but they did. As the guests tried to find the silver sixpence hidden in the pudding, which would bring them luck, a shout went up as Amelia was the one to find it.

When everyone retired to the drawing room where presents were handed out, John made his way below stairs with a bag of presents, each labelled for the servants. These presents were usually given out on

Thursday's Child

'Boxing Day' traditionally the day servants would have off, often returning home to visit family. 'Now please, enjoy your dinner.' John told them. 'And enjoy your day off tomorrow.' Having thanked him, they tucked into their meal, all excitedly talking about seeing family the following day or just having a day of rest.

With no servants, Selena and Amelia helped Mr and Mrs Johnson pack their belongings, ready for an early start the following morning for their journey back to London. Mr and Mrs Johnson had been overwhelmed with the hospitality they'd received and said so, thanking John over and over.

When William brought the coach round the next morning to start loading the luggage, Gerald was able to snatch a quick goodbye with Selena who looked him in the eye and coquettishly whispered. Until we meet again.' But Gerald wasn't the only one to have a twist of the heart. As John said goodbye to Mr and Mrs Johnson, who thanked him profusely yet again for a wonderful Christmas, he realised how much he was going to miss the company of Amelia.

John stayed in Yorkshire for the next few weeks whilst he made arrangements with the Finishing School which Selena had chosen to attend. During his stay, he busied himself at his Northern factory. Joseph was pleased when he was told they would need to employ more staff both in the carding and weaving factory and to train machinists.

Selena and Sarah spent the first few months of eighteen-eighty-two with trips to the London house and back to Yorkshire. On her London visits, Selena purposely avoided, where possible, meeting up with Gerald. Although she frequently encountered Jane Simpson-Wardour who she soon came to view as a rather silly, spiteful woman, who seemed intent on making snide remarks about Gerald, and bragging about her up and coming marriage to a Lord.

At the beginning of September, Selena and Sarah travelled to London, and after a couple of days rest, set off with Selena's father who would see them safely to Switzerland.

All three, John, Selena and Sarah had mixed feelings over this period of waiting, sometimes concern at others excitement. John was particularly anxious for the two women not to be making the long journey on their own.

CHAPTER 6

SWITZERLAND APRIL 1883

Selena gazed out onto the now familiar scene. The snow was still heavy on the mountains but less so further down. If she thought Yorkshire was cold, it was nothing like Switzerland, although it was a dryer kind of cold, and the sun seemed to shine more often even in the winter.

She had settled well into the routine of the school, made friendships, but her two best friends, a German girl Heidi, and Marie-Lore, who was from France, both spoke English. This was an immense help as when Selena started her language course, both girls were able to help her. At first Selena thought she'd never get to grips with these strange foreign sounds, and Sarah didn't help as she muttered away that it was a lot of hocus-pocus, and as she saw it, a waste of time.

Selena grew quite angry with her and after a quarrel during which she'd told Sarah if that was how she felt then she shouldn't have come, found Sarah crying. It appeared the elderly lady had become quite homesick for Harrogate and wished she'd never agreed to accompany Selena, who seemed equally fed up with her companion. Selena felt guilty at her behaviour and apologised for her outburst, suggesting to Sarah that if she wished to go home, Selena would write to Papa and arrange it. But Sarah declined Selena's offer, feeling it would have been a dereliction of duty. So, the pair called a truce with Selena promising to be a bit more understanding.

There were all sorts of classes, some of which Selena found interesting, some rather silly and unnecessary. Most of the girls had moved in aristocratic circles so a lot of the etiquette was already known to them, however, some of it sounded silly and over pretentious to Selena, a down to earth Yorkshire girl. She wondered if she even wanted to make her home in London and mix with so called Society, she thought that life in the North appeared more straightforward, more normal, but then if she envisaged a life with Gerald, she was going to have to mix with Society, especially as her father and Gerald's business seemed to be gaining strength.

The classes she liked most were flower arranging, and menu planning, though she was disappointed she wasn't allowed to cook, one would be expected to employ a cook and a housekeeper. True, they had a cook in Yorkshire, but her Mama had often helped in the kitchen, and Mrs Harris had helped Selena when she was a little girl make and decorate small cakes and biscuits. She was beginning to see there were two different worlds, three if you counted the poor.

She also enjoyed the dance classes, but not the singing, it appeared Selena was tone deaf and had her giggling uncontrollably with her class pals, much to the annoyance of the music tutor, a rather strict, fussy little German man. She was also hopeless at painting and drawing and her efforts at painting the goats that roamed the mountain sides, unrecognisable. She was able to walk well, and out shone all the other girls when they had to walk about with books piled on their heads.

Selena wrote regularly to her father and to Amelia, who wrote back. She was pleased the fashion show had been a great success and hoped there would be others that she would be able to attend.

Most of the time, her life at the school went fast, mainly because there was so much to learn, so many classes to attend and when they were not in class, they spent many hours in their rooms studying.

One of the things Selena did enjoy was the time spent in conversational German or French. This was when she, Heidi and Marie-Lore would get together in the sitting room and practice their language skills. Selena was surprised how quickly she'd picked these up and was soon speaking the two new languages like a native. She'd even started writing home in her new languages which although her father was proud of her achievement, asked her to send a translation otherwise he would have to give all her letters to Gerald to translate. This surprised her as she had no idea Gerald could speak any other language, what a dark horse my Gerald is she thought. And when she thought of him, a little thrill, as well as fear, ran through her, would he still feel the same about her? She was even more convinced that Gerald was the man for her. Despite the years between them, or maybe because of them, Selena knew she loved this man with all her heart and longed for the end of the year so she could be with him again. Next Christmas, Selena had set her heart on announcing their engagement, but what would dearest Papa say to that, should she start to hint at her feelings in her letters? Or would that put Gerald in an awkward position? No, she would have to restrain herself, content herself with learning and be patient.

One of the recreations they had, was the occasional ball. These were held at various homes of wealthy Swiss families, and always in attendance were young men from the universities, officers, or the sons of the families looking for potential matches. Although Selena enjoyed these occasions, she didn't always like the attention of the young men, often finding some of them pompous or boring. All too often she would compare them to her beloved Gerald and find them sadly wanting.

As Spring moved into Summer, and Summer to Autumn, Selena started to count the weeks. She realised she would miss Heidi and Marie-Lore, but the girls vowed to keep in touch. Selena had been lucky enough during the summer break to spend time at Heidi's home which was a castle called a Schloss in German. It was in a beautiful part of Germany, called the Black Forest. Later the two girls travelled, with their companions, to spend time at Marie-Lore's home in the Loire Valley region of France. Marie-Lore lived in a château which reminded Selena of a fairy castle.

Sarah had been overwhelmed at the grandeur the two girls came from and hoped it wouldn't have made Selena discontented. She needn't have worried, Selena was still the down to earth, typical Yorkshire lass, nothing, it seemed was going to change her.

In September, Selena celebrated her seventeenth birthday, and although the school made the day special for her, as they did for all the girls, Selena missed her father and of course a sadness thinking of her dear Mama came rushing back. Would she ever come to terms with her loss? Perhaps in time when she married and had a family of her own. This inevitably brought her thoughts back to Gerald, which made her smile to herself, and fleetingly wonder if he still felt the same about her as she did about him.

There were times when she almost confided in Sarah but held back thinking her companion would not approve. She would have been surprised if she'd known Sarah already had her suspicions in that quarter, and she did not approve. In her opinion, Mr Gerald was too mature for Selena and too worldly wise.

Back in London, the business of Carney-Tompkins and Elliott was taking the capital by storm. Since their Spring fashion show the previous year, there had been others, and the stores were clamouring for their designs. Amelia was also becoming a notable name in the industry for neither Gerald nor John had tried to hide the fact, the designs were hers, with a little input of theirs of course!

At first, some Society Ladies had looked down their noses at such a notion of 'Off the Peg' garments and stoutly refused to entertain them until their husbands got wind of the reasonable cost of such garments. Their argument was for the price of one personally made dressmaker garment, they could get two of these 'Off the Peg'. This idea started to take off, although the original idea backfired when wives and daughters took to the stores and the husbands and fathers received the bills!

Jane Simpson-Wardour was not persuaded especially as her attempts to attract Gerald Carney-Tompkins had failed and she was forced to accept the hand of Lord Cornelius Du-Barry.

When Gerald appeared at her engagement party, she'd made her last-ditch attempt to sway him, but it appeared he was more interested in gleaning information about Finishing Schools for that silly little

Northern girl. Surely, he wouldn't stoop so low as to be thinking seriously about her. Or perhaps it had something to do with his business partner, the girl's father? Whatever, Jane's parents, she knew would not have welcomed such an alliance, but for Gerald, Jane would have defied them.

By now, wedding plans were well on the way, again. Originally it had been planned for June, but Lord Du-Barry had been taken ill and after an operation, needed convalescence. So, everything was postponed. The wedding would now take place in December, but as long journeys were out for his Lordship, the wedding would take place at his Castle in Scotland, much to Jane's disappointment. She was hoping to make a big splash in London, make it the Society wedding of the year, but this was not going to be, so she would make sure Scotland knew how the English did weddings. If her parents were so eager for their daughter to marry for a title, then they could jolly well pay for it.

The invitations had gone out and Gerald was surprised to receive one. Mr & Mrs Simpson-Wardour did not object when they saw Jane had added his name to the list, as they thought it would let Mr Carney-Tompkins know, despite his having some blue blood in his veins, he didn't have a title and was therefore not good enough for a daughter of theirs!

Gerald had already accepted the invitation when John came in one morning to say that he had received a letter from Selena to say she would be travelling home the first week in December and should arrive in London on the twelfth. Gerald's heart dropped like a stone. He wouldn't be here to greet her. Selena should have returned in September but had accepted invitations to spend time in Germany and France with her two new friends. Jane's wedding was on the fifteenth and it had been arranged he would travel up with a party on the tenth. All he could do was leave her a letter explaining. Although they had written to each other during her absence, the letters had been friendly and without any suggestion of romance. Clearly Selena did not wish her father to guess her intentions, so if he saw the letters, which Gerald never attempted to hide, he would have no idea. Gerald just hoped when it was made clear to John their intentions towards each other, he would not object.

It was arranged that once again they would all go to Harrogate for Christmas and Amelia and her parents had been invited for the second time and accepted, as they'd had such a lovely time before. The Christmas Selena was in Switzerland, John and Gerald had been invited to spend it with Amelia and her parents, John was pleased as he was not looking forward to being without Amelia for so long, but he'd missed his daughter badly, Christmas just wasn't the same without Selena. These past few months, John and Amelia had become increasingly easy in each other's company, and John had begun to worry about what life would be like when Selena married as some day she would. True, he had the business, but what of the future? It could be a lonely life for a man on his own, and he was still only a young man at forty-eight.

Gerald was off to Scotland but would come down to Yorkshire on the seventeenth for Christmas. He too was looking forward to Christmas in Harrogate, not to mention seeing Selena again. He didn't dare risk leaving a letter for her, instead he said to John on the morning he left.

'You will apologise to Selena for me won't you, tell her I'm so sorry that I wasn't here to welcome her home and I look forward to seeing her in Harrogate. Tell her.... tell her I have a special present for her.'

'Oh......?' John said, but the query in his tone was not answered.

'See you on the seventeenth.' He said gaily and went to climb aboard the hackney carriage which arrived to take him to the station where he would meet the rest of the party heading for Scotland.

The London servants were more than happy when they knew they wouldn't be required at Christmas. It meant that those who had family nearby could return home and Mrs Bailey could have a nice quiet Christmas. She would just have to cook the odd meal for the servants who were staying. William and Kitty were thrilled to be going back to Harrogate, and although they'd had to give up their cottage when they'd moved to London, would be staying with Kitty's parents, and William would be on hand if Mr Elliot needed him.

In Harrogate, Mrs Harris and the staff were looking forward to having everyone back, and plans were already being made for the festivities, and guest rooms being given an extra airing and cleaning. Selena was almost sick with excitement when the train pulled in at Euston station on the morning of the twelfth. Leaping from the train, she rushed into her father's arms.

'Papa, Papa!' then burst into tears

'Whatever is it?' he cried.

Sarah caught up with them. 'Now't to worry about Mr Elliot, it's Selena, she's been that excited, she's almost made herself sick. Now calm yourself Miss, or your Papa will wonder what on earth's 'appened.'

'Sorry Papa, Oh I'm so sorry, I didn't mean to frighten you, it's just as Sarah says, I'm just so excited, I've missed you so much.......' Looking about her, she realised Gerald was nowhere to be seen. 'Where's Gerald?' she blurted out.

'Ah, he sends his apologies but said to tell you he'll see us all in Harrogate on the seventeenth.'

'The seventeenth? But why Papa, why isn't he here?'

John was a little perplexed at his daughter's concern as to why his partner was not there to meet her.

'Well, he'd accepted an invitation to a wedding before he knew you were coming home and couldn't very well cancel.'

'A wedding? Who's wedding and where is it?'

'Ah, well, you see that's the thing, it's in Scotland.'

'Scotland!'

'Yes, Scotland. Apparently, it was supposed to happen in June but had to be cancelled due to Lord somebody or other had to have an operation, then he had to get better, and anyway it's going ahead now on the fifteenth of the month, and Gerald will travel down to Harrogate on the seventeenth. Oh yes, and he said to tell you he has a special present for you. Now come along, let's get home and get out of this cold.'

'When are we going to Harrogate Papa?' Selena asked after greeting William and climbing aboard their carriage.

'The day after tomorrow. Mrs Harris and Anna are expecting us, and Amelia and her parents are coming up on the twenty first.'

'Oh goody, I do like Amelia, and her parents are such lovely people. I think they like the bit of pampering they get when they come to Harrogate.'

'I am sure they do. Now you must tell me all about your time in Switzerland.'

'I think I told you everything in my letters Papa.'

'Yes, well you certainly sounded busy. But did you find it useful?'

'Yes, I think so, though I do think some of the etiquette a little pompous, but I suppose if we have to mix with Society as your business status grows, at least I won't show anyone up.'

'I do not think for one moment you could ever show me up not now or before. And what about you Sarah, how did you find the experience?'

'Well, it was certainly that Sir, an experience. Especially when we went to stay with Heidi in her 'Schloss' and Marie-Lore in her 'Château', my, my, you should have seen the size of 'em, and the rooms, dozens of 'em.'

'Yes, well, we do have some rather large houses in this Country.' John reminded her.

'True, but I like our homes in Harrogate and Knightsbridge, they're big enough for me.'

All the staff were lined up at their Knightsbridge home, to greet Selena and Sarah on their return. They eagerly awaited their chance to have a good old natter with Sarah about her experience. Sarah on the other hand just wanted a cup of tea and a rest, the journey had been long and tiring, but she promised to catch up with them the following day.

With Gerald away, John had to go into work the following morning but left instructions what was needed for their journey home to Harrogate. William and Kitty set about organising themselves but when Sarah entered the kitchen, she was told to sit down and tell them all about Switzerland. Mrs Bailey promised to send Brenda to help pack for Yorkshire after she'd told them about her adventures. Secretly, Sarah was rather enjoying the attention. She told them about the journey to the Finishing School and when they got there all the different things Selena had to do. And when she described her visit to a German 'Schloss', Castle, she explained, and then the French 'Château' not to mention her visit to the wine cellars as Marie-Lore's father owned a vineyard, their mouths dropped open, and their eyes were out on storks.

She didn't bother to mention her homesickness, just the good bits, the balls they'd attended, and the German and French languages Selena had to learn, now speaking it like she'd been brought up to it. Neither did she mention the horse meat she'd eaten in France thinking it was beef, until she was informed by the French cook otherwise. She told of the magnificent pastries the cooks in both Germany and France made but again didn't bother to mention the frogs' legs and snails the French were partial too, though thankfully she'd not been offered those.

She described the scenery, the snow-covered mountains in winter, visited by skiers and in the summer, those same mountains where goats and cows with bells round their necks, roamed freely. By the time she'd finished, she was quite proud of herself for sticking it out, when at the time she would have given anything to come home, but she wouldn't tell them that!

Their reactions had spread from being scared and admiring of Sarah's bravery to envy and feeling that she was inclined to show off. None the less, when Mrs Bailey sent Brenda to help Sarah get ready for their return to Harrogate, the housemaid was so full of questions, it made Sarah's head spin.

With everyone busy, Selena noticed a couple of letters addressed to her, sitting on her dressing table, one had a foreign stamp on it and when opened, she was delighted to see it was from Heidi who had written in English and asked Selena to reply to her in German. Selena decided to reply to her friend that morning and also send a letter in French to Marie-Lore. The second intrigued her as she did not recognise the writing but was thrilled, when opened to discover it was from Gerald, and this letter had a tinge of mystery and dare she believe it, romance?

My Dearest Selena,

I hope I may address you as such. It has been such a long time, over a year. I do admit, you have been sorely missed, not only by myself but by your Papa and your friends.

I hope you enjoyed yourself in Switzerland and the instructions were not to gruelling, but knowing your cheerful disposition, you would have found some humour in it to get by.

Your two friends sound delightful, you must stay connected with them and perhaps one day, we may be able to return their kind hospitality.

I am so sorry I was unable to greet you on your return but hopefully your Papa will have told you I had accepted a previous invitation before I knew the date of your return. I expect he told you it was to the wedding of Jane Simpson-Wardour, and I thought, from a business prospect, it would be impolite to refuse, especially as arrangements had been made to travel with a party of others. However, I look forward to another happy Christmas.

Yours Truly
Gerald {*PS. I have a special surprise, I hope you like it*}

Selena read it and re-read it six times. Excitement bubbled inside her. The surprise? What could it be? And his reference to the friends she had made, he had written, *WE* when talking about returning their hospitality! She searched the page for other clues of his intentions, his feelings. He had written, *My Dearest!* He'd never addressed her so before in his letters to her. She hugged his letter to her, dreamily staring into space until there was a knock on the door and Sarah entered.

'Why lass, whatever ails you?' Sarah said as she entered. Selena realised that she'd jumped when Sarah had entered.

'Oh, it's nothing Sarah, honestly.... I was just.... thinking about my time in Switzerland. I have had a letter from Heidi. She's written in English and asks I reply in German, which of course I will do, and one to Marie-Lore, I must write to Marie-Lore, in French of course.'

'Is that it?' Sarah asked nodding towards the letter Selena was clutching to her chest.

'Mm....Oh...yes, Now, did you have a nice talk downstairs? And are they envious of your travels Selena asked, eager to change the subject. Sarah was soon drawn from asking further questions as she chatted about her tales to Mrs Bailey, and the maids. There was another knock on the door to announce Brenda who had been sent to help Sarah as promised. Selena took the opportunity to make herself scarce saying she would be in Papa's study writing to her friends. Quietly picking up the letter from Heidi which she'd discarded on her dressing table, she slipped out of the room leaving Sarah and Brenda to the packing.

In Scotland, Gerald was already getting board. He'd been there for four days, and all the gentlemen wanted to do was hunt and ride. The riding was fine by him as he enjoyed the beauty of the area, but hunting was not for him, perhaps it was because he was a city boy and although some of Society's blue blood ran through his veins, he had never been one to mix socially with them, especially after his family's attempts, and almost succeeding, in ruining the family business. Where once Gerald's family had been the owner of a large estate and Country houses, they were lucky to have retained the present home in Mayfair. If it had not been for Gerald's quick thinking and grasping the remnants of his family's wealth in the wool industry, they certainly would have been destitute. On the death of his parents, at the age of eighteen, Gerald had no knowledge of the family's dire position. But the quick-thinking young man had soon learnt. He'd thrown himself into the industry, asked questions of those who worked for him and soon gained their respect. His interest in the workers lives, their living conditions, poor pay and worse, their treatment by employers such as his father, were sickening. Gerald's determination to improve things for them initially was disbelieved but over time when they saw that by working with him, he would pass the success on to them and improve their lot. His words and deeds had come true, he was now a well-respected and highly regarded man of business, though some in Society disagreed with his methods, saying he was belittling the ruling classes and warning him he would rue the day he started molly-coddling his workers. And when he'd teamed up with a Northerner, one John Elliot, they threw up their hands in despair, whatever next! They screamed.

Through all the insults, the snubs he'd had to endure, Gerald continued to treat his workers as human beings, he'd come too close to poverty and degradation not to know that in life, every human being was important. Because of this, he was never without workers, good, loyal workers.

He'd accepted this invitation as all acceptance back into Society he felt, should not be refused if he wanted to continue building his business. His Jewish contacts had been a wise move as they and he had gained recognition and reputation for highly regarded garments, with many members of parliament now regular clients. However, these sorts of gatherings, important though they could be, could soon become hard going as he often had to turn a deaf ear to some of the unpleasant, often sarcastic remarks aimed at him.

It was the eve of the wedding and Gerald had escaped into the grounds of the castle. Despite the cold, he'd wandered out to look around, shaking his head in despair at the run-down condition of what had once been an incredible building. An owl twit-ta-wood in the night air which made him smile. Footsteps caused him to turn suddenly, only to come face to face with the bride to be, Jane.

Gerald always felt uncomfortable in her company, as she had made no secret in the past of her intentions towards him, though these had been repeatedly rebuffed, much to her anger. Her behaviour bounced from charming and flirtatious to anger and sarcasm when her advances had been ignored. He sighed heavily, surely, she wasn't going to try and coerce him at the last minute.

'Dear Gerald......so pleased you could come. How are you?'

'Jane.' he inclined his head. 'Already for your big day?' The girlish smile she had, slid from her face. He felt her cold eyes boring into him as her mood changed. Gerald took a sharp intake of breath and stepped back.

'Don't worry.' she said with a harsh edge to her voice. 'I'm not about to throw myself at you. Why would I? After all, why would I give up all this and a title for a washed-up little factory owner.' she smirked, her laugh spiteful.

Thursday's Child

Gerald looked at the crumbling castle walls and couldn't hide the smile as he looked up critically. 'No, I see what you mean.' his tone of sarcasm didn't escape her as she rounded on him.

'Oh yes, you can sneer, but it won't always be like this. You wait. Once I am in charge and Lady of the Castle Du-Barry, it will soon be knocked into shape, it will be the talk of London. All of London's Society will be itching to receive an invitation, I shouldn't wonder if the Queen will enjoy a visit.'

'The Queen aye, oh well, you will be walking in extremely high circles. I won't expect an invitation for myself and my new bri......' he stopped himself in time, but not in time for Jane to pick up on his last uncompleted word.

'Your new WHAT!'

Gerald could have cursed himself for being so flippant. 'I think it's late and you need to get to bed, catch up on your beauty sleep, big day ahead Jane. And seriously my dear, I do wish you all the happiness in the world, I think you are going to make a wonderful Lady Du-Barry, Cornelius is going to be a lucky man to have you by his side. Now my dear, I bid you goodnight.' and before any further exchanges could be made, he turned and walked swiftly back to the Castle.

Jane stood staring furiously at his back as Gerald strode away, cursing herself for being so transparent in her affection for him. But she'd show him, she'd make him regret turning her down. Wait until he saw how lavish her wedding was going to be, and heard her name mentioned by societies gossips. And in a year's time, Scotland's Castle Du-Barry would be the talk of London, and why shouldn't the Queen visit? After all, Balmoral wasn't so far away. Mm, what a pity John Brown had passed away earlier that year, he was said to be a favourite servant of her Majesty, though some would say he was more than that!

The morning of the wedding was dry, cold, but sunny. Servants ran hither and thither and there seemed to be mild panic as news filtered through of his Lordship's inebriated behaviour the previous evening. Cornelius had been staying at the home of the Duke of Arbroath as had some other male members of the wedding party. Gerald had not been invited to join them, in truth, to his relief. As he took a solitary breakfast, he wondered what on earth had possessed him to accept the wedding invitation, then he remembered it was not to offend, and to further his and John's business. Well, he'd done his bit and now he couldn't wait to leave. Just get through the day and then he would be on his way to Yorkshire first thing in the morning.

Cornelius looked very green around the gills as he stood, ever so slightly swaying at the altar of his private Kirk on his estate. He really was quite a repulsive man. Overweight, with an obnoxious aroma emanating from him if you got too close! What were Jane's parents thinking of? All for the price of a title, and a rundown castle! Gerald shook his head disdainfully, if ever he was lucky enough someday to have a daughter, she would marry for love, like he himself intended. This thought conjured up a picture of Selena and brought a smile to his lips.

Suddenly he realised the service was over. The wedding party and guests were starting to move. Now would come the photographs, then the wedding breakfast, oh when would it all be over.

And then it was over, and he was on his way to Yorkshire. At last, away from what he would consider a disastrous day. As the groom had got drunker and drunker on his wedding day, and he and some of his cronies made lewd comments, much to the embarrassment of Cornelius's new in-laws, Gerald was pleased to see Mr Simpson-Wardour, taking his new son-in-law, not so gently by the arm, to have a word in his ear. Cornelius had looked uncomfortable and had calmed down on his return. But what sort of a life was ahead for Jane?

But all that was over now and he, Gerald, was on his way to Yorkshire and to an enjoyable Christmas.

CHAPTER 7

HARROGATE, YORSHIRE
DECEMBER 1883

Selena had been watching out of the windows since the moment she'd got up. She knew Gerald wouldn't arrive until later in the day, perhaps not until evening, but that didn't stop her from continually looking out for him.

She tried her best to put him out of her mind by helping to ready their home for Christmas, but everything appeared to have been done. Mrs Harris and Anna had been thrilled to have Selena and John back in their Harrogate home and couldn't believe what a year had done to Selena. 'Why she's gone from a little girl to a young woman.' Mrs Harris exclaimed. 'Next thing we'll be hearing is wedding bells.' she said.

'I hope not.' John laughed. ' I would like *My Little Girl'* with me a bit longer.' which, when Selena heard this remark, looked concerned, a look that Mrs Harris didn't miss.

'Well Sir, …....who knows when love will strike.' and was gratified as Selena smiled quietly at her, as if she knew it was Mrs Harris's way of saying, I'm on your side lass, did that mean she knew? Had Mrs Harris guessed? Oh well, time would tell.

Gerald arrived at mid-day having made a stopover for the night as both horses and driver were cold and tired.

John greeted him enthusiastically as did Selena and the staff. Gerald was a popular visitor. They all wanted to know about the wedding and although he did not go into too much detail, he couldn't help but be honest and repeat that it wasn't the sort of wedding he'd want, rather too boisterous was how he described it.

Selena did not have much time alone with Gerald over the next few days, much to her annoyance and when she petulantly mentioned this to him, he replied. 'All in suitable time little one, all in suitable time. First, I must attend to business with your father.'

'But what about my surprise? You said you had a surprise for me?'

'And so, I have. Now you run along and just be a little patient, and soon all will be revealed.' he laughed lightly. Tight lipped, Selena almost stamped her foot, then remembered her training, it wasn't ladylike to behave like a spoilt child, so instead, gave him a restrained smile and went to find Sarah.

There was more excitement when a few days later, William took the carriage and went to collect Amelia and her parents from the train station. Selena decided to go with him to meet their guests, which was much appreciated. The Johnson's loved coming to the Elliot's, as they'd been made to feel so welcome previously, and it was a beautiful part of England, even in the winter.

Once again. over the next couple of days, Selena took them to visit friends of hers in the village, and just like the previous time, they were made welcome and, on this occasion, more like old friends. Everyone was intrigued to hear about Selena's time in Switzerland but by now Selena was getting a bit fed up with repeating it but steeled herself knowing that to those who'd never experienced abroad, and not likely too, it was fascinating, so she took a deep breath and once again described her months away. All agreed that she might have come back an elegant young lady, but deep down she was still Selena, still their down to earth lovely Yorkshire lass.

On the afternoon of Christmas eve whilst everyone was taking afternoon tea, Gerald managed to slip away with Selena without anyone noticing. Gerald had thought they could take a couple of horses and ride up to Beckton, a particularly beautiful spot, but unfortunately it had begun to snow again and become dark. Instead, he took her into the orangery and no sooner entered, turned, and went down on one knee before his courage failed him. Selena jumped back at this unexpected turn of events and when Gerald pulled from his pocket a small square box, she put her hands to her mouth and giggled with excitement.

'Selena, my dearest, darling Selena, will you marry me.' he said opening the box where sat an oval shaped emerald surrounded by tiny diamonds.

'Oh! Has Papa consented?' she asked, her eyes shining with happiness. Her question halted Gerald. She was right, he had done this the wrong way, he should have asked John first, but what if Selena had said no, how foolish would that have made him feel. Closing the box, he got to his feet. Smiling he held out his hands for hers.

'You're right of course. I had no right to ask you before your Papa, but I was so worried in case I had misunderstood. I had to be sure you see.'

'Oh Gerald.' she said stepping towards him and placing her hands in his. 'Of course, I'll marry you. I've thought of nothing else all the time I was away. But please, speak to Papa. Now, go now, I can't wait any longer.'

Gerald laughed at her excitement. 'Very well, I will ask him now and hopefully we can announce it at dinner this evening,'

'Gerald?' Selena asked hesitantly.

'Yes, my love?'

'Papa.......do not take no for an answer.'

The pair stood looking at each other, knowing the objection to their betrothal was the age gap. Gerald nodded in agreement, then turned and went in search of John.

John's smile slid from his face. The two men faced each other in John's study. 'You want to do what?' John asked Gerald incredulously. Gerald felt his stomach had turned to stone.

'To marry Selena.' he repeated.

'Yes, I thought that's what you said.' If it had been any other man, John would have been angrily asking him what the hell he thought he was playing at, but this, this was Gerald, his partner, and his friend. 'How old are you, Gerald?'

Gerald took a deep breath; he knew this was coming. 'Twenty-nine.'

'Twenty-nine.' John muttered 'And you know how old my daughter is? she is seventeen Gerald, seventeen! That makes you twelve years her senior.... twelve years Gerald!' Just then the door burst open and in walked Selena, startling both men.

'Selena, we're busy, and please knock in future........

'Papa! I know exactly what you are talking about and I had to intervene as I knew what your reaction would be and I have to tell you that it was your idea to send me away, and it was my decision to go knowing that if I still felt the same about Gerald on my return, then it would be a sign that what we felt for each other was true!'

'What *WE* felt for each other? How long has this been going on?' John spluttered.

Gerald felt it was time he interrupted as he could sense things were starting to get a little out of hand. 'John please, I can assure you nothing has been going on. It's just that before I suggested to you the idea of a finishing school for Selena, I admit, my feelings towards her were changing.'

'Oh, so you thought a spell at finishing school would train her up ready to make you a good wife?'

'No John, no. Please, hear me out. I knew that when Selena was ready to make her new life in London, whether it be with you or myself, she would at some time or another, encounter Society and I did not want her to feel uncomfortable at any time. And it is true, it also made me realise it would be a sensible thing for her to experience, meeting other young ladies, seeing something of the world and yes, meeting other young men, which I understand she has done at the many balls and parties she's attended. When I realised Selena had feelings for me, I was concerned.'

'So, you should be.' grumbled John.

'Papa!' Selena ran to her father who had sat down heavily. Kneeling before him, she clasped his hands, quietly, appealing to him. 'Papa, please don't be harsh with Gerald. It is true, it was I that first admitted my feelings for Gerald, and too be honest Gerald did try to discourage me, concerned about our ages. It was he that made me see sense and accept my time in Switzerland, reminding me not only would I learn a lot, but it would mature me for life as not only the daughter of a businessman, but of a wife of a businessman. And Papa, be aware, that I will always be your daughter and hopefully present you with grandchildren.'

John shuddered at the last remark. 'Oh please, your growing up is one thing, thinking of you as a wife is another, but children, no, please, one thing at a time.' All three were silent for a time until Selena said.

'Papa, how old was Mama when you married her?'

John looked down at his daughter and knew the battle was about to be lost. 'Seventeen.' he said quietly. Selena smiled.

'And if Gerald and I were to marry next year, I will be almost eighteen. And Papa, how old were you when you married Mama?'

John cleared his throat, looking into his daughter's eyes and thought, you crafty little minx, but he had to smile. 'I Know, I know. But it still was not twelve years difference.'

'How old Papa?'

'Twenty-four.'

'Twenty four. I make that a seven-year age gap.'

'It's still not twelve.' John insisted. Gerald went to assist Selena up off the floor and continued to hold her. 'But John, you know me. Am I not a clean-living man? Am I not hard working, honest and caring? And do you not think, that like you and your late wife, a man with some years of life experience would be an ideal one to place your daughter into his care. Especially to one such as I, who.... cares....no loves her dearly and would spend the rest of his life protecting and caring for her?' John heaved a heavy sigh.

'I suppose you are right. But let me think about it. We will speak about it again tomorrow.'

'Tomorrow is Christmas day Papa.'

'Mm, so it is.'

Christmas day dawned to a snow-covered scene just like the

Christmas cards Queen Victoria had introduced. Despite the cold, the sun shone, making the snow glisten and sparkle as if thousands of diamonds had been scattered.

Selena had hardly slept, tossing and turning and thinking about the answer her Papa would give the following morning. Selena wasn't the only one who'd had a troubled night. John swung from being angry at what he saw as subterfuge on Gerald's part and manipulation on that of his daughter. In the end he decided to talk to Amelia, she was a sensible young woman and at least it would clear his head, help him think straight. Breakfast was a busy affair with everyone talking excitedly about the day, the weather and the trip to church. John had asked William to take the ladies by carriage as he felt it much too cold for them to walk especially Amelia's parents. He and Gerald would ride, and two horses had been saddled for them.

The servants, having prepared Christmas day's feast, lit fires in all the rooms ready for their return. Wrapped up in coats, capes and shawls, they all headed towards church for the Christmas day service.

As Gerald and John rode side by side, their initial conversation was frosty to say the least until Gerald made it clear he was not going to allude to the previous evening's conversation. John relaxed and was soon his usual affable self.

With the service over, the servants made their hasty retreat to be back at the house before anyone else. The Elliot's and their guests took their time leaving church as neighbours, acquaintances and workers from John's factory, exchanged greetings for the festive season. Selena was in dreamy mood and the buzz of conversation around her went ignored as she thought what it would be like to stand in this church, as a bride.

'Sorry, sorry, I was far away.' she said as she realised, she'd been spoken too.

'I heard you'd bin ta some special school, to learn ta be a lady, I says to my 'arry, she already a lady, don't need no schoolin' Miss Selena.' the woman cackled away at her joke. Selena smiled.

'Well, that's very nice of you to say so Mrs Brown but I confess we did have fun.' Selena giggled conspiratorial.

'Meet any nice young men?' Mrs Brown asked, winking.

Selena pulled a funny face. 'They were a bit too fancy for my liking, but fun. And I did make two lovely friends, Marie-Lore, who is French and Heidi who is German.'

'Ooh, like our Queen's late hubby!' she laughed. This conversation was interrupted when John called for Selena to say their carriage was waiting. She wished Mrs Brown and her family a happy Yuletide and went to join the others.

Everyone was glad to get back home and gather round the fire with glasses of warm, spicy mulled wine. Mr and Mrs Johnson were in conversation with Gerald when suddenly Selena noticed her Papa and Amelia were not in the drawing room. She was about to remark on this when the door opened and in they walked. John went to the sideboard and picking up a decanter, poured two glasses of mulled wine. After giving one to Amelia, he turned to his guests, offering to top up their glasses. Amelia felt Selena's eyes on her and returned her stare with a little smile and a slight wink of the eye. Selena could not make out what that was all about. Had Papa been talking to Amelia? And if so, what about? She hoped he was asking Amelia's advice and if it was, could it be about a possible engagement, she hoped her friend had been in favour.

Anna came in to say luncheon was served and everyone trooped out. As like in previous years, John was carving, and everyone helped themselves to the array of vegetable and Mrs Harris's delicious gravy.

John suddenly looked up from his carving. 'It doesn't seem like it was a year ago since we were all together, celebrating Christmas, only then we were without my dear daughter. Where has the time gone?' Everyone muttered that yes, time did indeed fly, and so many changes. At the mention of changes, Selena and Gerald glanced at each other, and realised that John was watching them and to their relief, he smiled.

The meal continued, plum pudding consumed, and Mrs Harris and the maids were congratulated and thanked for yet another excellent Christmas luncheon.

As everyone patted their full stomachs, laughing and preparing to leave the table, John tapped his glass, calling for silence. As they re-seated themselves, Mrs Harris entered, pushing a trolley on which was placed several champagne flutes and bottles of Champagne in ice buckets.

'Before we adjourn to the drawing room to open our gifts to each other, I have a rather important announcement to make. Yesterday I had a rather hard lesson to learn, it was that your children do not stay children forever. Little girls grow up...........they fall in love and discover Papa isn't the only man in their world.' There were gasps and a few nervous, muffled giggles. Selena blushed with excitement and confusion. Papa didn't sound angry, but she dare not look in Gerald's direction. You could have heard a pin drop as John walked over to the trolley and proceeded to pop the first of the bottles, pouring the sparkling wine into glasses ready for Mrs Harris and Anna to hand out. 'So, I would like you to join me in congratulating my daughter on her engagement and welcome the gentleman who has asked for her hand in marriage. To Gerald and Selena, may they forever be happy.' Gasps of joy and shouts of well done, congratulations and what a surprise.

Gerald and Selena were so taken aback, they just stared, but smiling, Gerald left his seat and made his way around the table to take Selena's hand in his and having retrieved the box from his pocket, placed the emerald and diamond ring on her finger.

Toasts were made and then questions about the wedding, where, when and how, to which Selena laughed and said. 'All in good time, all in good time.' But she already knew the when, eighteen eighty-four, and the where? Harrogate!

The rest of Christmas day passed in a blur of excited conversations. Below stairs, on instructions from John, all the servants were treated to a glass of champagne with their Christmas meal.

Upstairs in the drawing room, presents were exchanged, and Selena went to her Papa. Slowly she put her arms round him and burying her head in his shoulder had a few gentle tears to thank him. She knew exactly what it had taken for him to recognise the time had come to let go. However, she wanted to assure him that no matter what, he would always be her beloved Papa.

Thursday's Child

Gerald too approached John, thanking him for his understanding and promising, he would never regret his decision and that he, Gerald, would make it his life's work to make Selena the happiest lady alive. The two men shook hands and patted each other on the shoulder. Selena sidled up to Amelia.

'Did you have anything to do with Papa's sudden capitulation?'

Amelia smiled and whispered. 'As your Papa said, there comes a time when every Papa must realise, you have to let go!' Selena squeezed her hand and replied.

'Thank you.'

The weeks that followed Christmas flew by. It was strange how quiet it was when they had all returned to London, all except Selena and Sarah of course. At first there was all the clearing up to do after their guests had departed and decorations to be taken down and put away for another year. The weather had continued to be cold with snow falling intermittently. Just when you thought a thaw had set in, down came another deluge of snow. Then one day in April, it really did feel that the Winter had gone, and Spring was on its way.

As Selena looked out of the window one morning, she remembered doing exactly that three years previously only that time she had been watching the last of the mourners departing. So much had happened. Papa had accepted the partnership with Gerald, she had been to a Finishing School where she'd made two very special friends, and she was now fluent in French and German. Which reminded her, it was her turn to write to Marie-Lore and Heidi. They had been thrilled and excited at the news of her engagement, and wrote they hoped to get an invite. Selena had a better idea and replied they were both required to be bridal attendants.

Preparations had started in earnest as soon as Papa and Gerald had returned to London. Before returning, Selena had told both Gerald and John, that she wished to marry in the Harrogate church and did not want a London wedding where she would know hardly anyone. If Gerald wanted to invite anyone from Society, then so be it, but they would have to travel to Yorkshire. On laying down this rule in front of them, John raised an eyebrow at Gerald saying. 'Well lad, Madam has spoken. Do you see what you're in for? Sure, you don't want to change your mind?' They all laughed, and Gerald assured him that no, he did not want to change his mind.

Selena had not been back to London, firstly because of the weather and later she was busy making plans with Mrs Harris about the wedding, who would be staying at the house, and who would be staying at the hotel. Before returning to London in January, John, Gerald and Selena had been to see the Vicar and arranged a date for the wedding. It was to be on Saturday the twenty-ninth of September at eleven o'clock. Armed with this information, Selena asked William to take her and Sarah to the Royal House Hotel in Harrogate where she had arranged an appointment to discuss with the Manager, details for the wedding breakfast. Selena had taken the precaution of getting Papa to write to the Manager assuring him that as John was busy in London, his daughter's wishes were to be adhered to.

She had written to Amelia and asked if she would design and make her wedding gown and two bridal attendants' gowns for her friends. Amelia was over the moon at her request and said that yes, she would be thrilled, and suggested Selena come to London to choose design and material. This was arranged for May.

Having had the meeting at the hotel, Selena had another request. One afternoon, she knocked on Mrs Harris's sitting room door. 'Cookie, am I disturbing you?' Mrs Harris swung her feet off the stool she'd been resting them on.

'Of course not Miss Selena, come in, sit down, is everything all right?'

'Yes, everything is fine. The Royal House is a beautiful hotel the room where the reception will be held is beautiful. The manager was so extremely helpful, probably had something to do with the letter he'd received from Papa.' she giggled. Mrs Harris smiled in agreement. 'I have a favour to ask you. I wondered; would you be so kind as to make our wedding cake for us?'

'Why Miss Selena, I would be honoured. But are you sure you

wouldn't prefer to have it made by a professional baker?'

'You are a professional Cookie, look at all the wonderful feasts you have produced for us over the years.'

'Yes, but a wedding cake......' Mrs Harris said uncertain of her ability.

'Yes, a wedding cake, my wedding cake, mine and Gerald's, and I could not think of anyone better to make it. And I will know it has been made with love, and that's most important. Anyway, I have already informed the Manager at the Royal that the cake is in hand.'

'Well Miss, then in that case I'd better look sharp, sort out recipes and start buying the ingredients. And thank you Miss Selena, it will be such an honour to make something so important, I hope I won't let you and Mr Gerald down.' she said, rummaging in her pocket for a hanky with which to wipe away her tears of emotion.

'You won't, I know you won't.'

In May, Selena decided to go to London for a few weeks. Apart from anything else, Selena ached to see her beloved fiancé, and of course Papa. Everything that could be done for the wedding at this stage, had been done, and she needed to see Amelia to start on her dress. Amelia had written to Heidi and Marie-Lore as she'd suggested to Selena, requesting their measurements. The girls would be arriving two weeks before the wedding but in time for Selena's eighteenth birthday, which on this occasion would be celebrated at their London home in Knightsbridge.

She'd planned this as she felt Cookie and the others had enough to do in Harrogate preparing for the wedding. When they heard the news, all the servants sighed with relief. Two celebrations of such magnitude coming one on top of the other would have been exhausting.

So, in the first week of May, Selena and Sarah, accompanied by William and Kitty, boarded the train from Manchester Piccadilly, heading for London.

Selena was quiet on the train journey and was happy for the others to converse amongst themselves. She just wanted to lie back and daydream of being once again with her darling Gerald, and of course Papa!

They'd had to change at the station called Crewe and had a devil of a job gaining the attention of a porter to help them take their luggage to another platform, as William was unable to cope with the luggage of four people. Eventually, they were settled, and the train set off. The ladies were so tired by now that they all fell asleep, almost until they arrived at Euston. As the train pulled into the station, they were all hoping they could find a porter, but nobody had reckoned with Gerald. As Selena leant out of the window, holding desperately onto her hat, Gerald's lovely face was the first thing she saw, and beside him, a porter with a trolley. When she reported this to the others, they all sighed with relief.

As she alighted, Selena walked and waved as swiftly as her ladylike composure would allow, but the youth in her was abandoned as she drew near, and she threw her arms around Gerald. His reaction was of sheer joy as he threw back his head laughing and hugging his future bride.

The others eventually reached the young couple and Gerald having greeted everyone helped William and the porter load the luggage onto the trolley. Outside, a carriage stood waiting and as soon as everyone was aboard and luggage safely stowed, they were off.

'Where is Papa?' Selena asked.

'One of us had to stay in the office today, we had a gentleman coming to see us, and as I had not been here the last time you came back to London, your Papa, thought I should meet you this time.' Selena beamed at him and squeezed his hand.

When they reached twenty-two Park Avenue, Selena was surprised at how happy she was to be back in Knightsbridge, it already felt like home. As soon as the carriage drew to a stop, the door of twenty-two was flung open and Ben, the footman, walked swiftly down the path, followed by maids Cilla, Clary and Brenda, all happy to help the travellers and welcome everyone home. Capes, hats, and gloves were taken, and Brenda announced that Mrs Bailey said that tea and refreshments would be delivered to the drawing room at once. 'Her words not mine.' chuckled Brenda who disappeared presumably to do Mrs Bailey's bidding. As soon as she had divested herself of her outer garments and washed her hands and face, Kitty went straight to the kitchen to offer her help. This was met with grateful thanks and confirmed Kitty's acceptance as "One of them!"

Sarah, William and Kitty now reverted to servant status and joined them below stairs. They were all eager to hear about the wedding arrangements and pleased they would be organising Selena's eighteenth birthday, though with a wedding only a couple of weeks after, it would be a smaller party than usual for an eighteenth. There was to be no "Coming Out" for Selena, and they doubted it would have been any different if Selena had not been engaged. Being the Northerners they were, London Socialising was something they found a little overwhelming, though of course it was something they would have to get used to, if they were to survive in business.

Later when Papa had arrived home and John, Gerald and Selena were at dinner, talk turned to the wedding plans.

'Amelia wondered if it would be convenient for her to call on you tomorrow, to show you some designs she's come up with and bring some fabrics for your opinion. She also wanted to know if you had any preferences regarding colour for your attendants. The next issue is of course, your birthday.'

Selena smiled. 'Dearest Papa, I have no wish to have anything extravagant for my birthday, not with the wedding so close.'

'Well, if you don't mind me putting in a suggestion.' Gerald said. 'I wonder, would it not be a good idea to hold your birthday at Browns Hotel? They have a rather nice drawing room where we could have afternoon tea, or if you would prefer to make it a little more of a celebration, how about we hire one of their dining rooms for dinner and perhaps a small dance for later? We could make the invitations special, say fifty or so? I'm more than happy to arrange this, if it would help.'

Initially, the idea was pure rejection on Selena's part but as she was about to say, she hesitated. Surely this is the very reason she'd attended the Finishing School, and with Heidi and Marie-Lore arriving in time for her birthday, what better way to entertain them, it could be fun. Smiling, she turned to Gerald. 'Do you know, I think you could be right. And with my friends coming from the Continent, it would be a lovely event for them to enjoy. If you are sure you would be happy to arrange it? As I think we already have enough to think about with the wedding.'

'I agree. And I promise you, you will have nothing to organise except for choosing a gown to wear, and I will also send out the invitations, after I have shown you the suggested guest list. I think, as we are having the wedding in Yorkshire, we ought not to ignore London Society altogether, especially as in business, we do need to court them.'

'I know, and I think you are right.' Selena agreed. 'I was also thinking that perhaps an after-wedding party, when we return from our honeymoon, in London of course.' Selena suggested.

Gerald nodded thoughtfully. 'You are getting the idea my dear.'

'Em, sounds like my daughter is going to be a social butterfly.' John quipped.

'Well, she may as well put her Finishing School training to good use.' Gerald teased her.

'After meeting me, they will all be clamouring to go the same school.' Selena said putting on a posh voice and a haughty expression, to which John and Gerald burst out laughing.

'Don't ever lose your sense of humour.' Gerald said getting up from the table.

'I think it's time to adjourn to the drawing room.' John said.

Whilst Selena sat sewing, the two men chatted about business before Gerald took his leave.

CHAPTER 8

SCOTLAND TO LONDON
MARCH 1884

For the past week, Jane had been feeling distinctly off colour, so much so that she'd instructed Cornelius to stay in his own room, although not happy about having his marital rights curbed so early in the marriage, when she was violently sick, he soon agreed.

Jane's illness seemed to go on for some time and she was sure it was the food the Scottish cook prepared, especially the ghastly porridge that she insisted on offering up for breakfast, complete with salt! for goodness sake. In the end, she convinced herself she was being poisoned, Cornelius sent for the Doctor, who roared with laughter and having examined her, shouted in his ridiculous accent, that she was with child!

The news sent Cornelius in a spasm of ecstasy. He puffed out his already, overweight chest, and bloated stomach, and went on a drinking spree in the name of celebration. A celebration that often ended up in Morag's bed!

Jane however, neither knew nor cared, she'd done her bit, the first part of the plan, heir number one was on its way.

Although the Doctor assured her this sickness would pass once she'd passed the three-month stage, Jane was having none of it and immediately made plans to return to London to stay with her parents until after the birth. Cornelius was delighted with this plan until he heard he was to accompany his wife. When he tried to object, Jane informed him that her father wished to discuss his finances.

'My Finances!' he screamed at her. 'How dare he! Has you father forgotten who I am? I am Lord Du-Barry of Castle Du-Barry, I own land, I have tenants, I have...I have...'

'You have no money.' Jane told him.

Cornelius stopped in mid flow; spittle ran down his flabby mouth as he glared at his wife. She turned her head away, the sight of him made her feel sick. 'Yes, you can turn away ya cold, frigid coo!' Jane turned back to him, and although it took all her strength, she stood up and made for the door.

'We will leave in two days' time, and if you want to save your crumbling Castle from further destruction, I suggest you behave with a little more servility in front of my father.

'I've still got ya dowry!' Cornelius shouted at her.

'According to my father, you've spent it all. So now you will be reliant on him to save your precious Castle. And don't forget, I am carrying your heir, so you should be grateful to us both.'

Jane left the room swiftly as she didn't want him to see the smile spreading across her face. And knowing that she and her father were now in control of Du-Barry Castle more than Cornelius realised.

The journey back to London was longer and more uncomfortable than Jane realised it would be. The coach seats were hard and despite it being March and supposed to be Spring, it was very cold. The stop overs in the various Inns on route, were draughty and noisy although Cornelius was in fine form, drinking himself stupid most nights, and suffering headaches from hell the next morning.

By the time the coach arrived in Kensington town, Jane could have cried with exhaustion. Thankfully, her mother and father were waiting with their coachman to take them home.

As soon as they walked through the door, Mrs Simpson-Wardour issued orders for a bath to be made ready for Lady Du-Barry, she had to get her daughter's new title in, and a doctor to be called, though she gave no indication as to why.

Cornelius was shown to his room, as he would not be sharing with his wife, that much was obvious. He was then expected in the study of his father-in-law, before dinner he was told, after he'd washed and freshened up, he was informed by his mother-in-law. This last was delivered with a sniff, indicating that he had an odour about his person.

Cornelius was furious but knew he would have to curb his temper if he was to put Castle Du-Barry back on its feet as it were. But at the meeting later that day, he almost threw caution to the wind when he discovered that Bertram Simpson-Wardour not only had friends in high places, but those friends had furnished him with all the details of Cornelius's financial and personal situation. Then, to add insult to injury, he introduced Andrew Darling, who, he was informed, would be returning to Scotland with him to oversee the renovations to the Castle, and to investigate how the estate was being run and advise on changes and improvements to be made.

It appeared that any money being spent on the Castle was in the form of a loan and not Jane's money. That! Bertram informed him, was in consideration of the dowry he'd received, and gone through like a dose of salts! From now on, Bertram had hold of the purse strings.

At dinner that evening, Bertram, Andrew and Sybil Simpson-Wardour, conversed about politics, the weather and Bertram's recent elevation to partner in the firm of solicitors he worked with. He beamed when Andrew spoke the new name of the firm, McCarthy, Samson & Simpson-Wardour.

'They tried to get me to cut out the Simpson, but I refused. Simpson-Wardour or I cannot accept, I told them, and of course they acquiesced.' He failed to mention that McCarthy and Samson had only caved in when Bertram threatened that a recent wealthy Duke who'd just become a client, might easily change his mind about joining as a client, if Bertram advised. It irked McCarthy and Samson that although Bertram was now a solicitor, he'd managed to brush off the fact that he himself had come from trade, his late father having been in leather, and had done very nicely thank you out of it.

Throughout dinner, Cornelius was ignored, not that he was bothered as he was deep in thought wondering how the hell had he got into this mess and how could he get out of it?

'Lord Du-Barry.............'

'Sorry, sorry, I was deep in thought. What was it you said?

'Your wife, Lady Du-Barry, I understand she is not well.' Andrew Darling asked.

'Em, yes, yes, I think she's having her dinner upstairs, the um journey took it out of her. She'll be alright in a day or two just needs the rest.'

As it was, Jane stayed in bed for a week, and would have continued to do so had it not been for her mother. When she did come down, Jane was restless and wanted to go out, call on some old friends especially now she had a title. She wanted to rub it in to those who'd previously looked down on her. What she didn't realise was, title or no title, it was Jane herself they didn't like more than her being a commoner.

'Do you really feel up to calling?' her mother asked

'Certainly!' Jane snapped. 'After all, in a few weeks from now I shall be obliged to stay out of sight until my confinement is over.'

'That's true.' her mother agreed.

The first two acquaintances they presented their calling card to was greeted with. '*Sorry, Madam is unavailable today,* and on the other occasion, *Beg pardon, but her Ladyship is not receiving today.*' Jane was furious, her mother embarrassed. The third, an even higher-ranking member of the aristocracy, surprised them by not only accepting their card but welcoming them.

Peony, the Duchess of Grantham was originally from Holland, and related to some faction of the Dutch royal family. She had been married to the duke for three years and in that time had given birth twice, on both occasions' boys. Unlike many of the English aristocracy who found any talk of pregnancy vulgar, Peony couldn't wait to entertain with details of her experience and even asked how soon Jane expected to be in the same position! Jane didn't know how to reply and looked to her mother for guidance. Sybil was very adept at these situations and managed to change the subject by discussing Jane's recent wedding in Scotland, the beauties of the area and its people, neither of which they really cared for, and lastly the Castle, which they described as some sort of fairy Castle, not the crumbling, draughty, ruin it really was.

The Duchess was soon making overtures for an invitation to the castle, to which Jane agreed, Autumn would be an excellent time. Talk turned to the Queen, and the demise of John Brown, and when asked, Jane reminisced about the times she'd entertained the gentleman, all lies of course, but she certainly made it sound as if she really had known him, even embellishing her story with a tale of how she'd written a condolence card to the Queen! Sybil sat there astonished and wondered how she could stop her daughter fantasising before she said something so outrageous, she would be caught out.

It ended with Jane inviting the Duke and Duchess to dinner, and Peony delightedly saying she would look forward to receiving the invitation. They parted the best of friends.

'Now let those Society baggage's deny me when I go calling.' she said angrily in the carriage on the way home. Her mother was thoughtful.

'Yes, but I do think you should curb your exuberance when talking about who you've entertained.' she suggested.

'Mm? Oh that, John Brown. Yes, rather clever of me don't you think.'

'Well, not if anyone was acquainted with the gentleman, especially as you were not in residence at the Castle that long before he passed.'

'Oh well, if anyone ever corrects me on the matter, I will say the Duchess misunderstood, English not being her first language. I must say there were times when I found it hard to understand her. She has an awful guttural accent, quite dreadful.'

'Yes dear.' was all Sybil was able to reply. After today's performance, she was beginning to hope the sooner Jane had to retire for the duration until confinement, the better. But first, there was this dinner party.

Later when Jane informed her father, she wished to hold a dinner party and had already extended an invitation to the Duchess of Grantham, who had enthusiastically accepted on behalf of the Duke, Bertram was thrilled. This was just what he'd envisaged when he'd encouraged the marriage to Cornelius. By now, Cornelius was safely tucked away in Scotland where there was no chance of him embarrassing the Simpson-Wardour's.

A date was chosen, list of guests made, and invitations went out. They were to be a party totalling twenty, and Jane knew as soon as it was known the Duke and Duchess of Grantham had accepted, the others would not dare to decline. With the dinner, they would be in, Jane was sure of it and so was her father. Sybil on the other hand made Jane promise not to talk of entertaining the late John Brown, or boasting of a connection with the Queen, which of course she did not have, Jane reluctantly promised.

The only refusal they received was from Gerald, who stated that he would be expecting his fiancé to return that week, this was a lie of course as Selena was not due until May, but Gerald did not want to get involved, especially as he'd heard Cornelius had been sent packing back to Scotland.

The dinner party was surprisingly a remarkable success, but then came talk of the growing success of Gerald and John's partnership and inevitably, talk of the forthcoming wedding.

Lady Dalgleish said, 'I understand the nuptials are to be held in Harrogate, Yorkshire, with a party later in London.'

'Well, what do you expect? She's hardly top draw!' Jane said sharply. There was an uncomfortable silence as everyone around the table looked at Jane. Lady Dalgleish gave a sly smile and was heard to murmur. 'And neither are you my dear.' Suddenly everyone was talking at once in the hope of covering up what had been an impolite exchange.

When the last guest had departed, Sybil took Jane to one side. 'I do not know what it is you have got against Gerald's fiancé, but you should be careful of your remarks. This young woman appears to have made a good impression in certain quarters; I have had the pleasure of her company.

CHAPTER 9

KHIGTHSBRIDGE, LONDON
SUMMER 1884

From May until the end of August, Selena was so busy, Sarah said she was whirling through the year like a whirlwind.

'That's because I am eager to celebrate my birthday, and even more eager for my wedding.' she laughed gaily. At the mention of the wedding, Sarah took a sharp intake of breath. Her wedding night! A young girl like Selena, with no Mama to talk to her about her wedding night, oh well, Sarah thought, even girls with mothers often were left uninformed, and it was certainly not Sarah's job to discuss such a delicate subject, especially by one such as she who'd never been married. This was really a case of letting nature take its course.

John and Gerald were starting to get invitations to dine by some members of London's Society, curious to see if Carney-Tompkins & Elliot, were a force to be reckoned with. Many were intrigued as to how this partnership had sprung up, after all Gerald did come from an aristocratic background, all be it a damaged one, but like the Phoenix, he appeared to be rising from the ashes! As for this strange little Northern man? Perhaps it had more to do with the daughter? Then again, a man of Gerald's stature and background, if he'd wanted the girl, any father, especially John Elliot, so they thought, would surely have been pleased as punch for his daughter to have an opportunity to make such a marriage. Luckily for those who spoke in such vein, their talk never reached the ears of John or Gerald. To this end their curiosity was such that invitations included Selena.

The ladies were intrigued, some a little envious as to how this young girl had captured the heart of such a handsome and charming man, but all were surprised when they met Selena, at her poise, graciousness and intelligence. All except for one, Lady Jane Du-Barry. Although Jane had met Selena on a few rare occasions, it never occurred to her that the ladies would praise this newcomer. But they were all aware of Jane's infatuation with the man whose heart Selena had stolen and cruelly enjoyed Jane's discomfort when they praised young Selena.

Gerald wondered if his decline of the dinner invitation to Bertram Simpson-Wardour's in late April, had been a mistake, and said so to John, who suggested that now Selena had arrived, he could make amends by inviting the Simpson-Wardour's to a dinner, hosted by John. This they did and the Simpson-Wardour's accepted, delighted. Unfortunately, their daughter Lady Du-Barry, would be indisposed due to her condition. Gerald was pleased to hear this, but Selena was disappointed, as though previous meetings with Jane had been sparse, Selena wanted to be friends and couldn't understand why Jane had been so hostile.

By now the news of Jane's condition was common knowledge and Selena wondered if she might try calling on the lady. She'd already heard whispers and comments, not always nice, about Lady Du-Barry. Apparently, she and her parents had got a reputation for social climbing, but surely as one went up in the world of business, was it not taken for granted, one automatically mixed with all walks of life. When Selena mentioned this to Amelia her reply was, *"Since marrying a Lord, she thinks she's above us"* came as a bit of a shock to Selena.

After her parents had attended the dinner at John's home and reported back to their daughter the names of other guests included many of which were titled, Jane was apoplectic with rage. And when Sybil went on the say that Selena had asked if she may call on Jane, her mother thought she'd blow a gasket. As Jane spluttered her spite about 'that jumped up little up-start, and how she was a 'Lady', her father suddenly roared at her. 'Be quiet! Who do you think you are? Has it not dawned on you that if you are not careful, you are in danger of making yourself a laughingstock!'

Jane's lips trembled and tears came to her eyes, never before had her father ever spoken to her like that. Where his wife and daughter were concerned, he'd always been the mildest mannered of men, though he could be quite a tyrant with outsiders, as his newfound partners had discovered. Even Sybil jumped at his furious outburst, though what he said next she understood, and it worried her.

'You have only become a 'Lady' because you've been brave enough to wed this pathetic, penniless, lazy, good-for-nothing aristocratic cast-off, who had no choice but to marry you, a commoner, to gain an heir and a spare!' he stated, only this time he did not shout but his words, so crudely spoken, made not only Sybil wince but Jane also. 'And stop blubbering, pull yourself together, we have work to do.'

At this, both women looked up. Jane ceased crying, dabbing her eyes and cheeks and blowing her nose loudly, in a most unladylike fashion which caused her mother to frown angrily.

'Now as you know, I have sent Andrew Darling back with Cornelius, with strict instructions to oversee every aspect of the repairs, keeping a strict eye on the finances and reporting back to me on a regular basis. He is also looking into and making recommendations regarding the estate and tenants. To this end he has visited and spoken to them, and assured them that repairs to their properties will be made, wages owed, to be settled and did you know the estate had its own hostelry?' When both woman looked surprised, Bertram nodded and laughing slightly, continued. 'Oh yes, and in an extremely poor state of repair it is. So, the landlord was thrilled when Andrew imparted the news of repairs and settlement of outstanding remuneration owed, but even more thrilled when he was told under no circumstances was he to hand any further takings to Lord Du-Barry! In future, Andrew would be collecting these, and wait for it, this will be on behalf of instructions from the new Lady Du-Barry!' At this the two women gasped then started to laugh. Bertram joined them adding. 'So, this part of Scotland is now under no illusion, that from now on, Lady Du-Barry, not only holds the purse string, but rules the roost!'

Sybil threw up her hands in delight, and Bertram sat back smiling at the delight his announcement had caused.

'So, what now Father?' Jane asked.

'Well, my dear. You will start to behave yourself in a manner befitting a 'Lady'.' He made marks with his fingers in the air when he spoke the word Lady. Jane visibly bristled at his criticism. 'And you will begin to make yourself personable. We will excuse your previous behaviour as discomfort caused by your condition. Some will be understanding, others not so. And of course, there will always be an element of society, to whom we will never be acceptable. However, money talks, and lots of money speaks even louder, and I intend to make lots of it, so in time, even those who wished too, will not be able to ignore us as with riches comes power.'

Sybil and Jane exchanged glances. Sybil felt quite uncomfortable, she just wanted a quiet life. Yes, she had yearned to be accepted, wanted to join the socialising of the upper classes, but so far the toe dipping she'd managed had not made her as happy as she thought it would. Jane, on the other hand, welcomed the challenge. So, her father intended to become rich, extraordinarily rich and in doing so, would soon put those who currently looked down their noses at them, take a step back. Jane could not wait. In the meantime, she was going to have to do what her father instructed and appear more demure, that was not going to be easy. Perhaps she should take a leaf out of the Northern girl's book.

'So how do we go about this?' Jane asked her father. 'And how has Cornelius taken Andrew's intervention?'

'For your part, you will accept the calling card of Miss Elliot, in fact you will go further and invite her to tea. You will be very solicitous, apologising for past coolness, and make a conscious effort to befriend the young woman. As for your husband, he will not give you any trouble as I intend to keep Andrew in Scotland even after all the repairs have been completed. Andrew has agreed that after overseeing his work on the castle and estate properties, he will be made Estate Manager and will have complete control, under my direction of all aspects.'

Though Jane relished this outcome, she didn't see how Cornelius was going to allow it and said so to her father who smiled. 'He will have no choice. It is too late. To save Du-Barry castle and his estate, he has already signed over the complete control of both to me. The contract is both legal and binding. I am now in charge, although to all intents and purposes, you are.'

Jane beamed. 'Father, that is amazing.'

'It is isn't it. However, you too have a part to play in all this, and I expect you to obey me.'

Jane nodded her head, leaning eagerly forward to listen.

'First, as I have said, you will make yourself available and befriend Miss Selena Elliot, they are becoming accepted by certain factions of Society, not surprising as Mr Carney-Tompkins already had his foot in the door. Second when your confinement is over and you are safely delivered, we will instruct Cornelius to return and you will present a united front to society, him being a Lord will soon give us access to invitations. You will put on a good act and show no revulsion towards your husband. He in return will be the epitome of excellent social graces.' At this both women raised their eyebrows in disbelief. 'You can make faces, but I am telling you, Cornelius will be well and truly under no illusion to his expected behaviour. After a period, when I am satisfied the name Du-Barry is starting to regain respect, the changes to his good behaviour attributed to you my dear Jane, you will return to Scotland and make sure you are soon again with child.'

'Oh No! Father, No!' Jane cried. Horrified to have to undergo not only discomfort of carrying said child, but worse still, was what went before, to get her into that condition.

'It is important that we strike while the iron is hot.' Bertram remonstrated with her.

Sybil felt compelled to intervene. 'Husband, dear, please, I beg of you, why so soon? Can you not see it will take time to recover from her confinement.'

'Poppycock!' Bertram exploded 'The lower classes produce them one after the other. It is imperative Jane produces a spare as soon as possible, and what if this one is female? Aye? What then? Cornelius must have a son, he has too!' Jane burst into tears and Sybil looked concerned. 'Pull yourself together girl, once this is done, the next part of the plan can be put into action.' he said.

'And what is that? Sybil asked meekly.

'The divorce woman! The divorce!' Bertram stormed out of the room.

A week later, Selena was surprised to receive an invitation to take tea with Lady Jane Du-Barry at her parents' home in Kensington. Gerald was wary and suspicious of Jane's motives. True, they'd had a pleasant evening when the Simpson-Wardour's had come to dine, but then Jane hadn't been with them, now all of a sudden Jane was issuing invitations to tea.

As he didn't want to make Selena feel uncomfortable, he said nothing to her but did mention his concerns to John, who said that probably her parents had spoken to Jane. As it turned out, Selena returned having had a warm welcome from the Simpson-Wardour's and giggling at some of the rather risqué gossip imparted to her by Jane. The latter of these, Amelia advised her not to repeat. Gossip like this, she informed Selena, could be dangerous if it was not strictly true, and in any case, it was not really ladylike to gossip, you would be much better thought of if you did not gossip, especially if it was of an unkind nature. Selena thought about this and decided Amelia was right. She made a vow to herself that from now on, she would not be a gossip, and furthermore would dissuade others not to impart such to herself.

Heidi and Marie-Lore had arrived, complete with their chaperones and been met by Selena, Sarah and William, and to the delight of all, had been taken on a whistle stop tour of London. With the promise that after Selena and Gerald had left for their honeymoon in Italy, Sarah would accompany them with William on a more in-depth tour before they returned from England to their respective homes.

The girls were delighted when they met Amelia at Selena's home and shown the gowns, she had created for them. Even more delighted when told they could take them when they returned home. Although the accommodation was smaller than they were used to, nobody mentioned this and the two chaperones accepted this but agreed, they couldn't fault the hospitality.

Selena's birthday on the fourth of September was a party of just fifty but John and Gerald had thought it expedient to send out invitations for a belated wedding party for one hundred quests, to celebrate the marriage of Mr and Mrs Gerald Carney-Tompkins, again at Browns Hotel, on their return from Italy on Saturday the twenty-fifth of October. This solved any disgruntled remarks about Selena's eighteenth, and the wedding being held in Yorkshire.

Selena's dress, veil and shoes, had all been sent on ahead to be looked after by Mrs Harris and Co who had also been sent a list of requirements to be ready to pack for the honeymoon.

Two days after her birthday, Gerald said goodbye to his bride to be, and saw the large party, John, Sarah, Selena, Heidi, Marie-Lore and their two chaperones, off to Yorkshire on the train from Euston. William and Kitty would travel by coach as they were taking all the luggage required by the ladies.

There had been excited goodbyes from the servants in the Knightsbridge house, but this was heightened as they would all be following in ten days' time as they made their way to Yorkshire having also been invited to the wedding. Who would have thought it, they marvelled when they'd received their gold embossed wedding invitations, having been instructed to close up the house and come to Yorkshire!

On arrival in Harrogate, one might have thought it was chaos that greeted them, but much to the amusement of Heidi, Marie-Lore and their chaperones, the Yorkshire house in a place called Harrogate, was even smaller than the London one. However, size it appear did not matter to these strange English people, some with funny accents, hospitality was once again superb and they were made to feel so welcome as if they'd known each other for years.

Maids and male man servants were on hand to help, guide you in the direction of where you wanted to go, and the scenery was breath taking, all agreed.

The tiny church where the wedding took place was heart-stopping. As requested by Selena, an archway of bronze, gold, yellow and white, chrysanthemums framed the entrance. When approached, the guests gasped, they'd never seen anything like it.
Gerald and the servants from Knightsbridge had been staying at the hotel where the wedding breakfast was to be held, and Joseph, the Yorkshire factory's manager, had been asked by Gerald, to be his best man, an honour, which when put to him had him almost bursting with pride.

On the day of the wedding, John proudly walked his daughter down the aisle. He was hard put not to cry. Not just because Selena looked so beautiful and was such an unspoilt, lovely girl, but because Mary, his beloved late wife and Selena's Mama, was not there to see their beautiful daughter on her wedding day.
As Selena glided down on her Papa's arm, she too was smiling through her tears for the same reason, but also looking with such love and longing at the man she had loved from the first day she set eyes on him.

Everything on the day had gone splendidly. The service, the wedding breakfast, the guests and even the weather had held a balmy warmth.
The newlyweds were to spend their wedding night in an hotel in York, making it easier for them to catch a train to London the following morning. From there, they would set off on their journey to Italy. The servants from Knightsbridge offered their help in clearing up the Harrogate house before departing to London, this was accepted gratefully.
Eventually everyone was gone, all except John and Amelia who were going to spend the week at the Yorkshire factory before returning to London. But this wedding, everyone agreed, would be the topic of conversation for months to come.

Thursday's Child

If Gerald had been concerned about consummating his marriage with his innocent, motherless bride, he had no need. On the contrary, he smiled to himself, she really was quite the little minx. He'd been careful not to rush her, waiting a couple of days just romancing her with kisses and caresses until one evening as they lay on their bed, Selena lent over him and comically asked.

'Is this it? Is this all there is to this marriage thing?'

'Er......no.....'

'Then what comes next? Because I have this feeling, a feeling of excitement and I don't know what it is. What am I missing?' So, he showed her! Now they both knew what bliss could come from the marriage bed.

Their days were spent together exploring the beauty, culture and museums of Italy, it was tiring but they were heady with happiness. Gerald often wondered if it wouldn't be nice to spend the rest of their lives just like this. They visited the Trevi Fountain, the leaning Tower of Pisa, the Colosseum and Vatican City. They ate and drank in small cafes on Piazzas and people watched. They rode on Gondolas and were serenaded softly as the boats glided silently through the waters of Venice. All too soon they were packing to start their return journey, though this also was going to be exciting as they were to spend three days in Germany and three days in France as the guests of Heidi and Marie-Lore's parents.

Back home in England, two other people had had a little jolt of their own, though neither hinted nor eluded to it.

Amelia had always enjoyed her visits to Yorkshire, but on this occasion it felt like she had come home. The servants had all treated her with respect and a familiarity which was not disrespectful but seemed to carry a fondness for her. She felt at ease with them especially when walking out, and when she entered the shops she'd frequented with Selena. She was greeted with such friendliness, it made her smile. Not for the first time it occurred to her how she would love to live in Yorkshire and said as much to John one evening.

It was after dinner when John had been telling her about his visit that day to the factory and how much he missed living in Harrogate, to which Amelia said, laughing. 'Oh I know just what you mean, I felt like I'd come home this time, so if you ever need a housekeeper you only need to ......'trailing off as she realised her remarks might cause embarrassment. Seeing her discomfiture, John jumped in.

'Well, I take that as a great compliment Amelia, and who knows, perhaps we'll end up together, here, in our old age.' he laughed kindly.

Amelia blushed, quickly changing the subject, asking how the ladies at the factory were getting on with the modern designs she sent recently.

The rest of the evening passed companionably until Amelia said she would go and start packing as she knew they would be leaving early in the morning to return to London.

John stood up and taking her by the shoulders gently placed a kiss on each cheek before saying. 'I want to thank you Amelia for everything you have done for my daughter.' When she started to deny her help. John would have none of it. 'No, no. I don't know what we would have done without you. You have been such a comfort to Selena, and to me, and for that I thank you. And..... may I say that I hope with all my heart, you will remain with us for a long time to come.' Amelia didn't know what to say, she was overwhelmed with emotion but quickly pulled herself together.

'Thank you John, it's been my pleasure. Selena is a lovely girl and I'm sure she and Gerald will make a very happy marriage. Now, I must away to my room, and thank you for making me so welcome not only in the business but also to your family, and for also making my parents so welcome, Goodnight.'

After parting, both would go over their last conversation, trying to read between the lines. Was it just friendship they were eluding to? Or could there be another possibility? Only time would tell.

Gerald and Selena arrived back in London with only a few days before their belated wedding party at Browns Hotel. Luckily for them, Amelia had taken it upon herself to ensure everything was in order and any queries were quickly dealt with.

John and Amelia had both received postcards from the happy couple which surprised them to learn this tradition had started some years previously in Austria and was gradually making its way across Europe. Even Mrs Harris in Harrogate and Mrs Bailey in Knightsbridge, received one to be read out to the other servants.

William was at Euston to meet them and take them to Gerald's home in Mayfair. There was a message from Selena's dear Papa, that she would see him in the next couple of days, when she had time to draw breath. Gerald told William to tell John he would be in the office the following morning. The only servants Gerald had were Mrs Pritchard, his cook/housekeeper, Maids Emma, and Gertrude and two gardeners come handy men, Stan and Benjamin. When his parents had been alive, there had been many more, much needed to run the ten-bedroom mansion and five acres of garden. But after their death, as servants left or passed away, Gerald did not replace them as he had lead a quiet life. Any socialising had been done at other people's homes or if Gerald was hosting, he would hire a room in an hotel. But now things were different, he had a wife who would no doubt enjoy entertaining, and one day, hopefully, children. The thoughts of this new life ahead of him brought a smile to his lips.

Selena, he was pleased to see, was greeted with much enthusiasm by all his staff who'd gathered on purpose to meet their new Mistress. Thankfully, they had all, at different times, met her so they all knew she was no threat and was not the sort to start throwing her weight about, not like a certain Lady Jane Du-Barry, whose servants had been quick to pass on her behaviour since becoming a "Lady", down the servant grapevine. Gerald realised there were sure to be some changes Selena would like. For a start, it had been years since any of the rooms had been decorated, and as he looked about him now, he saw how shabby the whole place was looking. Turning to his new bride who was deep in conversation with Mrs Pritchard he said. 'Dearest Selena, I have just been looking around my home and ashamed to say how embarrassed I am that I have allowed it to become so shabby.'

Selena smiled and looking at Mrs Pritchard she replied. 'Not to worry husband dearest, I'm sure Mrs Pritchard and the maids will help me with some ideas to smarten the place up.' The two women laughed conspiritedly.

'Well, my dear, I give you carte-blanch to rectify the place, within reason off course.' he added good humourlessly. 'Now Mrs Pritchard, may we have tea in the drawing room in say, half an hour? It will give us time to freshen up and settle down for the evening.'

'Of course, Sir, Madam, Stan and Benji have taken your trunks upstairs, would you like me to send Emma and Gertrude up now to unpack?'

'Perhaps later on.' Gerald said.

'Of course Sir, and may I say again, on behalf of all of us, welcome home.'

Over the next few days, Selena had no time to give thought to refurbishing her new home, as her time was taken up with visiting her Papa, catching up with Amelia and getting ready for their big celebration at Browns.

Amelia had created a beautiful gown of white satin and embroidered it with gold thread in a flower and leaf design. It came as a complete surprise to Selena when she realised a gown for this celebration had completely slipped her mind and she was horrified, until as if by magic, Amelia left the room, returning seconds later and revealing her new creation. Selena burst into tears of surprise, laughter and excitement as she gazed on this beautiful, sparkling gown, fit for a Queen.

On the evening of the ball, they lined up to greet their guests in the grand ballroom of Browns Hotel. John couldn't help wondering how this all had happened; it was like a fairy tale. He shook his head slightly as he remembered, a chance encounter after being dismissed from tailor after tailor, to end up lunching with a gentleman out of the blue and look at the result. He looked to the side, and smiled proudly as Gerald and Selena greeted their guests and he too shook hands with not only nobility, but with the employees of the London factory. This honour was unheard of, but then John Hadley Elliot was a force to be reckoned with, a man who refused to recognise the class system. This evening, Dukes and Duchesses, Lords and Ladies, politicians and solicitors, tradesmen and workers rubbed shoulders. They drank the same wine, eat the same food, danced on the same floor, some even conversed with each other, especially when they observed Peony, the Duchesse of Grantham and her husband the Duke, in deep conversation with the factory foreman, and later introducing the Duke, at his request, to John. This, it later transpired was to request a business meeting with the owners of Carney-Tompkins and Elliot to discuss, garments for export to Holland, his wife's suggestion.

Of course there were some of the die-hard who refused to bend and left soon after the banquet ended. Of those, neither Gerald or John were concerned, and Selena did not notice.

Sybil and Bertram Simpson-Wardour enjoyed the company of Mr and Mrs Johnson, Amelia's parents, and were enthralled with tales of the beautiful landscapes of the Yorkshire Dales and Moors and their Christmases spent there with Mr Elliot. Sybil almost burst with pride when Selena approached them and introduce them to Lady Dalgleish, who, when offered a chair by Selena, graciously accepted, and conversed easily with all four of them, even asking after their daughter Jane. Sybil left the hotel at mid-night, walking on air, she had arrived! At last, she had arrived and mixed with aristocracy, it was a night she would never forget.

After the success of the belated wedding celebrations, Gerald and his new wife were the talk of London. Some were amused he'd mixed the classes, some affronted but it mattered not which side you came down on, there was no doubt, the Carney-Tompkins and Elliot's, Selena now included, were here to stay, and rise they would.

Jane was glad of her condition, at least it kept her out of the way of hearing the constant praise of the Carney-Tompkins.

Two weeks into November, Jane had other things to worry about when at mid-night one November night, she was awakened by a warm, wet sticky feeling in her bed, and realised she had started her labour.

Her mother called the doctor, who called the midwife who called an assistant. Then the four spent two days of hell as Jane screamed, kicked and swore at them in a most unladylike fashion, and cursed her errant husband who was still in Scotland, on her father's orders.

The baby was huge and when weighed everyone felt sorry for Jane, no wonder she'd had such a terrible time. Cornelius Rory James Du-Barry Junior was the size of a six-month-old and weighed as much, nine pounds in all. He had a shock of bright ginger hair, enormous blue eyes which seemed to glare at you in a most dis-concerting manner, and he was fat! His face was fat, his belly was fat, his legs, his arms, every single bit of him was fat! And on top of all this, he was ugly.

Jane took one look at him and said. 'Take it away.' She refused to feed him so it was suggested they express her milk and bottle feed the child but after three attempts to express her milk, Jane also refused this claiming it was too painful. As a last resort they sent out for a wet nurse.

After six weeks, Jane was still refusing to get out of bed. Cornelius Senior, husband and father, had arrived within days of the birth of his son, thrilled when the child was placed in his arms. Unlike his mother, his father adored him and thought him the handsomest child on the planet and couldn't wait to take him back to Scotland.

If Jane had had her way she would have sent both father and son packing back to the Highlands and been happy never to set eyes on either of them ever again, her parents had other ideas. As far as Jane was concerned, she'd produced the heir, as far as her parents were concerned, there was still the spare to come!

As was the custom, Jane could not return to the marital bed until she had been "churched", a religious service carried out at the local church. When Jane heard this, it made her even more determined not to get out of bed. In the end her father threatened to take her to church in a chair, a humiliation one step too far. Reluctantly, Jane agreed to go on the promise that her parents would tell Cornelius that she would be unable to travel back to Scotland until after Christmas, and that whilst he remained in the home of her parent's, he would remain in his own bedroom at night.

Cornelius was furious, had he been back in Scotland, it wouldn't have bothered him, there was always Morag. The thought of Morag's comely body brought a stirring to his groin. How was he expected to go without his marital rights for the next few weeks? especially over Christmas!

Jane was so pleased with herself for pulling off this arrangement, she started to accept the calling cards that were presented. Of course, everyone who visited, wanted to see Cornelius Junior, who would be called by his second name of Rory to avoid confusion, though Jane couldn't for the life of her see why they should be so interested.'

As the weeks went by, Cornelius Junior, Rory, seemed to appear a little less gross to Jane, though whether that was her imagination or just that she was getting used to seeing his ugly face and fat body, though to be fair, he did seem slightly less large.

It was a few days before Christmas before Selena and her companion Sarah, presented their calling card, bringing small gifts for the family at Christmas, and a special one for the baby.

Jane had started to refer to him now as Rory, saying that Cornelius Junior was too much of a mouthful. Cornelius Senior was delighted at this and guffawed loudly at his own joke when he said. 'Well, there is only one Cornelius, ME!'

When Rory was brought to the drawing room that afternoon, at the request of Selena, she was rather shocked when she saw the size of him, and when he was placed in her arms, she almost dropped him, unaware of his weight. Jane didn't seem in the least concerned at Selena's struggle to hold him and when he suddenly opened his eyes and stared malevolently at Sarah, she let out a gasp of horror at which Jane's comment of. 'Mm, ugly little brute isn't he.' left Sarah and Selena speechless.

Selena was glad to hand Rory back to the nanny and spent the next half an hour trying to make small talk which was difficult as Jane seemed particularly uncommunicative. Jane realised she was being rather sullen and sulky and remembered her mother's words about making herself personable, so when Selena and Sarah made to take their leave, Jane made the effort and apologised for her lack of conversation, explaining that she was still finding herself very tired and hoped Selena would come again. To Selena, Jane's excuse was plausible, never having been with child, but to Sarah, Jane was still a young woman she would never trust.

Christmas for the Carney-Tompkins was to be spent at their Mayfair home. They were joined by Selena's Papa, Amelia and Amelia's parents. The servants in Harrogate and Knightsbridge were sorry that their employer would not be spending Christmas as usual but understood and although they would miss the hustle and bustle, appreciated theirs would be a relaxing Christmas when they could visit their relatives at leisure.

Selena was keen to get Amelia's advice on refurbishing her new Mayfair home, and having had a tour of the house spent many hours discussing colour schemes, furnishings and sketching ideas. The weather that year was particularly bad being wet and damp so the family were more than happy to stay around the fire after church and their Christmas luncheon on Christmas day.

As soon as her husband was back to work, Selena and Sarah, with the help of William whom she'd borrowed from her father, were soon scouring the shops, checking out decorators, and speaking to upholsterers who could also make new drapes for the windows.

Gerald smiled indulgently at his wife's enthusiasm and reminded her that perhaps she might give a little thought to engaging more servants. This, she thought, would be an ideal time to seek help from Mrs Pritchard who no doubt would appreciate Selena's consideration.

Whilst all was happiness in the Mayfair house, in Kensington, at the home of the Simpson-Wardour's, there was tension.

There had been truly little entertaining over Christmas as with Jane's confinement and after the birth, Sybil had had her hands full trying to keep a calm atmosphere which sadly had not been achieved. So in January Sybil, with the help of Bertram, had decided it was time Jane and Cornelius made a start to emerge back into society. This thrilled Cornelius as he'd been cooped up for weeks, but Jane was horrified until her father put his foot down and told her to pull herself together and make a grand presence of Lord and Lady Du-Barry, being temporarily in Town! For as soon as Spring came, Jane would be returning to Scotland.

Thursday's Child

Hearing this, Cornelius started to bluster that it was too long to be away from his beloved Scotland. 'All right, all right, calm down!' Bertram shouted at him. 'You will return to Scotland in February, after you've made a good impression with your wife. Andrew will go ahead in the next few days to continue the work on the castle and the estate....' He was interrupted by Jane who'd suddenly had an idea.

'And you can take Rory with you!'

'Do What?' her mother spluttered. 'You can't do that! Whatever will people think?' Jane had another idea.

'Well, the estate workers will be longing to meet the new, future heir, and he can take the wet nurse and nanny.' she announced, triumphant in her idea which seemed perfectly reasonable to her.

At the thought of the nanny, Cornelius licked his lips, she was a comely little wench, not as rounded as Morag, or experienced but he would enjoy teaching her, yes, Jane had had a good idea, he would have to be especially nice to her and do her parents bidding in showing a united front to London society over the next few weeks.

Jane was surprised at how solicitous Cornelius became over the next few weeks, she even began to think that she had been a little too harsh on him, it was almost like being wooed all over again. And when he mentioned taking Rory back with him as she'd suggested, she almost exploded with gratitude and even allowed him to visit her in the marital bed for one night, though that had only brought back distasteful memories, and she vowed she wouldn't be repeating it any time soon.

Andrew had gone back to Scotland and reported to Bertram that in the year since Bertram had taken over the reins of the estate, especially the Inn, both had started to turn a profit. Of course, the money spent on the castle and the estates properties were slowly being repaired, but at least things were going in the right direction, and productivity was up. The workers were not only happy but proud of their newly refurbished properties, keeping them clean and tidy. Wives cleaned windows, watered flowers in the gardens and the men turned their back gardens over to growing vegetables.

When Cornelius returned in the middle of February with Rory, the wet nurse and Nanny in tow, all the tenants sighed with despair. Would things return as they were before with wages not being paid and repairs required being ignored, but they were pleasantly surprised when Andrew made it plain, he still held the purse strings on behalf of their new benefactor, Lady Du-Barry. Only Andrew knew that was a ruse to make sure, when the time came for Jane to take over, there would be no hassle to her being a woman, after all, wouldn't they be grateful for all she'd done for them? It was unlikely Cornelius would contradict him as he would be even less likely to admit it was his father-in-law, an Englishman at that, who had the power.

Cornelius was pleased to be back, though not so when he discovered Morag had been dispatched to the Inn as a live in barmaid under the strict guidance of its tenants, Blair and Annis Campbell.

As Laird and owner of the Black Falcon, Cornelius was annoyed that he hadn't been consulted on this move but was swiftly put in his place when Blair informed him if he had a complaint he should speak to Mr Darling and then possibly Lady Du-Barry. Cornelius was speechless especially when Morag refused to meet him secretly in the forest.

With Andrew and Cornelius back in Scotland, and Sybil and Jane being made welcome in the houses of London's society, life was looking up for the Simpson-Wardour's. Rory's removal to Scotland with his father and Nanny, did not raise the eyebrows as Sybil thought it would, she had yet to get used to the idea that societies children should 'be seen and not heard' and Mama's of their class did not clamour for their children to always be around.

Now Bertram could embark on his next move to help him up society's ladder, politics!

CHAPTER 10

MAYFAIR, LONDON
SPRING 1885

One morning when Sarah entered Selena's bedroom, she was surprised to find the young woman sitting on the side of her bed gently rubbing her stomach and looking rather green about the gills.

'Are you all right dear?' she asked concerned. It was not like Selena to stay in bed so late and she looked distinctly unhappy. Screwing up her face, she shook her head slightly.

'No Sarah I am not. I feel awful. I'm just wondering what I could have eaten to make me feel so queasy. Gerald has gone to work so obviously it can't have been anything he has had, but we both have eaten the same. I'm trying to think where I have been that I may have had something to upset me.' The penny began to drop for Sarah, but how to approach this delicate subject. Sarah sat down beside her. Suddenly she'd become all emotional. Taking Selena's hand in hers, she smiled as tears of joy and sadness overcame her.

'Why Sarah, what is it? You are crying.' Selena cried in alarm; her queasiness forgotten.

. 'They are actually tears of happiness and yes, impart tears of sadness that your own lovely Mama is not here to comfort and guide you.'

'What do you mean?' Selena asked, and Sarah smiled, still the innocent despite being married for what? Almost eight months.

'Selena dear, I must ask you a delicate question, please forgive my intrusion. When did you last see your monthlies?' Selena stared at her, then thoughtfully she suddenly gasped.

'Oh! What does it mean.... I mean do you actually think......Oh my goodness.' then she started to giggle, and the giggle turned to uproarious laughter which brought one of the new maids rushing to the room wondering what all the commotion was. 'It is okay Jemima, Sarah and I were just laughing at something.' Selena told her.

'Very well Madam, as long as you're alright.'

'Oh, I'm fine Jemima, I'm fine.' When the door had closed behind her, Selena had turned back to Sarah. 'So, what happens now?' she asked

'Well, can you remember when you last, you know.' Sarah nodded towards Selena's nether regions.

'Oh, you mean when did I last see.....Mm, it was......end of February... end of March.....Yes that was it towards the end of March.'

'And we are two weeks into May. So, it's my reckoning that you may be about six weeks. Early days but maybe we should see a doctor, though we cannot be sure for at least another month.'

'So, what do we do?' Selena asked.

'If I were you, I think we should keep it our secret for just another few weeks, just to be sure. It could be a false alarm what with all the excitement of the wedding and moving to a new home, and then there's all the refurbishing you've been doing. And talking of refurbishing, if you take my advice, you'll slow down a bit, take things a little easy, rest a bit and whatever you do, don't pick up anything heavy or stretch up to reach anything, ask for help.' Selena nodded in agreement, then hugged herself and giggled.

'Oh Sarah, wouldn't it be wonderful? Can you imagine?' Suddenly Selena was thoughtful.

'I wonder what Mama would have thought?'

'Your Mama would have been as proud as proud, and for me it will be like history repeating itself.'

'You will be with me Sarah, just like you were with Mama? Selena begged beseechingly. Sarah smiled her affirmation.

'Of course, I will.'

Selena decided to delay speaking to her doctor as she knew she wouldn't be able to keep her possible secret from Gerald. After a light breakfast of dry toast, and weak ginger tea, Selena felt better. Sarah had gone to the kitchen to prepare it, making out that it was for herself as she felt a little out of sorts, she was not going to allow any suspicious gossip to go on below stairs.

The days went into weeks and Selena caught Gerald looking at her quizzically once or twice, even asking if she was all right. He knew it could be nothing to worry about as she seemed excited, happy as if keeping a secret or some surprise for him, but Selena was saying nothing. So, Gerald decided not to probe, whatever she was up to she would tell him when she was ready.

Gerald's birthday was approaching, and he wondered if he should do something special to mark the occasion, he would after all, be thirty years of age. But Selena had other ideas. She had decided to make her announcement in private to him on the eve of his birthday, that way he could still celebrate in style.

Selena spoke to Mrs Pritchard and together they began making plans for the party. As the twentieth, Gerald's birthday fell on a Saturday, they decided on a garden party, a little less formal than a banquet. Selena gave Mrs Pritchard permission to hire extra servants to help both with the preparations before the big day and for extra waiting staff on the day.

Selena had taken on Jemima, who'd settled in with the other servants, and Gerald had engaged a young valet who was keen to act as butler. William and Kitty, who still worked for John at his Knightsbridge residence, were now shared with Gerald as he saw no reason to have a coachman and housekeeper of his own. William and Kitty not only enjoyed working for him, but they also enjoyed the extra wages they earned and for the first time in their lives they were able to save for their old age. Gerald made a list of people to send invitations too, and asked Amelia if she would see to that task.

On the eve of Gerald's birthday, he'd wondered if John would like to join them for dinner as he often did on a Friday night, but was surprised when Selena said, rather sharply that No, as they would see him on the

Saturday. But when they sat down to dinner that evening, and the maid had left the dining room, he knew Selena had something to tell him.

'What is it my love? You seem agitated?'

Selena blushed, and putting down her knife and fork, she slowly lifted her head to look directly at him, a broad smile sweeping over her face, lighting up her eyes with excitement. Gerald held his breath.

'My darling Gerald...'

'Yes, my love?'

'In a few months we may have to employ another ……..Mm person.' she finished.

Gerald frowned. 'Really? Why is that? of course if you feel we need someone else, then by all means.......'

Selena started to giggle, then laugh heartily and getting up from her chair, ran to throw her arms around her husband. 'My darling Gerald, we will soon need a Nanny!'

'A Nanny?'

'Yes dearest, a Nanny! I am with child! We are to have our first child!'

'Really! Oh, my goodness, oh my darling, please, sit down, we must take great care of you and.... oh......and when do we expect this miracle?' Gerald was beside himself with joy. 'Oh, we must go to your Papa, he needs to be told. I will call William; he will take us there now.'

'But dinner?' Selena protested laughing.

'Dinner can wait my love, this is far more important, and anyway, I couldn't eat a thing, oh my darling I am so excited. When did you say it is due?'

'I did not. You did not give me time. But it will be December, a Christmas baby.'

Gerald rang for a servant and when Emma appeared he said. ' Emma, please ask William to bring the coach round, we have to go to see Mrs Carney-Tompkins Papa, and please ask Sarah to bring a cloak down for Madam.'

'Yes Sir.' Emma said glancing at the table and seeing their meals hardly touched. When she reported this to Mrs Pritchard and passed on the messages, Mrs Pritchard whipped off her apron and went swiftly to the dining room. Knocking gently, she entered when the call came.

'Sorry to trouble you Sir but is everything all right with your meal? Emma said you'd not touched it.'

'Nothing to worry about Mrs Pritchard, we just have to go and see my wife's Papa rather urgently, but like I say, it's nothing to worry about. But thank you for your concern, the maids can clear.' As he seemed in good spirits, excellent spirits one might say, Mrs Pritchard returned to her kitchen mystified but none the wiser. Sarah, on the other hand, seemed neither concerned or surprised so Mrs Pritchard had an inkling she knew what was going on, but if she did, then it was in confidence and Mrs P would not dream of asking her to break a confidence.

John was surprised when he heard the doorbell. He'd been pottering in the garden, which George, the gardener/handyman allowed him to do, though George made it known he kept a watchful eye on what John did. Brenda had come out to him to say that Mr and Mrs Carney-Tompkins were in the drawing room. John frowned and went quickly to the cloakroom to wash his hands, then to the drawing room, whatever could have brought them over at this time of the evening.

Looking from one to the other he said. 'My dears, whatever is it?' then he noticed, both had beaming smiles.

'Papa, we have great news for you.'

'Really?'

'Tell him Gerald.'

'No, you tell him my love.'

'No, you Gerald.'

'Oh, for goodness' sake, will someone just tell me!'

So together they told him in unison. 'We are with child!' they shouted.

'What both of you?' John joked then hugged them. 'Oh, what a clever young couple you are! Well, well, well. So! I'm to be a grandfather, am I? Well, well. Now that does make me feel old. Well, congratulations. Oh, dear we should celebrate.'

'We can do that tomorrow, though we prefer to keep this bit of news quiet for a little while.'

'Of course, of course, I understand. So, who does know?' John asked.
'Just us three, and the doctor of course.' Gerald answered.
'And Sarah.' Selena said. 'Well, it was Sarah who told me when she found me one morning feeling distinctly queasy.'
'Ah, Sarah yes. Well, she would have recognised the signs, good old Sarah. Well, she won't say anything, safe as houses is Sarah where secrets are concerned, never a gossip. So, when is this little miracle due to appear?'
'December. Oh, and Papa, we have no objection to you telling Amelia, after all she's almost part of the family.'
'Part of the family.' John muttered thoughtfully 'Yes, she is isn't she,'
When they returned to Mayfair later that night, Sarah and Selena exchanged quiet smiles with Sarah giving Selena a wink of the eye, which made Selena giggle.

Gerald's garden party to celebrate his thirtieth was well attended. John and Selena were now well acquainted with many of the aristocracy and conversing with them was no longer an ordeal. Their easy-going Yorkshire charm, delighted company wherever they went and many still compared Selena with Jane.
Selena always asked after Jane when in the company of her parents, and being told she was now back in Scotland busy helping her husband with estate matters and the final changes to the castle, said to pass on her regards. The Simpson-Wardour's appreciated Selena's friendship, as she was the only one who seemed amenable towards their daughter. Despite Jane and Cornelius courting society earlier in the year, and it seemed with some success, interest when Sybil mentioned their names, seemed to be ignored, the conversation changing direction.
Bertram thought his entry into politics would make some impression, especially as he'd been chosen to stand for a constituency in the coming election for the Liberals. On the contrary, his continued name dropping of Mr Gladstone, only seemed to irritate whose ever ear he was bending at the time. Similarly, Sybil's continued reference to her daughter as 'Lady Du-Barry' irked their wives.

Thursday's Child

Gerald was pleased he'd agreed to a garden party for his birthday as this meant it wouldn't go on all night, and now he knew of Selena's condition, he didn't want her getting tired.

John had not enlightened Amelia of his daughter's condition as he felt it a 'delicate matter not for a gentleman to discuss with an unmarried lady' so he told Selena, who giggled and said.

'Oh Papa, you are funny.' then went to seek Amelia out from the crowd and taking her to one side, told her privately. Amelia was thrilled. So now Selena had two ladies she could confide in, Sarah and Amelia.

It wasn't long before Selena had to withdraw from socialising, though she thought this a ridiculous tradition, and not one she was aware was adhered to in Yorkshire, If it was, she was not aware of it, but then as Sarah pointed out, she was mixing with a different class now. Oh class! Selena threw up her hands in horror, there was the stupid word again. Yes, she knew the same existed in the North, but somehow it didn't appear to be so noticeable, but again, Sarah was able to point out why. The Elliot's had lived and moved in different circles before they'd moved to London, and she had married Gerald. Gerald may have moved away from society, or been pushed aside by some, but he still had what was known as having 'blue blood' in his veins. Similarly, now his and John's partnership was the talk of the town, especially since receiving a summons to visit Buckingham palace with their samples, suddenly 'Trade' no longer was a word to be sneered at.

In Scotland, life was becoming almost unbearable for Jane who couldn't wait to get pregnant again just so she would have an excuse to return to her parent's home in London and she'd be free of her loathsome husband's attention in the boudoir!

The castle's renovation were complete and she had to admit, it looked very impressive indeed, so with her father's blessing and encouragement, Jane set about entertaining. Her first ball would be a masked mid-summer ball on Saturday August the fifteenth. All the invitations were for Lords and Lady this, the Duke and Duchess of that and Earls and

Baronets. There were few plain Mr and Mrs, one for her parents and one for Gerald and Selena. Others were for various clan Lairds Cornelius insisted they had to invite, to ignore them would have caused great offence.

When Gerald declined her invitation, and she read the reason for it, Jane was livid and in a fit of temper, smashed all her cut glass perfume bottles.

For days Jane fumed in the knowledge that Selena was with child, Gerald's child. At this thought she burst into tears of anger and despair. 'Why?' She asked herself over and over again, 'When it should have been me, I should have been the one to bear him a child.' she cried in the privacy of her room. And in her grief she started to pray, praying for the death of the child at birth or that of its mother. And that is when a plan started to take shape in her mind. 'There must be a way. Think, woman, think.' she admonished herself. As the weeks turned to months, her plan became increasingly bazaar, complicated, but feasible. She must find a way to return to London before the birth of Selena's child, the child that must die.

The masked ball held in August was a remarkable success, and everyone who attended, was impressed at the scale and grandeur of the castle. Jane also surprised her guests by being extremely hospitable and surprisingly happy with her Lord. Even Cornelius was surprised at his wife's sudden attention and friendliness. He wouldn't have described it as 'loving', that would be going too far and their coming together could not in any way be considered passionate. No, Cornelius understood the intimate side of things, was a matter of necessity if they were to have another child, 'The Spare, to The Heir! But despite all that, Jane did seem to be in good humour, although a little distracted.

She had taken to writing in a small notebook which she would lock away if anyone came too close. Not that Cornelius cared, as he had plenty of comfort from the nanny who had returned to Scotland with him. This hadn't gone unnoticed, and Andrew had duly reported back to Bertram and Jane, the latter greeting the news with relief, as it meant she should not have to put up with too many of Cornelius' visits, not to mention some of the bizarre and distasteful things he had suggested in the bedroom. However, it did leave Jane angry with the nanny who thought she'd got one over on Jane.

Jane rarely saw her son other than the obligatory daily visit at six in the evening before he was put to bed. If her mother thought that time would bring about any maternal feelings, she was to be sadly disappointed, if anything it was the opposite. The more Jane encountered Rory, the more revulsion set in, and she couldn't wait for the child to be returned to the nursery. Cornelius, on the other hand, continued to see his son as the most handsome and cleverest little chap that had ever walked the earth, not that at nine months he'd started walking, despite daily encouragement from both faither, (Scottish for father a term not used by Jane), and nanny. Although when Jane wrote to her parents in unsavoury terms regarding her son, they quickly wrote back telling her unless she bonded with the child, she would have no hope in gaining the castle in the divorce settlement as Rory would be the main successor.

With this in mind, guests attending the ball were amazed when nanny was instructed to bring Rory down to be shown off, and Jane made gushing overtures to her son, taking him from the arms of nanny and almost dropping him due to his weight and the fact she had not held him for months.

Having paraded him around, and declaring with delight, the future Lord Du-Barry, she eventually handed him back to nanny stating that her darling child must continue with his beauty sleep!

Even Cornelius was surprised but pleased with her action and said as much.

The morning after the ball, Jane awoke feeling so ill she wanted to die and spent most of the morning vomiting.

She sent messages to the kitchen accusing everyone and anyone of trying to poison her. On the third day, as no one else had been ill, Cornelius sent for the doctor who announced, this was no stomach upset, no poisoning, her ladyship was again with child!

Cornelius took off on a drunken spree in celebration, which lasted three days and included a long and lusty visit to a certain lady! Little did he know, but whilst Andrew nor Jane could have cared less, his behaviour in time, was to have a devastating effect on both their lives.

When confronted with the news, Jane was thrilled. Not so much with the pregnancy but that she was now able to return to her parents in London, away from these weird speaking peasants she was surrounded by.

Cornelius was pleased with her decision but not so pleased when she informed him she would be taking Rory with her. Nanny wasn't pleased either as she had high hopes of his Lordship's involvement with her and was sure she would eventually be in line for the title of the next Lady Du-Barry.

Cornelius had picked up on nanny's ambition, but as he was now tiring of her and beginning to dislike a certain arrogance in her behaviour, was quite happy to see her off with his wife. True, he would miss his son, but then again, and this brought a smile to his lips, it would give him a certain freedom to indulge with his recent paramour! Andrew could take a run and jump in Loch Tay!

However, both parties were to be disappointed when Sybil wrote, that her daughter was to stay where she was, as Sybil was on her way to Scotland!

Jane was furious. Despite still feeling extremely sick most mornings and not looking forward to such a journey, she had plans to organise, and must at all costs be back in London in early November. It was still only a few days away till the beginning of September, so that gave her two months to persuade her mother they should return at the end of October, beginning November if they weren't to get cut off in Scotland with bad weather.

When put like that, the battle was won. Sybil had no desire to be trapped in Scotland over Christmas, and in any case, Bertram was standing for the election which was taking place from the twenty-fourth of November to the eighteenth of December. Then there was Rory's first birthday, so yes, Jane's mother agreed, they would return to England at the end of

October.

Cornelius accepted all these arrangements stoically, knowing that with his wife and mother-in-law in unison, it was useless to argue. Whilst he was happy with the arrangement for the two females going back, he wasn't so sure about losing his son, whom he adored. But had he fought to keep him in Scotland, a fight he had no chance of winning, nanny would have remained as well, and he was beginning to look forward to seeing the back of her as well as his wife and her mother. He had just about come to accepting the idea when he received another jolt. He was expected to return with them! When he explained that as the Laird, it was his duty to be here in the castle especially at Christmas, he was told by Sybil that his duty was to that of his wife and son! Furthermore, he also had a duty, nay, gratitude, to his father-in-law for saving not only the castle, but the Du-Barry Estate! There was no arguing with that, they had him in an awkward position.

So, at the end of October, they set off for London. Because of the amount of luggage required, and the stops needed for Jane's comfort, it would take two coaches and six days to reach London. By the time they reached Kensington on the fourth of November, Jane was convinced she was going to lose the baby and took to her bed for the next week.

CHAPTER 11

LONDON
AUTUMN 1885

Their first year of marriage had been nothing but bliss. Gerald and Selena could not have wished for anything else. They had celebrated Selena's nineteenth birthday and their first wedding anniversary quietly with family and close friends. Neither of them were keen to overtly entertain, so were careful which invitations they accepted so they were not in the unenviable position of having to reciprocate too often. Of course, with Selena's confinement looming, this was as good an excuse as any.

She was surprised to hear that Jane had returned from Scotland with her husband and Rory and wrote to her, welcoming them back to London. She apologised for not being able to call on them, explaining her condition. So, she was delighted when she received a card from Jane requesting if Selena would be well enough to receive a visit from her, as she too was in the early stages of pregnancy? When Jane heard this, she was delighted and replied that yes, it would be lovely to receive a visit as they now had plenty in common. But when Gerald heard this, he was not so sure and confided in Sarah, who said not to worry, she would remain by Selena's side at all times. Afterwards, he wondered if he was becoming a little paranoid where Jane was concerned and reprimanded himself.

When the two ladies met a week later, onlookers could have been forgiven for thinking these two had been firm friends for many a year such was their greeting of each other. However, Sarah was not fooled. Although Selena was nothing but genuine in her pleasure at seeing Jane, Jane did not fool Sarah. Selena gave Jane a genuine hug, but Jane's response was a brief exchange of cheeks, something that past Selena by. Jane also showed her displeasure, as Sarah quietly took a seat over by the window and proceeded to knit.

Selena listened as Jane extolled the description of the castle's restoration, the entertaining she and his Lordship had done, but little about Rory.

'And what of Rory, he must be an immense joy? I can't wait for our child to arrive.' Selena said excitedly. The gaiety with which Jane had been conversing, suddenly slid from her face.

'Mm, of course motherhood is not it's all it's cracked up to be. Babies can be extremely smelly and noisy creatures, but of course that is why one has wet nurses and nanny's, how would we cope without them?' Jane laughed flippantly waving a lace handkerchief in the air.

Selena was struck dumb by Jane's comments. She was aching to hold her baby in her arms, cradle him or her as he or she nuzzled to her breast. Was Jane joking? She asked herself, but thought it wise to say nothing, instead she changed the subject. 'And what of your parents, are they keeping well? I understand your Papa is standing for election, how very brave.'

'Mm, well, yes, I suppose it is. I do know it's a lot harder work than I think even he imagined, all this campaigning.'

'Yes, I suppose it is.' There followed a silence when neither ladies knew what next to talk about. Jane it seemed was only happy when talking about herself or her achievements. Then a thought occurred to Selena. 'And how is your husband? Does he delight in returning to London?'

'Lord Du-Barry is only happy when in the Highlands. However, he does not like to be away from me when I am in a condition.' She answered, hoping to give the impression of a devoted, blissfully happy marriage, though Selena struggled with this having seen Cornelius and knowing him to be a rather overweight, uncouth gentleman, with a rather offensive odour about his person when she had met him. But then she hastily admonished herself for having had such unkind thoughts.

There was one rather interesting remark Jane made during their conversation regarding the birth and that was her recommendation of a midwife that she had had who was amazing, making the whole thing pain free and so easy.

'Oh dear!' Selena said, 'Is giving birth painful?' she asked. Sarah, seated within hearing distance, reminded herself she should have a little talk in private with Selena, to give her some advice of what to expect without frightening her. She was alarmed when she heard Jane's reply, and determined to put Selena straight as soon as she could.

'Well, it can be my dear, especially..' and here she turned her head slightly in the direction of Sarah, 'If those in attendance do not know what they're doing.....' with a slight inclination of her head in the direction of Sarah, it was obvious she had Sarah in mind. Selena was left open mouthed, and Sarah fuming at the accusation.

'Oh dear, but I believe we have a very good midwife haven't we Sarah?'

'Indeed, we have. She comes highly recommended by Doctor Martins.' Sarah replied haughtily.

Jane turned to look at Sarah, annoyed that she'd been brought into the conversation, but then thankful as this was information that she would need. Smiling through gritted teeth, she asked, 'And just who is this paragon of virtue? I may know of her?' Jane was thrilled at the reply. Not only was she given the name of the woman, but where she lived. With a smile, she returned her attention back to Selena, and soon took her leave. Luckily for Jane, as the doors closed behind her, she noticed a little maid heading to the back of the house. Checking that she was not being watched, she called out quietly to attract the girl's attention, and moved quickly towards her before she could disappear.

'Yes Ma-am?' the girl did a quick bob and Jane put her finger to her lips to silence her.

Jane quickly summed up that she wasn't too bright. 'I have a little favour to ask of you.' the girl raised an eyebrow in surprise. 'But you are not to breath a word, not now, not ever, do you understand?'

'Yes Ma-am.'
'I'm planning a little surprise for your mistress.'
'Yes Ma-am.'
'When your mistress starts her confinement, you are to come immediately to this address and ask for me, under no circumstances are you to speak to anyone else, only me, do you understand?'
'Yes Ma-am. But have I to ask Mrs Pritchard's permission?'
'Absolutely not! are you stupid girl? I said no one was to know!'
'Yes Ma-am.........so what's do I do?' Ada asked frowning, wondering how on earth she was going to leave the house unnoticed.
'You just slip away, and when you return, if asked where you have been, you say you have had an upset stomach and needed the lavatory, understand?'
'Yes Ma-am.'
'And if you do it correctly, you will receive a reward.'
This brought a smile to Ada's face. 'Yes Ma-am, thank you Ma-am.'
'But remember, you must never breath a word of this, ever!' As Jane handed a piece of paper with her address on it, she had a sudden thought.' I take it you can read girl?'
Ada looked at the paper. 'A little, yes Ma-am.'
'What does that say?' Ada carefully read out the address written. Jane nodded slowly and walked away.

As soon as Jane had departed, Sarah went to sit beside Salena. Reassuring her that the birth was nature's way for all creatures, human and otherwise. Why? she asked, would anyone ever have more than one child if the experience was bad. For one who had never experienced childbirth personally, it was easy to say! Reassured, Selena settled into the last few weeks of her pregnancy.

Jane was just about to retire when late one December night, there came a loud knocking at the door. She was up on her feet and down the hallway before their butler could get there, calling out that she was expecting someone. Opening the door, there stood Ada with the news she'd been waiting for. Snatching up her reticule, she took a coin from it and pushing it into the girl's frozen hand, told her to return and forget about it.

Glad that both parents had retired earlier, she collected her cloak and bag and hurried out. At the bottom of the road, she hailed a horse drawn carriage giving him an address to drive to.'

The driver hesitated. 'You sure?' it was late at night, and not the sort of place he liked to go to during the day let alone at night.

'I'm sure! Now drive.'

When they arrived, Jane instructed him to wait for her. The driver looked around nervously. 'You ain't gonna be long are yer?' but Jane had disappeared down an alley only to reappear in minutes with a scruffy woman who had something in her arms. Climbing aboard, Jane issued more instructions only now it was to a posh part of London.

On arrival this time, Jane pointed in the direction the woman was to take and said. 'Just remember, you are never to speak of this again.'

'When do I get me money?'

'When you deliver the goods and you have done the swap.' Jane then ordered the driver to wait.

Minutes later the woman returned, still carrying something. He was given further instructions to return to where they'd picked up the scruffy woman and she was no sooner out of the carriage than it was on its way back to where he'd picked is fair up the first time. The woman stepped down from the carriage, her face covered by a heavy veil. Pushing a bag of coins at him she told him not to speak about the evening unless he wanted to end up in the Thames with bricks tied to his feet, then she was gone.

Selena and Gerald were beside themselves with grief. How could this have happened? Sarah wanted to die as she felt she had not protected her darling mistress.

As Selena lay sleeping having been given a sleeping draft by the doctor, Gerald, the doctor and Sarah went over and over what had gone on. The so-called midwife had finally returned, after disappearing with the newborn, carrying a small wooden coffin in which she said the still born, disfigured, child lay. The doctor had wanted to examine the baby but was stopped when the priest from their local church arrived and advised the child be left in peace as it was now "in the hands of our Lord."

When Doctor Martin asked why the midwife he'd recommended hadn't been called, Sarah produced the letter this other midwife had given her, stating that Mrs Carson was unable to attend. No reason was given and Gerald and Doctor Martin, made an immediate visit to Mrs Carson, who was very distraught and said that she had not written any such letter, indeed, she'd received a letter stating that the Carney-Tompkins no longer required her assistance. It was signed Gerald Carney-Tompkins. Gerald stared at it and straight away declared he had not written the letter, it was not his handwriting or his signature and he quickly proffered his signature as proof.

The more they tried to make sense of it the more they went in circles. Sarah was convinced the child had not been disfigured, but had to admit, she'd only seen it at a glance, looking to see what sex it was and confirming it was a girl, and she recalled it had a birthmark on its left shoulder, that of a star, the star of Bethlehem as they called it, just like Selena and her late Mama.

For reasons of privacy, the Carney-Tompkins kept an exceptionally low profile, simply stating their expected child had passed, and Ginny made it her business to remove any notices she found regarding a foundling on the steps of the vicarage in Islington.

The family grieved for many months, and Selena sank worryingly into a melancholy from which no one seemed to be able to rouse her. That was until the Autumn of eighteen-eighty-seven, when it was discovered that once again, Selena was with child. The baby was due in the Spring of eighteen eighty-eighty-eight, only this time, the birth would be in Harrogate.

Although they were all thrilled about it, the family decided to keep it strictly to themselves, except for Amelia and Sarah, who'd guessed anyway.

Selena's pregnancy progressed well, this time without the morning sickness she'd endure during her previous pregnancy which Sarah said was a good omen. She thought about writing to Jane with her good news then for some reason felt reluctant to do so. It was then that she started to think about Jane's absence. Jane had apparently returned to Scotland immediately after the birth of her second son. According to the grapevine, few had seen the child and those who had reported he was quite a weak and sickly child, not as robust as Rory. But still, Selena was surprised she'd never received a sympathy card after her previous loss. Thoughts of Jane brought back the memory of her recommendation of midwife, their refusal and the subsequent mix-up over midwives in the end. Selena shuddered at the memory then pushed it from her mind, refusing to go back and wallow in the sadness.

Christmas was a quiet affair at the Mayfair home of Gerald and Selena with the only guests being Amelia and her parents, and Selena's Papa.

John had already written to Mrs Harris to inform her of Selena's desire to have her baby in Harrogate and to expect them at the end of March. He had also written to Doctor Saunders requesting his attendance at the birth, and also asking him to engage the services of a midwife. They were taking no chances this time.

As arranged, John Selena and Sarah travelled back to Harrogate at the end of March as John wanted to spend some time at the factory. Gerald would go up on John's return and would remain there with Selena until and after the birth

On April the fifteenth eighteen-eighty-eight at eight-twenty in the morning, Jonathan Gerald Carney-Tompkins, yelled his way lustily into the world to the delight of all. Below stairs servants stopped what they were doing, ears pricked and looked at each other before rushing into the main hall agog as to what the baby was, boy or girl?

Gerald ran onto the landing and leaning over shouted, 'It's a boy!' there were cries of joy and much merriment throughout the day.

Over the next few days the house was awash with messages of

congratulations. John and Amelia arrived from London and were over the moon when John held his grandson in his arms for the first time, John unashamedly shedding a few tears.

News filtered back to London society, and when Sybil heard, she ran to tell Jane the good news and was surprised at her daughters response.
'So why are you so full of Joy?' she snapped at her mother. 'It has nothing to do with us. What difference does it make?'
'Oh Jane,' her mother said sadly. 'Why are you so angry? Surely you can be pleased for her, especially after what she went through before, that must have been heart-breaking.'
'Not as heart-breaking as having a son with a fat, pink face which resembles a pig and this stick like sickly creature.' she said pointing to Ewan who lay passive whilst his nanny changed him as he was still in nappies.
'Oh Jane.' her mother said again, shaking her head sadly and walking towards the door.' Whatever has made you so spiteful? They are your children.'
'What indeed!' Jane muttered under her breath as she picked up a glass bon-bon dish, itching to throw it at the door her mother had just walked through, changing her mind at the last minute. 'Perhaps it was you making sure I didn't get to marry the man I loved and ending up with a fat, old, penniless slob with a title!'
Never did it occur to Jane that the man she loved, didn't care for her, that never registered, so she continually blamed everyone else.

A week after the baby's birth, John and Amelia returned to London. Gerald would return with Selena and Sarah and baby Jonathan, in early May. It was decided, with Sarah's agreement, that because of her age, a nanny should be employed although Selena told them in no uncertain circumstances, she would be Jonathan's main carer. The nanny was for backup only and Sarah would continue as Selena's companion.
When they eventually left to return to London, Mrs Harris, still Cookie to Selena, had a few tears as she said she would miss master

Jonathan growing up, never to have the pleasure of him running around her kitchen, sampling her biscuits and cakes as Selena had done as a small child. To which Selena promised they would take regular holidays in Harrogate.

PART TWO

NINETEEN HUNDRED

CHAPTER 12

MAYFAIR, LONDON.
JANUARY 1900

In twelve years, there had been many changes. Queen Victoria would be eighty in May and her obsession with Abdul Karim was no less. Karim had been her favourite of the two Indian servants sent to her in eighteen-eighty-seven in celebration of her Golden Jubilee. In that time, she had made Karim her "Munchi" which translated as clerk or teacher, and he in return had taught her to write in Urdu and Hindi much to the concerns of palace aids and many government ministers. She had also invited his wife and children to England and given them homes and land in India. She wrote letters to him signing them "Mother", but the more her advisers railed against him, the more stubborn she became.

Gerald and John's business had gone from strength to strength and Gerald's marriage to Selena had proved to have been the right decision. The couple now had four children, Jonathan born in April eighteen-eighty-eight, followed by Albert George in eighteen-ninety and then twin girls Sophia and Louisa in eighteen-ninety five. But Selena never forgot her first born and each time she gave birth, her thoughts drifted back to that awful night in December eighteen-eighty-five, and once again she couldn't help mourning her loss.

Amelia was still their chief designer and her parents, though still alive, were getting very frail and although Amelia now had extra care to help in her home, she worried that perhaps she should spend a bit more time with them herself and said as much to John.

It had been twenty years since he and Gerald had had that fateful meeting, and later lunched together. He often smiled at the memory. But for his visit to the same tailor where Gerald had been to order a new suit, they would never have met.

For some time now, John had been feeling tired. Not only that, he'd begun to lose interest in the business, with his thoughts regularly yearning for his home in Yorkshire, and a slower pace of life.

Gerald had noticed how listless his father-in-law sometimes appeared and worried if he was not well. One day when Gerald was enthusiastically regaling John with a funny story, he realised he was not listening and seemed to be staring off into the distance. When he stopped speaking, John didn't appear to notice.

'John, are you alright?' he asked concerned

'Em, sorry Gerald, I was far away. What were you saying?'

'I asked if you were all right? You haven't seemed yourself recently. Is there anything I can help with?'

John smiled at Gerald's kind concern for him. He sighed deeply. 'Fact is, I have two concerns at present, and one would affect you. But perhaps I ought to start with the one that doesn't affect you but may affect my daughter.'

'Oh?' The mention of Selena did concern Gerald as he was always very protective of her.

John smiled again, understanding Gerald's vocal concern. 'Nothing too drastic. I just wondered if you would have any idea how Selena would take my remarrying?'

'What! Good gracious John, I had no idea........do we know the lady concerned?'

John chuckled. 'Oh you do indeed, though nothing has ever been mentioned,.....and the lady concerned, well, I don't think she has any idea that my thoughts might lay in that direction, although I hasten to add that I think a certain amount of fondness for each other is a forgone conclusion. At least I hope it is or I'm going to look mighty foolish when I propose.'

'Propose!' spluttered Gerald who was also chuckling as his father-in-law certainly looked happy at the thought. 'Well come on then, tell me, who is she?'

There was silence for a minute before John said. 'Amelia. I wish to marry Amelia. There, I've said it. Now, what are you going to tell me, that I'm a silly old fool, wanting to marry a beautiful, intelligent woman who is far too young for an old man like me.'

The laughter from Gerald died away to be replaced with a look of wonder and pleasure. 'No, my friend, and dear, kind, partner and father-in-law. You're neither silly or a fool, and you are definitely not old. I think Amelia has loved you for a long time. And I am sure Selena would welcome her. I most certainly will.'

'Thank you Gerald, that is very kind and comforting for me to hear that.'

'So what was the other thing you wanted to talk about, the one which could affect me?'

'Retirement.'

'Ah...' Gerald said

'I' was forty-six when I met you, and that was almost twenty years ago Gerald, and I seem to have lost the appetite for business. I'm also missing my home in Yorkshire and yearn to return. I know Amelia loves Harrogate, and her parents are becoming very frail. They also love Harrogate so it is my intention, that when I ask Amelia to marry me, that she bring her parents with us, and together we will see they both end their days well cared for.'

'I think that is wonderful, and I'm sure you will all be very happy in Yorkshire. I for one would not dream of standing in your way. Might I ask that you remain as a silent partner, someone to whom I can come to for advice?'

'That would be my pleasure Gerald and thank you for being so understanding.'

Gerald said nothing to Selena about the conversation he'd had with John, when he later returned home that evening. John did not bring either subject up again until the end of March, when he suddenly announced they should all go to Harrogate at Easter.

It was left to Selena to write to Mrs Harris and warn her the family, all six of them plus Papa, Sarah, Amelia and her parents would be descending on them the week before Easter.

When Cookie received her letter, she was at first thrilled at having them all back home, then panicked at the thought of four kiddies and all the meals to be organised and cooked. When she read that William and Kitty would be retuning also to help, it was a huge relief and she soon had everyone rushing around in preparation. Bill the handyman was called in and issued with a list of jobs, Albert and Billy told to get tidying the gardens and let her know what vegetables she could rely on, and she hired another maid from the village to help Anna spring clean the whole house.

In Mayfair Selena and Sarah were busy with lists of packing their servants had to do, at the same time trying to keep the children calm as they were so excited at the thought of going to Harrogate.

Jonathan would be twelve when they were in Harrogate, so Selena asked Mrs Pritchard if she would be kind enough to make a birthday cake for them to take as this would be a great help for Mrs Harris. Mrs P was delighted as over the years, she had come to love her new mistress and adored the children as they'd been brought up polite and respectful to everyone, including servants.

Albert, or Bertie as he was often referred to, would be ten in the summer, and both boys attended a private school locally, but Selena insisted they would never be allowed to board, she wanted her boys home every night. The twins Sophia and Louisa would be five in September when they would start at an all-girls school, again, locally.

Despite having a wonderful healthy, happy family, Selena never forgot her first child and still mourned her death and the mystery surrounding it. This memory would also remind her of Jane, which on this occasion reminded her that she hadn't heard anything from her for ages, not that they'd ever been really close, and certainly not since Selena's family had grown. Sarah often remarked it was jealousy which kept her away, but Selena did visit Sybil now and again, especially as the elderly lady was not in good health, all the more reason for Jane to visit more often. Selena decided to make a visit before they left for Yorkshire, taking Sophia and Louisa with her as Sybil loved seeing the twins and was sorry she only had two grandsons. So one afternoon, Selena set off with the girls, and was surprised when they reached the house to see the drapes had been drawn. For a moment Selena stood staring, not knowing what to do. There was only one reason for drawing drapes during the day and that was when someone had died, but she had not heard anything. For a few minutes she stood biting her lips in a quandary, until Sophia, dancing up and down asked for the lavatory. Uneasy with this request, Selena felt she had no option but to knock on Sybil's door.

A butler opened it and bid her enter and take a seat. There was an awful deathly hush, and Selena shivered. Louisa gripped her mother's hand and nervously asked if they could go home. A maid appeared and Selena attracted her attention asking if she would be kind enough to take Sophia to the lavatory. No sooner had they disappeared than the door to the drawing room opened and a rather distraught Sybil, came towards them, dabbing at her eyes with a handkerchief.

'Oh my dear Mrs Simpson-Wardour, have we called at an inconvenient time?' Selena asked sympathetically.

Sybil shook her head. 'No, my dear, please come through '

'Em, one of your maids kindly took Sophia to the bathroom.' Selena told her.

'Oh, here she is.' Sybil said as the maid brought Sophia down the stairs. Sophia ran to greet them and did a little bob as she reached Sybil. Sybil smiled. 'What dear, dear children you have Selena, such a comfort they must be too you.'

'Yes, they are.' Selena said uncertain whether to offer to take her leave, but Sybil seemed happy for them to stay, ushering them into the drawing room and ringing for a maid, to which she ordered tea for themselves, and milk for the children.

'Please, be seated. I am so sorry to greet you like this. The fact is we received sad news two days ago, Cornelius, Lord Du-Barry, my son-in-law, has passed away.'

'Good heavens! ' Selena said shocked. 'Had he been ill?' At this Sybil seemed to take a step back, uncertain how to answer. Finally, she told Selena about the message she'd received, though it was difficult to understand.

'Em, we are not certain as to the cause, though he appears to have been poorly for some time and now it is Jane who has succumbed..........Em, well we are not sure. I suppose it could be grief. Yes, yes, it could be grief.'

'If you would prefer us to go......

'No, no. Please stay. The tea will be here soon. No, it will make a nice diversion. We have not seen anyone and......'

'You mean no one has offered their condolences?' Selena was shocked. A member of the aristocracy being ignored, even if it was in Scotland, surely......'

'Oh no, oh no, you don't understand. It is the way they wanted it.. Jane was going to return to London but then, well it was recommended, advised, that she stay there, in Scotland, with the boys you see. But Andrew has returned, you know, he was made Estate Manager and it appears he has spoken to my husband, oh, dear, oh dear, the whole thing I mean it is just so....' There came a knock at the door swiftly opened by the maid pushing a trolley loaded with tea paraphernalia, Jugs of milk and an array of tiny cakes.

'Cook thought you might like some cakes Madam. Would you like me to pour?'

'No Daisy, thank you. And please thank cook, it was thoughtful.'

Selena was totally confused. Sybil seemed very flustered and almost contradictory in her explanation. It was like she was trying to hide something however, she suddenly pulled herself together and changed the subject asking after Selena and the family. In the end, they spent a pleasant afternoon catching up. Sybil was especially vocal about Bertram's continued success in government and dropping into the conversation snippets concerning the Queen and her offspring. Selena noticed how she avoided speaking about her own grandchildren or Jane which was unusual. When she left, Selena asked to be remembered to Jane and extend her condolence for her loss.

CHAPTER 13

ST. MARY'S VICARAGE, ISLINGTON, LONDON

'Well, how did you get on?' Elizabeth asked Thursday. She was excited to hear all about her daughter's first day as a pupil teacher.

Thursday slipped off her gloves slowly, smiling with an air of sophistication which made her mother laugh. 'Come on.' she said. 'Stop teasing, and tell me, how did you get on?'

'It was good. Miss Cranford said I had a natural ability.'

'Oh, did she now. Well, that would be down to your father letting you teach in Sunday school.' Elizabeth laughed. But Thursday agreed.

'You are quite right Mother, and of course the boys have helped letting me read to them for practice.' The boys Thursday referred to were her three older brothers.

Thursday's desire to become a teacher had never waned, so as soon as she was fourteen, Elizabeth and Mark had approached the governors of the school and requested them to take her as a pupil teacher. The training was long and she would stay at the school until she was eighteen. During this time, she would receive seven and a half hours tuition a week from an approved Master or Mistress, of which Miss Cranford was one. This was to improve her education as she taught the younger children daily, and to give her practice in teaching. Throughout this period, she would be monitored by the education authorities, and reports on her progress held. Then at eighteen she would be eligible to take an exam, which could lead to a Queens scholarship which would finance her collage training.

Of course, this was not obligatory and many a pupil teacher, for one reason or another, chose not to go that route, but Thursday had other ideas, and was determined to complete her training no matter how long it took.

Of the boys, Harry was now twenty-four and a junior doctor, Edward was twenty-two and having completed his university studies worked in a solicitors office and Theo was nineteen and reading Religious studies at Oxford university. He wasn't sure what he wanted to do though he was rather leaning towards missionary work.

Mark was still Vicar of St Mary's and was wondering if he would ever be moved. Although he'd enjoyed working in the East End, he'd started to hanker for a country church. This had come about from reading some novels about a small village, purely the imaginations of the author, but it appealed to him, and he was sure that somewhere outside of London he could find the same idyll. When he told Elizabeth of his dreams, she laughed and teased him saying he was an old romantic, but still the vision persisted.

However, his dream would have to remain just that for the coming years, as until Thursday was old enough to go away to a teacher training collage, if that is what she wanted, he had four years to wait. It wouldn't be fair to uproot her, as finding another school that would take her as a pupil teacher, might not be easy.

CHAPTER 14

Travel to Yorkshire was long and arduous, especially with four children. Amelia's parents were finding it particularly gruelling but hid their discomfort as they didn't want to upset their kind hosts. William and Kitty had gone on ahead, taking all the luggage, and would meet them at the train station with an extra coach.

On arrival in Harrogate, Mr and Mrs Johnson were taken straight to their room and after cups of tea and biscuits were brought to them, advised to rest and not to come down until they were ready, there was no need to hurry.

They were grateful for everyone's consideration, and when Amelia popped her head in later to tell them dinner was but half an hour away, she found them both sound asleep. Selena thought it best to leave them and said so, they were obviously more tired than hungry, and in any case, Selena told her, if they wanted something to eat later, she would happily get it for them if Mrs Harris had retired.

As it was, the Johnson's slept round the clock, waking up at eight the next morning, embarrassed but well and truly rested.

As a treat, John said he had booked luncheon at the Royal House Hotel, where sixteen years before, Selena and Gerald had celebrated their wedding breakfast. Apart from treating his family, John had another reason for wanting to visit the hotel.

Gerald, Selena and the children had all gone for a walk, whilst Mr and Mrs Johnson and Amelia were in the conservatory reading. When John entered, Amelia looked up but the others didn't appear to have noticed. John put his finger to his lips, and beckoned Amelia to follow him.

In the study, he quietly closed the door and offered Amelia a seat.

'What is John?' she asked concerned. John smiled and sat down beside her on the sofa. Taking her hand in his surprised her, never had he in all the years they'd known each other made such a personal gesture. As he started talking about their friendship, his love of Yorkshire and his desire to return there her heart sank. If he were to retire, and that's what it sounded like, she would miss him terribly. For years she'd held a candle for this quiet, gentle man with the funny but attractive accent, but knew he'd had a beautiful and happy marriage and perhaps had no need for another. John had been talking but Amelia hadn't been listening as she was upset she would not be seeing him daily as before. He'd stopped talking and Amelia rallied herself. She shook her head to clear her thoughts. 'Sorry John, I was far away, I didn't hear what you said.'

'Which bit did you miss dearest Amelia?'

He'd called her "Dearest" "Dearest Amelia" had she heard right? 'I'm sorry John, I'm sorry. I lost you after you spoke about coming back to Yorkshire. I take it you mean, retire? I....I....well, I must be honest, I would miss you terribly but if that is your wish I....' Amelia got no further as suddenly John was down on one knee in front of her.

'Amelia, my dear, I'm asking you to marry me?'

'What! Oh, my goodness.' Then fearing he may have the wrong impression, she too sank to her knees and putting her arms around his neck, cried 'Oh yes, yes, yes, John. Oh yes I'll marry you.' but as they both made to stand up, they toppled over just as Selena opened the door to tell them they should be getting ready to go out to lunch.

'The laughing, crying pair was a remarkable sight and Selena didn't know what to make of it until Amelia burst out. 'Your father has asked me to marry him Selena, I hope that is alright?'

Selena started to laugh, and as she turned to run back and make the announcement she called over her shoulder .'And about time too Papa.'

That Easter was especially joyous for all concerned, and when Amelia told her parents they would be living in Harrogate and wanted them to join them, Mr and Mrs Johnson were doubly delighted.

When the news trickled down to the servants, they were also thrilled as they too had become very fond of Amelia and her parents. However, news of John's retirement plans reminded Mrs Harris that she was not getting any younger and wondered how she would cope having four people back in residence on a daily basis. There were only two options. Either she retired, or she had to have help. Mrs Harris decided to have a chat with Sarah and ask her advice as to whom to approach. Leaving the Elliot's after all these years would break her heart, but she also had to recognise she didn't have the energy of old, and tired easily. But if she retired, where would she go? She had a little savings so hopefully; she'd be able to find a small flat to rent. But in the end her worry came to nothing. When John got to hear of her plight, he discussed it with his wife to be and they soon had a plan.

One morning, after breakfast had been cleared, Selena appeared in the kitchen saying her Papa wanted to see Cookie in his study and it was nothing to worry about.

'Mrs Harris, please, come in and sit down.' John said kindly. Mrs Harris looked at Amelia who smiled encouragingly. 'Now, it has come to my attention that you are concerned you will be unable to cope with all the extra work we unthinkingly would be hoisting upon you with our future plans.'

'Oh, but please don't think.......I mean I am we are all thrilled with the news …....' she started but was interrupted when John held up his hand.

'It was remiss of us not to consider and talk to you before, but we would have eventually got around to it. Now, Amelia and I have been talking and would like to know your opinion on this. Amelia is keen, naturally to run her own home, and would like to assist in the day to day running of the house, which will include cooking but only with your approval.'

'Yes Mrs Harris, I only want to help, I have no wish to take over your domain, so I hope we can work together on this. We realise with four extra mouths to feed it's too much for one person.' Amelia added.

'And William and Kitty will be returning with us. They have been serving both myself and Mr Gerald, but it is time for them to also return to Yorkshire and Mr Gerald will employ a new coachman. This means

Kitty will be available, and if you are happy to work with her, she would be happy to work with you and perhaps you can teach her your skills so when it comes to your retirement, she will be able to take over. And when it does come to your retirement, you have no worries there either. Again, after discussion with Amelia, we will provide you with a small cottage, rent free, and a small pension. You will never be in difficulty. You have been a loyal, faithful, not to mention, hardworking servant and cared for us over many years, it will be our turn to care for you.'

Mrs Harris's eyes filled with tears and a small sob escaped. "Oh Sir, Mr Elliot, what can I say? It has been an honour and a pleasure to serve you and your family over the years. Many happy times, and some sad ones, but let us hope the future will be all happy, and I, we, all of us who have served you, wish you every happiness in the future. And thank you, thank you for being so thoughtful and so generous.'

Arrangements dealt with, everyone felt relieved, peace and tranquillity had been restored.

John and Amelia did not want a big affair, but he wanted to give her the day every bride deserved. He may have been married before, but she hadn't and therefore she would have a day to remember, he was determined on that, and so was his daughter.

The wedding was to be in June, as John saw no reason for a long engagement. They'd known each other for years, and although he didn't mention it, the years were not on his side.

Selena took her Step-Mama to be, in hand and sat her down to design a wedding gown. Amelia was touched when Selena suggested she be the Maid of Honour and her children, page boys and bridal attendants. 'As soon as we return to London, you will have to get our machinists sewing.' Selena told her.

Whilst in Harrogate, Amelia and John visited the church to discuss their ceremony. The vicar knew the family well. His late father, also a vicar, had officiated over John's first marriage, Selena's christening, and Mary's funeral. He had married Selena to Gerald in eighteen-eighty-four and later christened all their children, so he was delighted that once again he would be able to welcome the family into God's care.

The wedding breakfast had been booked when they went to have lunch at the Royal House hotel, and again manager and staff were delighted to see the family again.

Word soon spread about John and Amelia's forth coming wedding, so everywhere they ventured, congratulations were forthcoming. This wasn't surprising as John, and later partner Gerald, were highly respected and loved employers.

When the family returned to London after Easter, they left Mr and Mrs Johnson behind in Harrogate. It was decided that as they would be returning in June for the wedding, it was too much for the elderly couple to keep travelling back and forth. John told Mrs Harris to engage another maid to help Anna with the cleaning and washing and a temporary person to assist her with the cooking until Kitty returned in June.

Amelia was to pack up their home in London, giving notice to the landlord, and sell what furniture was not required. Then she would move in with Selena until her marriage. As soon as she was ready, John would arrange for her parents' personal belongings to be transported to Harrogate. Everything was going according to plan and with Selena's help, like clockwork.

One afternoon Selena popped out to post a letter, when suddenly a dog shot onto the road and attacked the horse which was pulling a cart loaded with sacks of potatoes. The horse reared in terror, its hooves flaying in panic. The old man driving tried desperately to control horse and cart but it was too much. As the horse continued to rear and the dog continued to attack, man and cart were turned over, one of its wheels caught Selena with a glancing blow across her back and shoulder. Selena went down and onlookers screamed fearing the worst. Police came running and another carriage drew to a halt. Everyone frantically looked around to see if the young lady was with anyone. When they realised she was on her own, still breathing but unconscious, the gentleman from the carriage, scooped her up and said he would take her and the old man from the cart to hospital. Before leaving, the policeman looked into

Selena's reticule and found a calling card with her name and address on it. At least they would be able to notify her family.

At the hospital Doctor Harry Milton was called to attend two people who'd been brought in from a road accident. The old gent was shaken but seemed okay and wanted the doctor to pay attention to the young lady who'd started to come round.

Selena opened her eyes and when her vision cleared, looked into the eyes of a smiling young man.

'Hello Madam, can you tell me your name?'

Selena frowned. Her head hurt, then she realised, both her back and shoulder hurt. When she tried to move, she cried out in pain.

'Don't move. I'm Doctor Milton and you are in hospital. Can you tell me your name?' he asked again.

'My name.' whispered Selena. 'My head hurts, and my back.......what happened?'

'Yes my dear, but I need your name, what is your name?'

'Selena, Selena Carney-Tompkins.' This was greeted by a few gasps as many of the staff in the hospital, including Doctor Milton, recognised the name.

'Are you any relation to Carney-Tompkins and Elliot?' he asked. Selena went to nod her head then regretted it

'Ooooo. Yes, Gerald is my husband and John Elliot my father.'

Harry Milton smiled. At least she knew who she was, so not too much to worry about as long as there were no broken bones. 'Well Mrs Carney-Tompkins, I will just have to examine you to make sure there are no broken bones.' Gently, with the help of a nurse, Harry began to peel back her jacket, then her blouse, when he stopped dead and stared. He put his hand to his mouth and stared, shocked at what he'd seen. Was it possible? In the brief time he'd been a doctor, he'd never seen another like it. Selena had closed her eyes again against the pain so hadn't seen the doctor's reaction, but it wasn't lost on the nurse.

'What is it Doctor?' the nurse whispered.

Milton shook his head. All sorts of thoughts were buzzing through his head. He was breathing heavily and knew he must hide his reaction from his patient, too late for the nurse, but what he had to ask his patient now should not be overheard by the nurse. He had to find some way of getting the nurse to leave. 'Oh, it's alright Nurse, I thought it was a broken bone but it appears not. Could you go and find someone to look up this lady's address, we need to inform her family as soon as possible.' As soon as she was gone Harry touched Selena gently to gain her attention. 'Mrs Carney-Tompkins, may I ask.....this birthmark..' Selena gave a little smile.

'Oh that, family mark you might say. My Mama called it the star of Bethlehem.'

'Your Mama had one?'

'Yes. So have all my children.'

'Your children?' Harry Milton went cold. 'How many children have you?' Selena smiled sleepily she was in pain and didn't really want to talk. 'Mrs Carney-Tompkins, how many children have you?' he asked again.

Selena closed her eyes but replied. 'Four, two boys and twin girls.' Hearing this, Harry did a quick calculation and relaxed before he was jolted back when she added. 'But I did have a baby girl, many years ago, but she died.'

'And did she have the mark?'

'Oh yes, according to my nanny, but I didn't see her.'

Once again, Harry went cold. 'And when was this?'

Selena had closed her eyes again. 'Oh, it was a long time ago, I can't remember, please can you help me it is so painful.'

'Yes, yes of course.' Suddenly there was a rush of people as in strode Gerald, John, Amelia and Sarah.

Two days later, Selena was sent home with a warning to rest as although there were no broken bones, she was badly bruised and would be for several weeks.

Harry Milton was stunned as his discovery. But what had he discovered? A young lady with a birthmark identical to his sister. But she wasn't his sister. He remembered the morning they'd come down to be told a baby had been left on their doorstep, a foundling no less. But what if?.........he could hardly bear to think of what if..... He told no one. His parents would be devastated if Thursday turned out to be.....No, don't think like that, it can't be, it's a coincidence. But was it? When had he ever seen a birthmark such as his sister and this patient had? And she'd said it was a family mark. Her mother and all five of her children, was it possible the first child hadn't died, was the first one their own......dear God no! It didn't bear thinking about. But he couldn't get it out of his mind. He would talk to Mrs Carney-Tompkins some more, maybe she could throw some light on it, reassure him that Thursday, that's a point! If she could tell him when she'd had this baby, the date, time, day, anything. But when he was next on duty, he discovered Mrs Carney-Tompkins had gone home. Put it out of your mind he told himself repeatedly, but every now and again, it popped into his head. It woke him at night, and he found himself looking for babies being born with birthmarks or patients. But he never saw another anything like it.

The weeks went by and just when he thought he'd forgotten about it, something would happen to remind him. He found himself watching Thursday, trying to see a resemblance with Mrs Carney-Tompkins, but it was fruitless. Just when he was beginning to despair, he decided he must go and see them, perhaps speak to Mr Carney-Tompkins.

Their address was easily found, so on his next day off, he made his way to Mayfair, and the home of the Carney-Tompkins. He stood for ages outside, walked up and down working out what he could say, how he could start without alarming them. In the end he walked up to the front door and pulled the bell-rope. It was sometime before a manservant opened the door and Harry was informed the Carney-Tompkins were away to Harrogate for a family wedding and he was unable to inform the gentleman the date of their return. The door swiftly closed so no further enquiries could be made.

As the weeks passed, the incident at the hospital gradually faded from Harry's memory, until he eventually forgot about it. That was until a chance remark by his brother Edward.

'You'd never guess who came into the office today?' They were all sitting at dinner one evening. Elizabeth looked up.

'Oh, who was that somebody famous?'

'Sort of. She recently married a very well to do gentleman, a rather famous gentleman, any ideas?' he teased.

'Well if he's famous and wealthy, we're hardly likely to know him.' Mark, his father said.

'Mrs Amelia Elliot! She's down from Yorkshire, came in to up-date the address on her parents Wills.'

There was a clatter of cutlery as Harry leapt up from his chair. 'Father, I must speak with you.'

Mark looked up at the urgency in his son's voice. 'Can it wait till we have finished our meal?'

The wedding had gone without a hitch. The weather had been perfect, the bride looked like a fairy princess according to Selena's twin girls, who'd behaved impeccably, and the church had been full to bursting as many of the workforce from the factory and surrounding villages, arrived.

The wedding party enjoyed a sumptuous reception at the Royal House Hotel, and Mrs Johnson shed a few tears seeing her daughter marry such a lovely man, something she thought never to see as Amelia had been so determined to care for them.

John and Amelia were to honeymoon for three weeks touring Italy, after which they would return to London until John retired at Christmas, though he hadn't informed Gerald of this decision. Gerald would not be surprised, as though John had not given him a date, nor had he mentioned his wish to retire since he first spoke about it, Gerald knew it would be coming.

Selena, Gerald, Sarah and the children stayed for a few more days, just checking the Johnson's were settled and Mrs Harris and the other servants were all happy. But as Sarah said the day they set off. 'Lovely as the children are, I bet the servants will be glad of the rest!'

'Until Christmas.' Selena chuckled as she'd made up her mind she would want to spend Christmas back in Harrogate.

Sybil was angrily throwing clothes onto the bed, as her maid tried scooping them up and folding them before they got creased and needed ironing again. Bertram entered the room.

'Well!' Sybil demanded. Bertram looked uncomfortable and glanced towards the maid as if warning Sybil not to say anything further. Sybil noticed his embarrassment and decided to use it to her advantage. She raised an eyebrow and glared at him, it said "do as I wish or else" Bertram caved in.

'Yes dear, you are quite right. I'll instruct my man to pack for me, and inform the House, (Parliament), that I have urgent family business to take care of'.

Since hearing Andrew's report concerning the cause of death of her son-in-law, Sybil had been in a terrible state of shame, terrified it would become known. Thank the lord he'd lived in Scotland and had made very short visits to England and mixing with society. So far, to her knowledge, society knew nothing of Lord Du-Barry's demise, only she, Bertram and Andrew knew the full details, though Sybil shuddered at the thought that probably half of Scotland would know. And what of her daughter? Could she have contracted it? Hopefully having had Rory and Ewan, there'd have been no further need for contact of the bedroom variety.

She had heard about the nuptials of John Elliot and his employee. Why on earth had he stooped to marry the girl? Surely a man of his standing could have chosen someone further up the ladder of society, with his wealth one would have thought so. Still, he was only a Northerner with a funny accent and from all accounts had quite a modest property up there in the wilds. But then look at Gerald, he too had married beneath him, true society had shunned him in the early days, but to be fair he had turned the fortunes of the Carney-Tompkins around, and although now society welcomed him back, he appeared to be unimpressed. And the girl, Selena, she too had to be admired as a charming little thing who'd produced four healthy offspring, though there was some mystery surrounding a baby which died or something. Strangely, Jane was quite friendly with her at the time, though showed no sympathy and had shot off to Scotland. Sybil shook her head mystified, oh well, she had her own problems at the moment.

The journey to Scotland was arduous, and although they'd gone by train most of the way, it didn't go as far as they required, so a coach and driver had been sent to meet them at the train station. The rest of the journey continued over heavily rutted roads which shook and threw them about. The driver, a course, a huge, frightening man, sporting a bright ginger beard which almost obliterated his facial features. He looked like he had just left his cave dwelling. He was wearing what all the men in this part of the country wore, a pleated skirt apparently called a "kilt", Sybil did not approve but said nothing.

When they arrived, the servants greeted them almost disdainfully. It wasn't until Bertram reminded them who paid their wages that they suddenly, reluctantly brought in the luggage and took them to their rooms. Sybil was surprised that Jane was not there to greet them and asked the housekeeper where her mistress was and received a sullen reply.

'Where she always is, in bed!' Sybil was lived and as the woman walked away, recalled her.

'Come back here!' Sybil roared. The woman stopped dead in her tracks and turned, obviously surprised and a little unnerved at Sybil's demand. 'How dare you speak to me like that! In future when I ask a civil question, you will answer with a civil reply, that's if you want to keep your position. Now, I am going up to see my daughter, but in one hours' time, I want every servant in this household, assembled in this hall, do you understand me?' The housekeeper gave a surly nod. 'I said, do you understand? to which you will reply, "Yes Madam", now do you understand?' For a moment there was a standoff as both women glared at each other.

'Yes Madam.' the housekeeper replied, only this time her attitude had reverted almost to civility, she had met her match. Sybil pointedly looked at her watch which hung round her neck on a gold chain. Then turning, made her way up to her daughters' boudoir.

When Sybil entered, she was horrified. The room smelt disgusting. It was so dark in there with the heavy drapes closed, Sybil could hardly see Jane. Going first to the windows, she swept open the drapes and flung open the windows letting in the late summer sunshine and fresh air. Then turning, she made her way to the bedside and could have cried at what she saw. Jane lay sleeping though just to look at her face, neck and shoulders, you could see she was all skin and bone, Dear God what had been going on. As she gently pulled away the covers, Jane opened her eyes. The smell emanating from her made Sybil take a step back. Tears filled her eyes. 'Oh, my dear girl, whatever has happened to you? How could they leave you in this state?'

'Mother? Mother is that you? Is it really you?'

'Yes, my darling it's me.' And despite the smell, Sybil leant forward taking her sick child into her arms, for she was her child, no matter how old, Jane was still her child, and who ever had left her like this, would pay for it.' 'Are you hungry?' Sybil asked.

Jane smiled weakly. 'I would love some of your broth, the food here is awful.'

'Don't you worry, Mother's here now and things will change, I will make you better. And your father's downstairs, he will not stand for any nonsense. Jane smiled again, closing her eyes.

'Thank you Mother, but I'm afraid you're too late, I'm dying.'

'Dying! Who said you were dying? All you need is some decent food and attention. Just you wait, you're the Lady of the house and we're here to get you back on your feet and in charge again.'

Jane's reply was a simple smile as she drifted off.

Sybil left the room, going in search of her husband who she found in the study. He was going through the accounts with Andrew.

'Andrew!' she said sharply as she entered. 'Why didn't you tell me how ill my daughter was? And how neglected?'

Andrew looked up, startled at her words. 'But, but I wasn't aware she was ill.' he said mystified.

'You weren't aware!'

'No Madam' he replied and looked genuinely surprised.

'Have you not seen her?'

'No Madam, and when I did ask after her Ladyship I was told she had no wish to see me, and I should get on with my work and they would get on with theirs. I'm sorry Madam, I had no idea. Is she very poorly?' he asked concerned and clearly worried.

'Yes, she is.' Sybil had Bertram's full attention and saw how his lips went to a hard line; such was his furry when Sybil described her daughters situation. 'I've told the Housekeeper to have all the servants in the hall at,' she checked her watch. 'In twenty minutes, time.'

'Right!' Bertram banged his fist down onto the desk so hard, the ink stand jumped. 'I thought it was too good to be true. Andrew has done a good job keeping the farm and Estate in order, and it is making a good profit, but it appears the household has been running amok!'

'I'm so sorry Sir, other than the finances, I felt I had no jurisdiction over the household as this was her Ladyships domain and I didn't wish to interfere. If only I had known, I swear to you Sir, Madam I would never have let this happen to her Ladyship.'

It was clear to them both that Andrew had had the wool pulled over his eyes and the housekeeper and the rest of below stairs servants had run rings round him. He was clearly very distressed. Bertram got up, patting the young man on the shoulder, reassuring him.

'Don't worry, I can see what's been going on here, but nobody, nobody ill-treats my daughter and gets away with it. Heads will roll!' he roared as he swung open the door, startling the servants who'd begun to gather in the hall. 'Right now. I don't know what you think you've been playing at since his Lordship passed, but it stops now!' He yelled out at them; some visibly shook with fright. His London accent and temper left them in no doubt, this man was not to be played with. The haughty accent he'd spent years practising, in an effort to try and replace his London one, had gone, he'd reverted to his London roots. 'Now 'ands up those who no longer want to work for the Du-Barry Estate which means my daughter, Lady Du-Barry?.........' Silence as servants eyed each other nervously. 'Mm, cats got yer tongues. You!' he pointed a finger at the housekeeper who now looked terrified, gone was her obnoxious manner of before.

'Me Sir...'

'Yes, you Sir. What's yer name?'

'Mrs Mc Donald.'

'Mrs McDonald SIR!' he screamed at her.

'Mrs McDonald Sir.' she repeated, her voice shaking

'Do you wish to continue in her Ladyships employ?'

Mrs McDonald nervously nodded, remembering to speak before being roared at again. 'Yes Sir.'

One by one each and every member of the household, was grilled and demanded of. None dare say anything which would see them out of work. As for the outside workers, they received a less severe talking too, even some gaining praise from Bertram as he told them Mr Darling was satisfied with their work and if it continued with enthusiasm, there would be bonuses for those come Yuletide. These men were then dismissed whilst the rest told to remain. It was now the turn of Sybil. Spurred on by her husband, she was ready to lay down the law with a vengeance.

'Right. Mrs McDonald, as housekeeper, you will do just that, keep house. And by that I mean I want this place cleaned from top to toe, the place is filthy. So take your maids and instruct them on how each room is to be cleaned and that it be done every day to my satisfaction and to her Ladyship's when she recovers. We will not be leaving until her Ladyship recovers and when we return, if we find it like this you will all be sacked immediately. Now, who is her Ladyship's personal maid?' one hand rose slowly into the air. 'Right, you and cook are to remain, the others are dismissed and can get started on cleaning. You, what is your name?' The personal maid who'd raised her hand, replied.

'Aileen ma'am.' She answered in a shaky whisper.

'Well Aileen, I wouldn't give you a reference as a Lady's maid after the condition I found her Ladyship in when we arrived. Do you know the duties of a Lady's maid?'

'Yes Madam.' She squeaked nervously.

'Then why didn't you carry them out?' Sybil barked at the now shaking girl.

'Mrs Mac, said wasn't necessary Miss, I mean Madam.' she was whispering with fear.

'Well now, from now on you won't listen to anyone other than myself or her Ladyship when she recovers. Now, go to her Ladyship, run her a bath, bathe her and wash her hair, gently mind, she is very poorly, then dress her and get help to bring her downstairs to the conservatory. You will perform these duties every morning and help her into bed at night. Is that clear?'

'Yes Madam.'

'Go, and hopefully a maid will soon be up to clean the room. You can spend the rest of your time, daily, sorting through her Ladyships garments, mending and sending any unclean items to the laundry.' The girl scuttled off so fast she left a draught. Now Sybil's attention was all for the cook. The woman looked unhygienic and slovenly. Sybil looked her up and down. Cook returned her stare belligerently. 'When did you last bathe?' Sybil asked.

'What's it to you?' Came the reply. What Sybil did next hadn't been planned, but she was so angry that despite everything that had been said first by Bertram and then by herself, this woman was still ready to treat her employers with distain. Furthermore, Sybil blamed this woman for Jane's ill health more than anything or anyone. She had obviously taken immense pleasure in serving her daughter muck! For this she would pay. It would also serve as a warning to anyone else who thought they could mess with the Simpson-Wardour's.

Staring at the woman, Sybil walked over to the bell rope and pulled it. A footman duly appeared.

'Take this person to her quarters and see she packs her personal belongings, then see her off the estate.

'But, but.'

'No buts. And if you ever step foot on this estate again, I shall order the gamekeepers to shoot on sight. Now leave the castle, you have half an hour.' As Sybil turned away, the footman grabbed the cook's arm as she yelled after Sybil.

'What about ma mooney?'

Sybil turned and looking coldly at her replied. 'Thank your luck stars I'm not calling the police and charging you with attempted murder. Now, get her out of here before I change my mind.'

Over the next few weeks, the castle was scrubbed, buffed, washed, dusted and polished within an inch of its life. Even the groundsmen had improved on their previous performance.

Bertram visited the tenants, farmers and the landlord of the Black Falcon with Andrew, whom he was pleased to see, everyone without exception, greeted them warmly, no doubt because since taking over, not only had they seen their homes repaired, watertight and cosy, but they had also been paid every week and on time.

Sybil, to the surprise of all the servants had taken over in the kitchen and after demanding a complete strip down and clean, ensured that good nutritious and tasty food was the name of the game. Nothing fancy simply good home cooking. She also noticed, over time, that the household expenses were less than before and realised that someone had obviously been on the fiddle. She made sure that all were aware of her discovery and informed Andrew for future reference and for when a new cook was engaged. Although the new cook would be made fully aware that Andrew and her Ladyship, when she recovered, would be watching.

But Jane was still a worry. Despite being looked after and fed well, there was little improvement. She was nowhere near her old feisty self. Sybil wanted to call a doctor but had no liking or trust for those in the area. In the end, after discussion with Bertram, they decided to bring a doctor from London to examine their precious daughter, though not one who had links to London's society. They didn't want any chance of a scandal. Bertram agreed but who? Who could be trusted, as now they were worried that Jane had somehow attracted Cornelius's disease.

'Who was that vicar you were talking to when you were campaigning? would he know of a doctor who could be discreet?' Sybil asked one evening,

'Yes, I remember. Can't think of his name though. Mayland, Maylord, Matlan, something like that.' Bertram wracked his brains but couldn't put his finger on it, it was so annoying, he had it on the tip of his tongue. 'It'll come to me.' He told Sybil. 'And if I can't remember, I know the church he served, hopefully he'll still be there, he's sure to know someone who can be discreet. I must return to parliament next week, so I will look him up and let you know.'

'Thank you Bertram. The sooner Jane's better, the sooner I can return to London, I'm really not wanting to stay here over the winter, and you know what it's like, if or should I say, when it starts to snow, that will be it, we'll be stuck here until the Spring.

In the meantime, Sybil had managed to engage a new cook. A nice widow woman who was an amazing cook. Not only that, she was thrifty, kind and eager to serve.

The morning Bertram left to return to London, Sybil thought a walk might not go amiss and suggested this to Jane. She also mentioned that perhaps at half term the boys might like to return for a holiday from their boarding school. Sybil thought it most odd that not only had the boys been boarders since they were five but were sent to some distant relative during their school holidays. This arrangement had only been since Cornelius had died and Jane had become increasingly ill. But as she seemed a little improved, her mother thought a visit from her children might give her something to look forward too. But apparently not, as when suggested, Jane seemed filled with horror at the prospect, which Sybil thought strange for a mother. That was until later that day when she was forced to understand her daughter's concerns.

It was around four-thirty, they were just finishing their afternoon tea, which consisted of some tiny sandwiches and cook's light, fluffy scones with her home-made jam and thick whipped cream, when they heard a carriage approach. Sybil frowned at Jane as neither felt like entertaining at this time of the day. They heard the bell go and expected one of the footman or a maid to enter with a calling card which they would decline stating that her Ladyship was indisposed today. Unfortunately, there was a loud commotion in the hall, followed by the drawing room door being flung open and the maid making a frantic grab on one large fat boy who flung himself onto one of the sofas, then lunging towards the scones and whooping with joy. Having snatched at one of the scones and plastering it with jam and cream, proceeded to shovel it into his mouth with great gusto.

'I'm sorry Madam, your ladyship, but they just burst in, there's a gentleman here to see you, says he's from the school.

Jane sat almost speechless but managed to say. 'Show him in.'

Sybil looked from Jane to Rory and back to Jane again before saying. 'Jane! Aren't you going to say anything? His manners are appalling! Rory, Rory, stop that at once! How dare you behave in such a manner, stop it I say, stop it.' Just then the maid ushered in the gentleman she'd spoken of. He looked uncertain at both ladies 'Lady Du-Barry?' he enquired.

'I am Lady Du-Barry, and just who are you and what are you doing with my son?' Jane spoke quietly as she still had little energy, but she did manage her old haughty voice.

The gentleman gave a slight bow. 'Your Ladyship, I am Mr Donald Mackie, Superintendent of the Strathclyde school for boys. Forgive this intrusion but we have only recently heard of your late husband's demise, please accept our sincere condolence for your loss.' He put his hand to his mouth and coughed. 'I only had the pleasure of meeting your husband when he enrolled the boys, but.... oh dear, this is rather a delicate matter, but I'm afraid the headmaster has sent me as escort to bring your son's home.'

Jane stared at him. Sybil looked uncomfortable as Jane had made no attempt to speak to Rory or Ewan, who having crept in behind his brother, was now sitting, hat in hand like a terrified waif.

'Their aunt was supposed to deliver them back to school after the holidays, for the new term. I have been and still, extremely ill. They cannot possibly stay here.' Sybil was shocked at the way her daughter dismissed her own children. But before she could say anything, Mr Mackie continued.

'I am afraid Madam that is impossible. You see the fees for the coming year are payable in advance and this has not happened.'

'That is not a problem, I will get our Estate Manager to give you a cheque to take back with you. You can take the boys at the same time. Now if you care to wait in the hall, I will arrange it. Rory! Go upstairs and wash your hands and tidy yourself.'

'I, I, you see the thing is....'

'Mr Muckie or whatever you call yourself, did you not understand me? Go and wait...'

Thursday's Child

'But Madam, you don't understand....'

'No! Mr Muckie it is YOU who does not understand...'

'Madam, the headmaster refuses to have the boys back, in fact I am under strict instructions on no account am I to return with them!' it was Mr Mackie's turn now to raise his voice. Sybil thought her daughter was about to burst a blood vessel as she went almost purple in the face with rage. She had to intervene. Getting up, she took over.

'Mr Muckie, Mackie, please, my daughter has been extremely ill, and I fear this situation could have serious consequences. Would you please follow me, and I will call Mr Darling to deal with this.' Pulling a bell rope on her way out she met a maid on her way to the drawing room. 'Please take the boys to their rooms and keep an eye on them and send for her Ladyships maid to attend her.' On reaching the study, Sybil reached for another bell rope to summons Andrew Darling.

The conversation that followed appeared to have nothing to do with the non-payment of fees. Rory's behaviour was so disruptive, he would have been expelled even if the fees had been paid. Strathclyde school for boys had wanted rid of him for years, it was only because of his father's name, "Lord Du-Barry" giving the school a bit of class, that the lad had been kept for so long. As soon as they'd heard of his father's demise, they felt able to act and the school fees not being paid gave them an excuse. Mr Mackie explained that although young Ewan was no problem, he was neither, athletic nor academic, so in their eyes, he was of no use to the school as he would not be amongst the achievers the school like to boast about.

As Andrew Darling said, 'There was obviously no more to be said.'

As soon as Mr Mackie had been shown out Sybil turned to Andrew, 'So, what do we do now?'

'We could find them another school, but it seems to me it would be a waste of money, that's if we could find a school to take them. I have a suggestion if I may?'

'Fire away Andrew, I'm at a loss.'

'One day, young Rory will be the Laird.....'

'If he lives that long.' Sybil muttered, thinking she'd happily strangle the so and so with her own bare hands. 'Sorry Andrew, I interrupted..'

'In my experience, there's nothing to knock a wild animal into shape as training, discipline and that young man is behaving like a feral dog. Give him to me and within six months you will start to see a difference. As for Ewan, well I think he is a different cut of cloth. He's a sensitive laddie but I do not think he's stupid. No, if I were you, I'd home school him at first, perhaps a governess or tutor, someone who could encourage the boy without bullying. We need to find out what his strengths are, everyone has strengths.'

'Gosh Andrew, you do talk a great deal of common sense. No wonder my husband employs you. I will discuss it with her Ladyship and write to my husband, but I think your suggestions are excellent and I see no reason not to implement them immediately. I will ask Mr Simpson-Wardour to find us a governess or tutor, then I can organise a school room and a room for whoever we employ. I will leave you to make plans as to how you will deal with Rory. Would you like me to send him to you?'

'Not yet. I will see him in the morning, that way it will give me time to work out a timetable. I will have to enlist the help of farmers, small holders, and the stable workers. Some time spent with the gamekeeper wouldn't go amiss, yes, leave him to me Madam and we'll soon knock him into shape.'

'Oh, that is such a relief. My daughter will be able to recover with this burden's taken off her shoulders.'

As Andrew went to leave the room, he hesitated. Frowning he turned to Sybil. 'Mrs Simpson-Wardour, may I make a suggestion regarding Ewan?'

'Of course, what is it?'

'I hope you won't think I'm speaking out of turn, but as I said, Ewan is of a sensitive nature, and I've a mind to think the boy could have potential, we just have to find what it is.'

'What are you suggesting?'

'Well....'

'Speak up man, I think we've known each other long enough to be frank.'

Thursday's Child

'I'm wondering if it would be possible for him to have some small interaction with his mother, if not her then yourself. It would mean perhaps, him reading to her. Do you think her Ladyship would agree, just for ten or twenty minutes of an afternoon? It may be good for both. I think the boy would grow in confidence with some small acts of.......shall we say affection?' There was silence for a moment when Andrew began to fear he'd overstepped the mark.

'I think you are right Andrew; I think you are right. However, at the moment, my daughter is ill, but her father is arranging for a doctor from London to visit to find the underlying cause of it. But in the meantime, I might take on that roll. Yes, leave it with me. Thank you, Andrew, I think our meeting has been very encouraging, peace, I hope will soon be restored.'

In London, Bertram was on his way to visit the vicar he'd been so impressed with back in his campaigning days. He still couldn't remember his name but did remember the church, so headed for the vicarage.

Knocking on the door, a young maid opened it, and Bertram offered his card, requesting to see the vicar.

'Sorry Sir, Vicar's not here at present, would you like to speak to Mrs Milton?'

That was it, that was the name which had escaped him. "Yes please if she can spare me a few minutes of her time.' The girl went off and a few minutes later, a smartly dress lady came towards him, smiling and ready to shake his hand.

'Mr Simpson-Wardour, how nice to meet you, do come through.' As they entered a pleasant day room, Bertram noticed all the photographs of the family.

'What a handsome bunch you have, I take it they're all your family?'

Mrs Milton smiled at the compliment. "Yes all ours, and all grown up sadly, it seems like only yesterday they were all playing, coming and going to school and now, well three are still at home, our youngest is away at university, but so far the others haven't seen fit to fly the nest.' she said laughing.

'Food's too good.' He replied joking. 'Sadly, we only had the one. And it's about her that I come here today to ask your husband for help, but you may be able too.'

'Oh? please take a seat, would you like any refreshment?'

'No, no thank you, I'm fine. It is a rather delicate matter, a matter my wife and I would like discretion with.'

'I can assure you Mr Simpson-Wardour, anything you speak about to myself or my husband, will never go further than these four walls.

'I don't know if you are aware of whom my daughter is?'

Elizabeth Milton frowned. She knew he was a member of Parliament, and vaguely remembered him when he was canvassing but couldn't for the life of her place the daughter.

'She is Lady Jane Du-Barry,.... she recently lost his Lordship.' Uneasy, he decided it wasn't necessary to explain what Cornelius had died from and continued.' Since then, my daughter has been extremely ill and seems not to be making any progress in recovery. She lives in Castle Du-Barry in the Highlands of Scotland, and I'm afraid my wife and I have very little faith in the medical men in the area, they all seem rather like quacks, mostly bearded, wearing skirts they call Kilts, and speaking with such strong accents, sometimes a language called Gaelic, which we can't understand. My wife is with her at present but we wondered if we could find an English doctor to go to Scotland, all expenses paid of course, and find out what ails her.'

'Could she not come to England?' Elizabeth asked.

'Sadly no, she is too frail to make the journey. As I said, we will pay all expenses, travel and his fee, but we do ask for absolute discretion.'

Elizabeth nodded thoughtfully. 'I may be able to help.'

'You can?' Bertram asked in astonishment.

'I think I know of someone, and discretion you can be assured of.'

'Oh, Madam that would be such a weight off my mind. How soon will you know?'

'This evening.'

'Really!'

Elizabeth smiled. Could you call tomorrow evening? My husband and the doctor I have in mind will be here. You can discuss all the details then.'

'Oh Madam! I could kiss your feet!'

Elizabeth laughed. 'Oh Mr Simpson-Wardour I do not think that will be necessary.'

At seven p.m. the following evening, Bertram was on the doorstep of the vicarage and shown immediately into the drawing room to be greeted by the Vicar, his wife and son Harry, Doctor Harry Milton, what luck, who better than a doctor who is the son of a vicar.

One hour later, an elated Bertram left the vicarage with all arrangements in place. He could now send an urgent message to Sybil informing her, Doctor Milton would be with her a week the following Thursday.

CHAPTER 15

ISLINGTON TO SCOTLAND

When Harry had leapt from the table telling his father he needed to speak to him all those weeks ago, the rest of the family stared at each other wondering what could have caused his sudden reaction. Edward thought back to what he'd been saying, all he said was that the new Mrs Elliot had come to the offices to make alterations her parents Wills, as they had moved to Yorkshire. Edward frowned.

'Was it something I said?' he asked joking.

'I have no idea. ' His mother said. 'Anyway, finish your meal, I am sure we'll be told about it all in good time. The family continued eating and discussing their day. In his father's study, Harry was pacing the floor, as his father stared mystified at his son's anguish.

'Whatever is it, Harry? For goodness' sake son, sit down, stop pacing and tell me, I'm sure it's not the end of the world.'

'Are you? Well, I'm not. Oh father, I don't know where to begin. It might be a huge coincidence and I could cause enormous upset, but then again.....'

Mark was now worried. His son was not a dramatist, so whatever he was worried about, was serious. 'Harry, sit down, take a deep breath and start at the beginning.' Harry did as he was told. He bowed his head for some time, trying to get the words in his head right, but whichever way they came out, it would still be confusing. When he lifted his head, Mark could see unshed tears in his son's eyes. 'Whatever is it son?' he whispered.

Thursday's Child

'Father, I think I may have found Thursday's mother!' There, he'd said it and he felt sick.

Mark sat like stone. It felt as though someone had punched him in the stomach. He too felt sick, as though his stomach had dropped from his belly, eventually whispering 'What?'

Harry proceeded to tell him about the accident which had brought in an injured patient, who on examination, not only had the identical birthmark as Thursday, but told him all her children and her late mother, had the same.

For several minutes they sat silently, Mark digesting what he'd just been told. 'Well.' he eventually said. 'It could be a common thing, lots of children have birthmarks, I see it a lot when I'm baptising.'

'That's what I'd hoped, but I've spent weeks looking at new-borns' and where a few have indeed had birthmarks, nothing like Thursday's.'

'You say this woman was upper class?'

'More than that Father, she is the daughter of John Elliot and the wife of Gerald Carney-Tompkins, the clothing company!'

'Oh well then it has to be a coincidence, they would hardly have left a baby on our doorstep.' Mark said relieved.

'No. But what if it was stolen?'

'Oh, now you're into the realms of fantasy.' Mark laughed.

Harry shook his head slowly. 'But father, there's more.'

'More? What do you mean more?'

'Mrs Carney-Tompkins told me she'd had five not four children but the first one had died, though she only caught a glance. It was a little girl, and she had the same mark on her left shoulder.

'But the child died, you said the child died.'

'That was what she was told, but there was some mystery surrounding the child's death, disappearance, what if.......Oh I don't know it's all such a muddle. What should we do? What can we do?'

'Go and see the Carney-Tompkins?'

'I did think of that. Some time ago I did visit their address, but they were away. Something to do with a family wedding in Yorkshire.' Harry told him.

'We must think very seriously about this. We can't go rushing in with our theories, it could do terrible damage. And don't forget, Thursday has no idea she is not our birth child. Dear Lord, what a quandary. I will go to church and ask for God's guidance; I know he will show me the way. In the meantime, we say nothing to anyone, not even your mother.'

When asked later by Elizabeth what had been Harry's problem, Mark told a fib he wasn't proud of. He told her, Harry had a difficult problem at the hospital, which needed discretion, Elizabeth asked no further questions.

Despite his prayers, Mark received no guidance from God, perhaps he too was considering the situation. But all that was swept away when one evening Mark came home and Elizabeth told him about the visit she'd received that afternoon from an eminent member of parliament. Intrigued, they agreed to put the request to Harry, asking if he thought he could get time off from the hospital to visit the lady in question.

Harry too was interested and said as he was due some time off, he could request it and agreed to meet Mr Simpson-Wardour the following evening.

Towards the end of October, Sybil realised she was unlikely to see her London home this side of Christmas, but then acknowledged she was actually enjoying her role being in charge. The servants had gone from being surly, awkward and aggressive, to civil and eager to please. This was due to Sybil's attitude. Since her arrival and giving them all a dressing down, she neither talked down to them or was harsh, unless they deserved it. The more they pleased her the fairer she became, and since Andrew's arrival, at least they had been paid regularly. The Laird had been okay, but he'd caused them a lot of work as he was slovenly and lazy. Then when he'd married, he'd got worse and her Ladyship lead them a merry dance, so her mother, they liked, long may it continue.

Having the boys dumped on her was another headache, but she soon knew the only way to handle this was to take the bull by the horns and show young master Rory she wouldn't put up with his behaviour. Having taken Andrew's advice she'd spoken to the gamekeeper, gardeners and grooms, and instructed them in their roles as tutors to the young Rory.

Thursday's Child

She was giving them carte blanch to "Knock the little blighter into shape"!

Well, it hadn't been six months and barley six weeks, but already one could see the difference. Rory was less surely, and didn't stuff food into his mouth at mealtimes, not since Sybil sat him outside on a stool next to the pigsty with his dinner plate.

And as for little Ewan, well now, there was a difference. When the governess chosen by Bertram arrived, Sybil was horrified. The young woman was just that, young! And with extraordinarily little experience. Sybil was not impressed, but four weeks later she could already see the difference, and had to admit, she'd been wrong. Miss Mary Pegatty had shown the boy affection, with firmness, and he'd responded immediately. Ewan no longer acted like a frightened waif, but was alert, eager to learn, and even wanted to inform his grandmother what he'd learnt that day. He'd even put on a little weight so wasn't so scrawny. Miss Pegatty reported to Sybil that young Master Ewan, as she referred to him, was a bright and pleasant little boy and she felt what he lacked in physical strength, he had in brains. In short, she thought Ewan could be academic, and a candidate for university.

Sybil almost fluffed up her feathers, if she'd had feathers, with pride at what she saw as her achievements. True, she'd had advice from Andrew, which she'd had the common sense to take, and look at the results. The servants turn-around was down to her. So, servants in line, boys on the right road, there was only one more person to sort and that was her own daughter.

Worryingly, Jane had taken a turn for the worse and taken to her bed the week before and refused to get up. She seemed confused, didn't want to eat but worse, she'd developed sores on her nether regions and her face which were discovered when they'd given her a bed bath. And when brushing her hair, her lady's maid reported several strands had come away on the brush.

Sybil was now sick with worry, so when news came the doctor was on his way and should be met at the Station on the following Thursday, she almost feinted with relief. They had just two days to go before help arrived.

In private, Sybil had her own thoughts and it terrified her. She didn't want to believe it, couldn't believe it, how could it have happened. No! It's not that! No, it can't be! she admonished herself.

On Thursday Sybil was so restless awaiting the arrival of the doctor, she'd sit down, then get up. Walk a few paces then sit, then get up. The anticipation of the doctor's arrival was nail biting, stomach churning, so when she heard the carriage approach, she was at the door before any of the servants.

As he stepped down from the carriage, Sybil had yet another heart stopping moment. Like the governess, this doctor was a mere boy, or looked like it. Then she thought about the governess. She'd had the same thoughts about her and look how she'd been wrong about that. Taking a deep breath Sybil stepped forward, offering her hand in welcome to the young man.

'Mrs Simpson-Wardour, I'm Doctor Harold Milton.'

'Doctor Milton, thank you for coming, I know it's been a long journey, but I am so grateful to you for coming. I'm nearly out of my mind with worry.'

'Well, I am here now. Shall we have a little talk first and you can give me some background?'

'Yes Doctor, yes, of course. Oh, where are my manners, would you like to freshen up, and something to eat and drink, you must be starving?' Sybil was all a fluster.

Doctor Milton smiled down at her in his usual placid manner. Touching her gently on her arm he said. 'Well perhaps I might just have a quick visit to a bathroom, then a cup of tea would be most welcome.'

'Of course, of course. Duncan, please show the Doctor to his room and make sure he has everything he needs, then bring him to the drawing room. ' Sybil instructed a footman, then turning back to Harry she said. 'And please Doctor, whatever you need please ask Duncan, he will be at your disposal for the duration of your stay.'

Harry gave a slight bow of appreciation. 'Thank you Mrs Simpson-Wardour, that is very kind of you.'

Duncan picked up Harry's portmanteau saying. 'If you care to follow me Sir.'

Thursday's Child

Half an hour later the door opened, and the doctor was shown in and greeted with tea and buttered teacakes.

'I hope this will suffice until dinner time?' Sybil said.

'It will be fine, thank you.' Harry said and dived in as he was starving. 'Now Madam. Can you give me some details of your daughter's illness?'

Sybil spent the next half an hour wringing her hands in anguish and telling Harry how she had found her daughter when she'd arrived in Scotland after her son-in-law's demise. 'I thought it was some sort of melancholy due to her husband, Lord Du-Barry's, ' she had to get his title in, 'death.' Though even she knew this would be stretching it a bit knowing what a wastrel Cornelius was, but appearances had to be kept up.

'And when did his Lordship pass?' Harry enquired, by now he was making notes in a small black book. Sybil told him. 'And in what circumstances did he pass?' Harry asked and then waited as Sybil continued to wring her hands but not answer. Harry was not sure if she'd heard the question.

'Madam......how...'

'Yes! I heard you.' Sybil snapped which shocked Harry. 'Let me think. Please, I must think.'

'Certainly, certainly, take your time.' Harry spoke softly, and kindly. It was obvious this lady was in a great deal of distress. 'Perhaps you could take me to see your daughter?'

Sybil looked up at him and he could see unshed tears in her eyes. Oh dear, this lady was clearly in a great deal of distress. There was something very wrong here. Despite her daughter being ill, Harry was sure her mother was hiding something, but if he was to get to the bottom of this, she would have to be honest with him. Suddenly he had an idea. As they both stood to go upstairs, Harry said. 'Do you have your son-in-law's death certificate?'

'What?' Sybil seemed surprised at the question. Harry repeated his question.

'Your son-in-law's death certificate?'

'Em, I'm not sure. I will speak with Andrew.'

'Andrew?' Harry asked not understanding who Andrew was and why they should speak to him.

'Andrew is, was his Lordships Estate Manager, still is. Now in the employ of my daughter. Well, my husband. It was my husband that gave Andrew the job as........oh it's a long story and not relevant, but Andrew can answer any questions you have.'

Harry nodded in agreement. 'That's fine, perhaps after I've seen the patient, I may have a meeting with the gentleman?' Sybil nodded and turned to go upstairs to Jane's room as Harry followed.

Jane's room was in darkness when they entered, as heavy drapes covered the windows. Jane's maid stood up from the chair she'd been sitting on at her mistress's bedside.

'It's alright Aileen, you can leave us now, the Doctor is here to see her Ladyship.' The girl did a slight bob and made to leave the room, halting as Harry addressed her.

'Would you wait outside please, I may need to speak to you about her Ladyship's condition, and behaviour issues.'

Aileen looked wide eyed and nervously at Sybil. 'That is alright Aileen, do as the Doctor says.'

'Yes Ma'am.'

Despite the cold outside, Harry was aware of the stuffiness of the room and went immediately to draw the drapes and open the window. A slight breeze of late Autumn drifted in, and Harry was reminded of a conference he'd attended where the speaker was Miss Florence Nightingale. She was very keen to encourage fresh air at all costs, accusing the many hot and stuffy rooms for the acceleration of disease.

The fresh air influenced his patient as she moved about the bed, opening her eyes, immediately shading them with her hands and crying out about the brightness.

'That's why we keep the drapes drawn.' Sybil said huffily and strode over, dragging them back into place angrily.

'I'm sorry, I didn't know.' Harry said apologetically.

'You didn't ask!' came the sharp retort.

'Well, I have to make some notes, so if I could have a candle?'

Sybil walked over to the dresser, returning with a lit candle which she placed on the table beside Jane's bed. Jane immediately turned her head from the light.

Harry removed his jacket and asked to wash his hands. When he was ready, he asked Sybil if she wished to assist him or prefer to recall Aileen.

'What are you going to do?'

'I need to remove the bedding and her night attire. I need to thoroughly examine your daughter.'

Sybil thought for a moment, then nodding, went forward and proceeded to remove blankets and sheet, then hesitatingly removed Jane's nightdress. Turning her head in revulsion, Sybil exposed her daughter's sore covered body. Harry stared in horror. There was little doubt in his mind now what ailed Lady Du-Barry. After the symptoms described by her mother, and what he saw in front of him, he was ninety-nine percent sure, Jane Du-Barry had Syphilis, and she was dying. Furthermore, he was sure her mother knew full well what was wrong with her daughter and when he spoke to the Estate manager, he was sure he would confirm that Lord Du-Barry also died of Syphilis.

Harry was angry. This dreadful disease was preventable if only people were more respectful of their sexual encounters, especially married men. He'd seen too much of this, where men casually disregarded their wife's health and ultimately, their lives, because whether it was weeks, months or even years, it would get them in the end.

'Well Doctor?' Sybil asked.

Harry turned slowly. 'Mrs Simpson-Wardour, do you still not wish to tell me what your son-in law died of? I can ask his Estate Manager if you wish?'

Sybil shook her head sadly. The game was up. 'Syphilis.' she whispered. Harry bowed his head and sat down on the bed. 'Can you.......Is there anything......?' Sybil's questions trailed off. Harry slowly shook his head. When he looked up, Sybil's tears were streaming silently down her face. 'No one should bury their own child.' She sobbed quietly.

Andrew confirmed Harry's fears and told Sybil that sadly he could do nothing for her daughter. There was little point in staying as there was nothing he could do. His only advice was to keep Jane clean and comfortable, with plenty of fresh air and water to drink. If she could eat fine, but not to force her. Harry knew that would only prolong her eventual death, better to let her go as the Lord saw fit. To prolong her life, was to prolong her suffering.

Harry stayed for a couple of days, overseeing her cleansing and comfort administrations. On his last evening, Aileen had just left the room when suddenly Jane opened her eyes and said with amazing clarity, which shocked him. 'Who are you?'

For one awful moment, Harry wondered if his diagnosis had been wrong. 'I'm Doctor Harry Milton, your father sent me.'

'I'm dying, I know I'm dying. ..'

'Well I.....'

'No, no, listen, you must listen. The baby, the baby....... it was a girl....' Jane closed her eyes but was breathing heavily, almost panicky.

'What is it? Your children are fine. The boys will be okay.' Harry waited. He could only hope the infection had been caught by Jane, after her pregnancies. Then just when he thought she had drifted off, she opened her eyes again. She stared at him, a wild look in her eyes.

'No, no not boys, the girl, it was a girl, workhouse told her, take to orphanage. Not dead.' Then she started to cry, great wracking tears, sobbing with such anguish, Harry felt he had to hold her to comfort her in her grief.

'Calm down, calm down. Tell me, can I help?'

'Baby, baby......with mark...'

'Mark? Mark who?' Harry asked, desperately trying to understand. Jane gave a weird gurgling noise almost a laugh, but it came as a cackle. 'No, mark, mark …. shoulder...' Jane attempted to point to her left shoulder. Harry started to go cold.

'What mark! Tell me what mark?' Right now, he felt he wanted to shake her. What was this woman trying to tell him! Oh my God, don't let her die! ' What mark? please tell me?' Jane slumped back in his arms exhausted. But when he thought it was all over, she suddenly took a huge intake of breath and her eyes sprung open. Grabbing at his shirt she said.

'The sword of Bethlehem.......'

'The sword?...... Do you mean the star? The star of Bethlehem?' he almost shouted at her. Jane slowly nodded. Harry froze. Are you telling me you took a baby, a baby girl with a birth mark like the star of

Bethlehem on her left shoulder and took her to an orphanage? Did you steel this baby from someone?' Jane nodded slowly. There was gasp as unbeknown to Harry, Sybil had entered the room.

'Oh, dear God!' Sybil stood with her hand over her mouth, tears running down her face.

'Did you know about this?' Harry demanded.

'No, no, I swear to you.'

'But you know something don't you?' He demanded again.

Sybil stared at him too horrified at the thoughts whirling around her head. Running to her daughter's bedside she knelt beside it. 'Jane, Jane, please I'm begging you. Has this anything to do with Selena's baby? The baby girl they all thought died?' For what seemed an eternity, Jane neither moved nor spoke until at last.

'Yes!'

That was the last word spoken by Lady Jane Du-Barry. She fell into a coma, later passing away peacefully in her sleep. Her mother said "peacefully" because she felt her daughter had made her peace with God by owning up to what had been an horrendous crime.

It was several hours as they sat by Jane's bed, that Sybil, told the story to Harry of Jane's obsession with Gerald Carney-Tompkins, finishing with 'I wonder what ever happened to that baby?'

It was then Harry's turn to tell the story of the baby girl found on the steps of the vicarage early one cold winters morning, and how that baby girl grew up, never knowing the truth, that the mother and father, and three brothers who adored her, were not her real family. At this point Sybil and Harry wept together.

The following day, Harry set off for home. Overnight, he and Sybil had talked and talked as to how they would put this terribly wrong, right, firmly convinced that Thursday was the missing baby. There would be dreadful heartache all round. Selena and Gerald discovering their daughter, John Elliot finding his granddaughter, and Gerald and Selena's children discovering they had another sister.

And for the Milton family, for Elizabeth and Mark, it would be like losing a daughter all over again, and for the brothers, losing their sister. And for Thursday, what a blow. To discover after all these years your family was not your family, and that you had a big family a few short miles away. How on earth would she be able to come to terms with that? How would anybody?

As agreed, Sybil had written a heartfelt letter telling the truth, as much as they knew it, that Jane in a moment of madness, had stolen or arranged to steel Selena's baby out of shear jealous rage, and planned to send it to a workhouse or orphanage. How Thursday had landed on the doorstep of the vicarage they would never know, but luckily, she had. And because of a series of incidents, Selena's accident, Harry being on call that day at the hospital and seeing the birthmark and his subsequent conversation with her, then this strange quirk of fate visiting Scotland, the mystery had begun to unfold. There's a saying "It's a small world" well isn't that just the truth.

Thursday had had a good life with a loving family and through her "brother", would be reunited with her real family.

Harry held the letter of proof in his hand to this strange tale, How or when he would deliver it, would be decided after he'd told his mother and brothers the truth. Would anyone be angry that he, Harry had had his suspicions and told his father some months previously but they had not said anything. Their only defence being, at the time, they had no proof. It was not a pleasant journey home.

After Harry departed, Sybil was left with huge problems. Firstly, what was she to do with the boys? She couldn't just abandon them, neither could she take them back to London. Du-Barry castle was their home, and although Rory was too young to perform official duties of the estate, Jane had at least seen sense and arranged for Andrew to be their legal guardian and mentor until Rory became of age. What she was later to find out when the Will was read, that Sybil and Bertram had also been made legal guardians.

Andrew was a major source of strength and confirmed that he would maintain his position and training of Rory whilst Sybil continued to organise the domestic arrangements and care for the boys.

Thursday's Child

Rory had maintained a stoical silence since his mother's passing, showing little of his feelings. This wasn't surprising really as Sybil remembered her daughter's dislike for her first born, for which she felt a great sadness for the boy. Ewan on the other hand, wept buckets and took comfort not only from her but more commonly from Miss Pegatty his governess or as he'd come to call her, Peg.

As Jane slipped away, Sybil immediately contacted Bertram. Now, she had long letter to write, informing him that the loss of their daughter meant life would never be the same again, at least not until the boys were adult.

The funeral had been a small, private affair, and Jane was laid to rest in the mausoleum in the grounds of the estate. Not what any of them would have wished for but time was of the essence, and under the circumstances, the quicker it was over the less likelihood of gossip. Plus, Jane had never gone out of her way to make herself popular.

Bertram's reply was that he would be with her for Christmas, Sybil felt relieved.

For the Carney-Tompkins, Christmas nineteen hundred was to be spent in Yorkshire, and despite the journey ahead, Gerald, Selena and the children were all looking forward to it. John and Amelia had popped back to Harrogate a couple of times since returning from honeymoon, just to check on Amelia's parents and John to check into the Yorkshire factory.

Mr and Mrs Johnson couldn't have been happier and told Amelia and John not to worry. They were being well looked after and even felt better especially as they had been taking regular walks in the lovely Yorkshire air. They loved the town and enjoyed making trips into the large stores and the smaller village shops nearby.

Before leaving London, news had filtered through about the demise of Jane, Lady Du-Barry. Many were shocked as she was still a young woman and would be leaving two young boys motherless, though some said, rather spitefully, they didn't think she'd been much of a mother. There was also some speculation about her death so suddenly after her husband. But Bertram would not be drawn, sidestepping any awkward questions. Getting away for Christmas would be a welcome distraction.

The welcome received from the Harrogate servants was overwhelming, they especially loved seeing the children and as Cookie said, it took her back to when Selena was, "Ney but a lass"

Christmas day started as always with a trip to church, and it amused Amelia to see how friendly everyone was, especially with her parents who it appeared were now regulars at the church. Her mother had joined the sewing circle who met every Tuesday afternoon, so it seemed the move had given her parents a new lease of life.

As they gathered in the dining room for their Christmas lunch, John laughed and said they would have to get a bigger table.

Selena looked with pride at her father and Amelia, so pleased he would not spend his last years in retirement alone. Gazing around the table, she thought how lucky they were, she and Gerald. They had a thriving business, a beautiful home and four wonderful children. A cloud drifted over her thoughts, as always when she thought of the children, she would think of the one she'd lost. Would she ever come to terms with what happened all those years ago? It seemed unlikely. Still, she mustn't be morbid, put it behind you she remonstrated silently to herself.

Christmas in the Milton household had been a quite different affair. On his return from Scotland, Harry repeated the stories Jane and Sybil had told him, to his father. This confirmed that Thursday was indeed the stolen daughter of Selena and Gerald Carney-Tompkins. Furthermore, he had a letter from Mrs Simpson-Wardour to prove it.

Despite knowing for months there was a strong possibility Thursday's parents had been found, and that she was not a foundling, but subject of a vicious crime, Mark Milton was still shattered. It was obvious they had to act on this knowledge, but not before Christmas. It would cause the most explosive upheaval, so a couple of weeks more was not going to change anything.

Mark worried about the law and said so to Harry.

'But you did everything you could Father.' Harry replied. 'I was only ten, but I do remember you going to the police, the magistrate and putting up notices all over London.'

'But why did nobody come forward? Surely someone would have investigated it, word must have spread?'

'But supposing someone went round taking the notices down? And don't forget, the Carney-Tompkins thought their daughter had died. No father, you did nothing wrong.'

Mark was silent for a moment as thoughts whirled around his head, had he done everything he could? Then he remembered something.

'The birth certificate! We lied, your mother and me! To get the birth certificate, we lied!'

'But weren't you told to do just that? By the magistrate? Didn't he tell you if you wanted to make sure nobody could take Thursday from you, to create a birth certificate?'

'Yes, you are right. But what if he denies saying that what if he can't remember or doesn't want to remember?'

'Father, you were protecting an innocent baby, a baby who'd been left on our doorstep, who would have died had we not taken her in and cared for her.'

'They might say we should have taken her to an orphanage.'

'They might, but for what? Hasn't Thursday been brought up in a God-fearing home, loved, protected and educated? Look at what a lovely, confident young lady she's turned out to be, a pupil teacher no less. No father, I do not think you have anything to worry about. But if you are still concerned, why don't we confide in our very own lawyer? We have one here in our very own home.'

'Yes, of course. We should ask your brother. He will have to be told the whole story and asked to keep it to himself until after Christmas, but he's a lawyer after all and used to keeping secrets.'

And so after dinner one evening, out of earshot of the family, Mark asked Edward, his lawyer son, to come to his study. Edward was mystified, something in his father's manner concerned him. He was even more mystified when having closed the door, his brother Harry entered and sat down.

Edward looked from one to the other. 'Is something wrong?'

Mark sighed heavily. 'Sit down son, we have a disturbing story to tell you and must ask you to say nothing when you leave this room. We will speak to your mother, Theo and Thursday after Christmas.'

Between them, Harry and his father began to tell the story, right from the start when Harry had met Selena Carney-Tompkins in the hospital.

During their telling, Edward had enquired about certain facts, incredulous though it was, after searching his thoughts about the law, he was able to confirm, that his parents had done nothing wrong as there were no laws to cover a situation like this. Furthermore, Thursday had been kept safe, well looked after, loved and educated and many would argue, better than had she been taken to an orphanage. Of course, had Jane lived after her confession, then that would have been a different story, she'd have probably ended up in prison.

It was difficult, but some members of two families that Christmas, the Milton's and the Simpson-Wardour's, had an uncomfortable time.

Sybil and Bertram in Scotland, worried if there would be a backlash when the Carney-Tompkins found out about the baby girl who had not died but had been stolen in a conspiracy planned and carried out by their own daughter. What would be the repercussions? Would they sue? Would it reflect on Bertram's position in government? How could they prove they were not party to any of it? There was of course Doctor Milton. Surely, he would confirm they were innocent of any wrongdoing.

They gave the boys the best Christmas they could, though Rory occasionally had a sullen strop. Ewan, seemed to have got over his mother's death and turned increasingly to Governess Pegatty, or Peg as he affectionately referred to her.

However, in the New Year, there would be a bigger, and a more urgent situation to attend to.

CHAPTER 16

LONDON
JANUARY 1901

As soon as they entered into the new Year, Harry and his father knew they could no longer wait with their dilemma. The situation had to be faced despite the devastation it would cause. First to be told was Elizabeth.

'I knew it, I knew it!' she cried in anguish. 'I knew there was something going on, I felt it in my bones.' For some minutes Elizabeth cried, broken hearted, she sobbed. As she dried her tears, she looked at her husband and son. 'And you are sure? Positive this woman was telling the truth?' Both men nodded.

'We only have one other avenue to go down. If Mr Carney-Tompkins confirms the midwife he'd engaged did not attend because she'd had a letter telling her not to, then there can be no doubt.' Mark said.

'But what of Thursday? She's our child. We've brought her up, we are her family. We are the only family she has ever known. How can you tear her away from us?' Elizabeth beseeched them.

'We don't know what is going to happen yet. But I will make sure that no harm will come to our daughter.' Mark declared.

'But she's not is she? She is not our daughter. How can we stop them from taking her? These people are rich! They have power.'

'True, but they are also kind and good people. I have met Mrs Carney-Tompkins, she's a nice lady. And when I was in Scotland, Mrs Simpson-Wardour told me a great deal about them. I made other enquiries when I returned. No one has a bad word to say about them.' Harry told his mother. Kneeling beside her, he took her hands into his. 'Mother, we must do the right thing. For Thursday's true parents, for her real grandfather and for the real brothers and sisters she has. She will always be our sister, but we have to be honest.'

Elizabeth let these thoughts sink in. Then with a huge, shuddering sigh, she said. 'How will we go about it?'

'Father has drafted a letter with my help, to Mr Carney-Tompkins, requesting a meeting with him at his offices, stressing the importance of discretion. We will meet with him, show him the proof we have and then, if he agrees and after he has spoken to his wife, we suggest a meeting here with Thursday, to see if there is any recognition, resemblance, after which, Thursday will have to be told.'

Elizabeth nodded sadly. 'Who else knows of this? Apart from the Simpson-Wardour's?'

'Only Edward.' Harry replied. 'Father was worried in case any laws had been broken, and Edward being in the law, we thought he was the best person to ask.'

But before anything further could happen, came the sad news of Queen Victoria.

On January the twenty-second nineteen hundred and one, it was announced, to the Nation, that Her Majesty, Queen Victoria had passed away. The Country went into mourning. This was followed by many Countries throughout the world.

Two days previously, a letter posted to Gerald and addressed to the factory, marked, *"Private to be opened by addressee only"* arrived and was placed on his desk.

With the announcement of the Queen's passing, and the sudden rush of black outfits being required, it sat where it had been left for another couple of days, unread.

John and Amelia rushed back to London. Despite now retired, John felt it prudent to offer his services to Gerald and likewise, although they now had a team of designers, none had ever had to design for a situation like this. Amelia knew she could be of help and Gerald was incredibly grateful to have them back. They had just finished a meeting, when shuffling through his tray of correspondence, Gerald noticed the envelope he'd previously missed.

As John and Amelia left to go to their offices, Gerald opened the envelope and read its contents.

> Dear Sir,
> I would beg of you to agree to a meeting at your office on Friday, January the 25th at 6pm.
> My son and I have recently come upon some very grave but important information which concerns both our families.
> Until we have spoken to you, I would ask you to keep this meeting a secret as we wish to cause as little distress as possible. Please be assured, we wish your family no harm but hope to right a wrong that was cruelly conducted unbeknown to both of us.
>
> Yours Truly
> Reverend Mark Milton & Dr. Harry Milton

Gerald stared at the letter and then read it three times more. 'What an extraordinary letter' he muttered to himself, then checked the date. Today was the twenty-fifth, and looking at the clock, saw it was four-thirty. Thank goodness he'd seen it, or he would have gone home, and these two gentlemen would have had a wasted journey.

As John and Amelia left that night calling out 'Goodnight', Gerald made an excuse for his not leaving at the same time.

The clocked ticked nearer and nearer to the appointed time, and it seemed to get louder as every minute passed. When the knock came, Gerald almost jumped out of his chair, but hurried down to open the door.

He was most relieved as he looked at the two men stood before of him. Despite the letter seeming genuine, he'd still had a slight worry it might be some kind of criminal hoax. But one of them clearly was a man of the cloth as Gerald took in the dog collar round his neck.

'Good evening, gentlemen.'

'Good evening Mr Carney-Tompkins, may I introduce myself, I am the Reverend Mark Milton, and this is my son Doctor Harry Milton.' They shook hands and Gerald ushered them in and up to his office.

'Please Gentlemen, take a seat. I must admit I almost missed your letter what with all the sad news of Her Majesty, I only came across it later this afternoon. I had to read it three times and cannot for the life of me think of anything that has befallen me that I have not noticed.'

Father and son looked uneasily at each other. Mark spoke first. 'I will leave my son to explain it to you Sir, as it was he who first came upon an unusual situation last summer. But before he does, I have a delicate question to ask of you and hope you will not be offended, but I can assure you, your answer is relative to the story.'

Intrigued, but smiling, Gerald nodded assent.

'Many years ago, I believe your dear wife gave birth to a baby girl, who.......you were informed, had died at birth?'

The smile abruptly left Gerald's face and tears sprang to his eyes as he was taken back to that terrible night. Unable to speak, he nodded.

'Sir, we do not wish to cause you any distress, but must ask, did you send a letter to the mid-wife you'd engaged telling not to attend?'

'No! I did not. But how do you know about that?' Gerald had jumped up and was shouting.

'Please Sir, we are here to help you unravel a dreadful wrong, which hopefully for you and your wife, could bring joy.' Mark said.

'We know about the letter as we know who sent it.' Mark said gently.

'What!' exclaimed Gerald

'You are, or were acquainted with a Lady Jane Du-Barry who recently passed away?'

'Yes, but what has she to do with this?' Again, the two men exchanged anxious glances.

'I'm afraid to tell you Sir, that it was she who wrote that letter, and she made the confession to my son who was in attendance on her death bed. It was the confession of a dying woman, the whole story, witnessed by her mother, who I must impress upon you had no part in the conspiracy.'

'What? I don't understand?'

'On the morning of December, the eleventh, eighteen-eighty-five, our maid awoke my wife and myself in a dreadful panic saying, someone had left a baby on the doorstep of our vicarage..........' Mark continued with the early part of the story until he came to the part of Selena's accident. 'I will leave my son to continue with the final piece of the jigsaw story. But first should you like a drink? I can see this has been a terrible shock for you.' Mark Milton looked around the office. Gerald stood up and going to a drink's cabinet said. 'I think we could all do with one.'

It took over an hour for Harry to tell the whole sorry story, with many stops as Gerald had a lot of questions to ask. When he ended, Gerald sat for several moments digesting all he'd been told and found it incredulous, but grateful to Mark, his wife and family for taking care of his daughter. There was no disputing that Selena, when she heard about this would be devastated at the thought that their own baby girl had been brought up by people who were not her parents. And what of John? good grief, what ever would he make of this story? And the Simpson-Wardour's? He would be making a visit to them, but not until he had calmed down. Despite being assured by the Milton's the Simpson-Wardour's had had no knowledge of their daughter's chicanery, he still felt angry, murderously angry at the trauma she had put them through.

As Mark had suggested a meeting, more in the shape of afternoon tea, be arranged so as not to alarm Thursday. This would be in the coming weeks. Concerns for both Selena and John lay heavy with Gerald as he walked home that evening. He declined his normal carriage ride as he needed to think, his head was pounding as he continued to try and make sense of the story. And what of poor Thursday? Even the name was bizarre, would she want to keep it? Would she even want to come to them, her real family? Gerald was no nearer the answers to his questions by the time he wearily walked up the path to his home.

Naturally, Selena was concerned at Gerald's lateness at retuning home, but even more concerning was that he seemed deeply worried. Selena immediately thought there must be a problem at the factory and enquired of him. Gerald smiled wearily and gently took her into his arms. For several moments they stood like this, locked in each other's arms, until they were noisily accosted by their four children who came hurtling down the stairs, ready for bed, but refusing to go before saying goodnight to their father. Gerald briefly pulled himself together, not wanting to alert them that he was worried about something. He jovially apologised for not being home in time to take dinner with them, but promised with the weekend ahead, they would all visit their grandpa John. Which surprised Selena as nothing had been arranged, but she kept quiet, surely this must have something to do with Gerald's late meeting, though why her father wasn't present was a mystery. Despite taking retirement, John would have always been available if there was a problem.

'Now children, off you go, I will be up in a minute to say goodnight.' As the children raced up the stairs, Selena said. 'Why don't you go and wash your hands and I'll pop down to let cook know you're home and we'll be ready for dinner in half an hour. How does that sound?' she ended brightly?

'It sounds wonderful.' He said, heading towards the cloakroom. Selena watched him go before rushing to the kitchen to alert cook.

Gerald was already seated and drinking a whisky by the time Selena returned. 'Gerald? What is wrong? I know something is, and it must be something serious, especially as you mentioned a visit to Papa. I know he came down recently, but I thought it was just a general visit, I know how he and Amelia like to visit London, especially since they know her parents are in safe hands in Harrogate, so what is it my darling?'

'You are right dearest. But please, may we first have dinner, and then I have a long and strange tale to tell you. But let us eat first.'

Thursday's Child

Selena nodded in agreement but had to ask. 'Just tell me one thing. Is the business in trouble?'

'No. Nothing like that. I'm pleased to say that both our factories are doing well, though at the moment, with all the orders for mourning outfits in respect of our own dear departed Queen, everyone is rushed off their feet.'

'So.....'

Gerald held up a hand to stop his wife from asking further questions. 'Please dearest, let us eat.'

Their meal was taken in silence, though neither of them could tell you what they'd eaten as both were deep in thought. Gerald with, how did he tell her, and Selena wondering what on earth it could be. Suddenly, she had a thought and her head shot up. 'Is it Papa?' she demanded. 'Is that why they have come to London? Is he ill? Tell me Gerald, tell me.'

'No, my dear, it is not your Papa, as far as I am aware, your Papa is in excellent health, in fact I'd go so far as to say his marriage, has acted like an amazing tonic.' Gerald flung down his napkin. 'It's no good. I know you are worried, and I cannot eat. Ring the bell dear and tell the maid there's nothing wrong with the meal, I'm just not hungry and do not want pudding. They can clear down and go to bed.'

Minutes later, Selena joined him in the drawing room. Sitting herself down opposite him she said. 'Now, no more delay, what has happened?'

'Selena, what I must tell you is the most bizarre, tragic and the cruellest act of deception I have ever come across. And the telling of it my darling is going to be the cause of much pain and trauma, but there is no easy way to tell you, only the way it was told to me tonight.'

Selena gasped and readied herself for shocking news.

'I was going to say it started on the night you gave birth to our first child, but I think it began before that, at least the perpetrator of the deed certainly started to plan her vicious act from the moment she knew you were with child......' It took several hours of telling, answering Selena's questions and drying her tears as she repeatedly broke down.

She was still in shock when they wearily climbed the stairs after midnight to go to bed. What Gerald had told her swam round and round in her head. One moment it was joy that her baby had not died, but the next, it was the shear horror of what had happened and continued to happen for fifteen years. Her own child, stolen and brought up by strangers, unaware those she called Mother and Father, were of no family to her, in any shape or form and her real Mama and Papa were a few short miles away. No, she just could not bear it. And what of Thursday? How would she take it when she was told? And Jane! It was a good job she was dead because if she had not been Selena felt she would have killed her with her own bare hands. What a wicked thing to do. And the planning of it and then to carry it out, drag other people into her vicious scheme. How did she manage that? But then money talks, and there are plenty who would do anything for money. All these feelings and emotions kept her tossing and turning in bed, unable to sleep until dawn broke and she eventually slept from shear exhaustion.

When Gerald woke, he saw the strain on his wife's sleeping face, the dried tears on her cheeks, and could feel himself welling up at the dreadful situation. Fleetingly he wondered if they'd have been better off not knowing, there was still much upset to come when they would eventually have to tell Thursday the truth, their other four children and John, her grandfather, the grandfather she'd never known. What a mess! Like Selena, his thoughts went to Jane and like Selena if Jane had lived, Gerald would have wanted to kill her for what she'd done. One thing he would do, first thing Monday morning, he and John would be making a visit to the Simpson-Wardour's, though what good that would do he had no idea, given, if they were to be believed, had no idea of their daughter's action.

Gerald bathed, dressed, and crept quietly out of their bedroom, asking the maids to organise the children but impressed upon them to be quiet as their mother had not had a good night and needed to sleep.

After breakfast, Gerald sent a message with one of the footman, to inform John the family would be calling that afternoon, although it wasn't entirely a social call as they had something of importance to discuss with him.

John, when he read the message, was not unduly concerned though intrigued and replied he and Amelia looked forward to seeing them, as they were thinking to return to Harrogate on Monday.

By eleven o'clock, Selena had still not put in appearance so Gerald went to their room, and gently woke her. He suggested her maid run her a bath and then a light lunch before going to her Papa's.

Selena agreed to the bath but said she couldn't eat a thing.

Downstairs, Gerald told his children they would be visiting their Grandpapa and step Grandmama after lunch, but mama was not feeling too well, so a little quiet would be appreciated. As always, his young family understood and calmed down.

Arriving at John and Amelia's home and being greeted, Amelia, having realised that something of importance was to be discussed, took charge of the children.

'May we go to your study, John?' Gerald asked. This surprised John who took another look at his daughter and to his horror saw how pale and distressed she looked. Suddenly he began to worry, was Selena ill? Please God, he silently prayed, he couldn't bear that. Losing her mother had been bad enough but to lose his daughter, it didn't bear thinking about. Losing the smile from his face which had greeted them, he lead to way to his study.

'Whatever is it? John asked. 'Are you ill?'

'No Father, not ill. But yesterday, Gerald was given some shocking news, we are still reeling from it.' John looked puzzled from one to the other.

'Sit down John, you are going to need to sit down, but first let me assure you, Selena is quite well, shocked, traumatised but not ill, no one is ill, but we do have something incredulous to tell you, and it will take a while.' John sat, and Gerald began his tale.

An hour later came a gentle knock on the door, entering quietly, Amelia asked. 'Would anyone like some tea?' John looked at the others who nodded.

'Come in Amelia, I will ring for a maid. We have something to tell you.' John said.

Later, at Amelia's insistence, the family sat down to dinner, though conversation was muted, and sparse, but the children made up for it seeming not to notice how quiet the grown-ups were.

John and Amelia delayed their return to Harrogate, as until the whole situation was resolved, John not only wanted to stay but felt it was his duty, not only that, but he too wanted to meet the granddaughter he thought had died.

The next few weeks was a blaze of discussion. First Gerald made a visit to Bertram's offices, accompanied by John, and later met with Sybil Simpson-Wardour at their home. It was obvious neither of them had had any idea of their late daughter's behaviour, though both admitted they knew of her obsession with Gerald. Bertram couldn't help showing his nervousness of the story getting out and ruining his political ambitions by association. Both Gerald and John assured him they had no wish to make any of the situation public, though how they would explain Thursday's sudden appearance was something they hadn't thought of. At present, no one knew how Thursday would react. That was the next hurdle, and two weeks later a Saturday by arrangement, Selena, Gerald and John met Thursday.

So as not to alarm her, Edward was in attendance as Harry had been unable to get away from the hospital, and Theo was at university, so Mark and Elizabeth had chosen not to tell him until everything was clearer.

When Thursday entered the room, all three of the visitors stifled a gasp. Seeing her was like looking back in time. It was like a young Selena walking into the room, the similarity was remarkable, even the Milton's had no doubt, Thursday was Selena's daughter.

Edward was keeping a watchful eye on proceedings, as he'd not met any of their visitors before, he was concerned that Thursday should not be upset should they start asking her questions. For some reason, he had the feeling Thursday would, from instinct, be aware there was something of importance in these visitors being received. But it appeared nothing seemed to phase her, on the contrary, she seemed perfectly at ease as she sat talking, mainly to Mrs Carney-Tompkins, though he noticed Mr Carney-Tompkins, hung on her every word.

Mr Elliot was also keen to talk to her, especially talking to her about his home in Harrogate. Edward wasn't the only one who was watchful. Mark and Elizabeth watched sadly, as they could see the daughter they'd thought of for years, as theirs, had to admit there seemed an invisible bond, and they knew it was only a matter of time before Thursday would have to make a decision, which could shatter at least one of the families.

Selena was fascinated at how mature her daughter was, far more than she had been at the same age. Although thinking about it, it wasn't long after at the same age, she knew she would marry Gerald.

Thursday not only spoke about her hopes and dreams of becoming qualified as a teacher pointing out that as all three of her brothers had been to university, it must be in their blood, so she was optimistic in following in their footsteps. This last remark was like a punch in the stomach, making Selena feel suddenly lost. It was a stark reminder, that this young girl had no idea the reason these strangers were visiting her home. Would she feel anger when she was told the truth? How would she feel looking back on this afternoon, realising she'd been the object of scrutiny. Would she feel excitement or devastation? She feared it would be the latter.

When they took their leave, it was with a certain amount of sadness, especially when Thursday shook hands with them in such a grown-up way and said.

'It's been lovely to meet you, perhaps next time you could bring your children.' And turning to her mother she said, 'Wouldn't that be nice Mother, as Mrs Carney-Tompkins has twin daughters as well as two sons.' Then turning back to Selena, she said. 'Brothers are all very well, and I love mine dearly, but it would be so nice to meet other young ladies, don't you think Mother?' Elizabeth was unable to speak she was so full of emotion at Thursday's word so nodded in agreement.

Sitting in the carriage on their way home, all three were silent, all thinking about the situation and what would be the next move.

Arriving home, they were greeted by four extremely excited children who exclaimed they too had had a wonderful afternoon with dear Grandmama Amelia. Although not that old, Amelia delighted in the fact they not only considered her in that role but called her "Grandmama".

Her parents were treated to the titles of Great Grandpa and Great Grandma, titles of which they were extremely pleased to receive.

There was no time to talk about the afternoon's visit as the children were constantly with them, so Amelia had to wait until they were in their carriage and on their way home before John could tell her all about it.

Likewise, Gerald and Selena had to wait until their children had all gone to bed, to discuss where they went from here.

'I think my dear, we have to wait for the Milton's to speak with Thursday, and to be fair, we have to let them do this in their own time' Gerald said and Selena had to sadly agree. But when and how? Just how long would they have to wait?

The following morning there was news of the late Queen's instructions regarding her funeral. She had left instructions in her Will, that despite having worn mourning black since the death of her beloved Albert, her funeral was to be a white one! The Queen had forbidden black. The streets of London were to be hung with banners of purple with white silk bows. In her coffin, Victoria was dressed in white lace and on her head she wore her wedding veil. The closed coffin was draped with a white satin pall and embroidered with a gold cross in the centre and the Royal Arms in the corners. The gun carriage which would carry her to her resting place in St Georges chapel, at Windsor Castle was to be pulled by white ponies.

As the Queen had died at her beloved Osborn house on the Isle of Wight, arrangements had to be made to bring her back in time for the funeral to take place on the second of February. It was said to be the largest gathering of European Royalty that had ever taken place. But as she had served the United Kingdom and Ireland as Queen for sixty-four years and held the title of Empress of India, it was not surprising.

As soon as the funeral was over, the royal household turned their attention on Abdul Karim. With the aid of royal servants and members of parliament, Victoria's son Edward had Karim and his family thrown out of the house the Queen had given him and deported back to India. Karim had served her Majesty, loyally for fourteen years, much to the jealousy of many closest to her.

With the sadness of Victoria's passing a new Edwardian period was declared. King Edward the seventh was yet to be crowned but he immediately threw himself into restoring the gaiety which had been denied to the country since the death of his father forty years previously.

It was now time for the Carney-Tompkins to resume their family problem. They still had not informed their children but unbeknown to them, the Milton's had confessed to their youngest son Theo, and together, the family had told the sorry story to Thursday.

At first Thursday thought it was a joke, though she did not take kindly to it. Then, as they revealed more and more graphic detail, and the Carney-Tompkins visit was included, the dreadful truth dawned. Over the days which followed Thursday was distraught. This emotion was followed with anger. Accusations went from being unwanted, first by the Milton's, then by the Carney-Tompkins. After many outbursts, tears and arguments, Elizabeth and Mark were able to start making inroads towards an understanding. But it was Theo who eventually broke through to his little sister when unaware she was sitting silently in his father's empty church, he entered.

He was due to return to his studies, but before leaving decided to go to his father's church and say a prayer for Thursday and perhaps ask God for some guidance on the matter. Thinking he was alone, he did not whisper his prayer or questions, but spoke loudly, as if God was sat beside him.

Unbeknown to him, Thursday heard every word as she sat hidden in an alcove. Listening to him, Thursday saw the whole episode in a new light. She heard about the deception, the theft of her as a new-born, the devastation of Selena, Gerald and her grandpa believing she had died. Although she'd heard it all before, now the details of that terrible night, took on a new meaning. None of these people were to blame for what had happened. The only person to blame was the woman who'd planned and carried out the plan, and she was dead. In a way, she, Thursday was the lucky one. She'd lived a happy and safe life with a mother, father and three brothers and it would always be like that for her The Milton's were her family. But she also had another family, another mother and father, and two more brothers and two sisters. Had she not always thought how nice it would be to have a sister? And now she had two.

Two families had suffered great pain and trauma, through no fault of their own. Now she, Thursday, could heal and end that pain. It would be like a marriage. When you married, did you not make your husband or wife's family yours? All this she had gleaned from listening to Theo talking to God.

'Theo.' she said. And as her voice echoed around the church, Theo jumped as he thought he was hearing the Lord actually speaking to him. He was mightily relieved as he turned and found Thursday coming out from the corner of the church where she had been hiding. 'I've been listening to you talking to God, asking him for advice. I think he has replied through me.'

'Really?'

'Yes. So not only has he made me see the picture as it really is and not the tragedy I thought it was, but I realise what I must do.'

'You do?'

'Yes. Oh, and Theo, I think you are going to make an excellent vicar, because God does listen to you. They say, "God moves in mysterious ways" Well he did today because he made me see through your words what I have to do.'

'Right. Well, no doubt you will enlighten us then?'

'Yes, and when better than now. Come, we must return home and speak to Mother, Father, and the boys.'

Mystified but pleased that somehow, it looked as if a miracle had occurred, Theo sent a silent prayer after which he added, 'Thanks God', as they left the church.

As soon as they returned home, Thursday ran up to her room saying she had something urgent to do. Elizabeth raised an eyebrow, but it was obvious Thursday was back to her happy, contended self. Turning to her youngest she asked. 'Has something happened?'

'I think it has Mother, I think it has, and I know Thursday will tell us all about it at dinner.'

'Is it good? She does seem a lot less unhappy'.

Theo nodded. 'Yes, I think it is and we have God to thank for her change of angst. I had a quiet word with him in church this afternoon. Thursday was there, though I didn't know, and it appears God had a word with her!' with his hands in his pocket he went upstairs whistling a very happy tune. Well, whatever has happened, it looks like Thursday is more settled thought Elizabeth.

Mark, Elizabeth, Harry and Edward were all talking to Theo about his coming departure back to university the following day, when Thursday entered the room. Everyone stopped talking and looked in her direction. The atmosphere had been strained for some weeks now, but tonight it seemed a different, a calmer and happier Thursday had entered. She smiled as she took her seat by the fire.

'Before we go to dinner, Mother, Father and boys, I have an announcement to make.' No one moved or said anything. 'As you know, we've all had a terrible shock these last few weeks and I know it hasn't been easy for any of us. I know, Mother, Father, that what you did all those years ago was a wonderful thing. You took me in, loved me, educated me and kept me safe with my wonderful three brothers. You could have handed me over to an orphanage, but you didn't, if you had it is highly unlikely I would never have known the truth, but now we do, and it is up to me to make all my parents, brothers and sisters happy. So, I've written a letter to......I wasn't sure what to call them, and I don't want to hurt you, because you will always be Mother and Father, and you boys will always be my brothers. I have thought about this and, if you are willing, I wish to stay with you...'

There was a gasp from Elizabeth as she turned to Mark hardly believing what she'd heard. Tears welled in her eyes but then she thought of the Carney-Tompkins. Thursday continued. 'But I feel I owe my birth parents something. It wasn't their fault what happened, and it must have been terrible to have a baby then have it taken from you, only to find out years later, it hadn't died. But, at the moment I don't feel I fit in with them, does that sound really bad?'

'Not at all.' Mark said and came to hug her. 'What have you in mind?'

Thursday took a deep breath. 'I've written to ask them, with your agreement, that I stay here, because it's what I know, but that I would like to spend time with them, perhaps a couple of days a week, get to know them, share myself with both my families, what do you think?'

Elizabeth beamed with pride. 'I think it's a wonderful idea. And Thursday if you ever feel that...you...want too...live..' Elizabeth couldn't finish, it was a gesture too far and one she secretly hoped would never happen, but Thursday instinctively knew what her mother was trying to say.

'I don't know if that day will ever come …..but if they don't mind sharing me, let's see shall we?'

The letter arrived just when they'd almost given up hope. When it was read, although there was some disappointment for the family, they all agreed it was a step in the right direction. After all, asking a fifteen-year-old to give up the only family she'd ever known was just too much, but hopefully, as time went by, she would come to love her real family and feel part of them but that could take time.

John and Amelia had returned to Harrogate, but Selena wasted no time writing to them with the news. They replied that they were thrilled with the news and said what a sensible, mature young girl Thursday was. And although it was not the news they had really wanted, time was needed to build confidence and a feeling of belonging for Thursday. John also issued an invitation and said if they thought it a good idea, he would write to Thursday and suggest she may like to visit them in Harrogate the next time her new family visited. John was pleased to receive, almost by return, a letter from Thursday, accepting his invitation and telling him about her first steps staying with Selena and Gerald whom she referred to as Ma and Pa.

Small steps, muttered John when he finished reading, small steps. For now, this would have to do. But what of the future? Thursday was growing up, she had her whole life ahead of her, and two families wanting her. They would have to be careful not to make too many demands or they might lose her.

So, the future would have to wait, and everybody wondered, how long and what would the outcome be?

Printed in Great Britain
by Amazon